The
Sleeping Angel

MARGARITA MORRIS

Margarita Morris asserts the moral right to be identified as
the author of this work.

Published by Margarita Morris at CreateSpace

Cover Design by L1graphics
Portrait of a beautiful young Victorian lady in white dress by
Raisa Kanareva
Teen couple running along road in countryside by
karelnoppe

www.margaritamorris.com

ISBN: 0-9927489-4-1
ISBN-13: 978-0-9927489-4-4

For my parents.

CONTENTS

When I am dead, my dearest,
Sing no sad songs for me;
Plant thou no roses at my head,
Nor shady cypress tree:
Be the green grass above me
With showers and dewdrops wet
And if thou wilt, remember,
And if thou wilt, forget.
Christina Rossetti, 1848

PROLOGUE

Saturday, 19th March 1870, 11 o'clock in the evening.

It is late but I am wound up like a spring and know it would be hopeless to attempt sleep for the time being. This evening we did not achieve the hoped-for results but it will happen tomorrow – I am sure of it. When Madeleine came out of her trance this evening she was greatly exhausted from her exertions. I revived her with a little brandy and hot water and she explained that, although we had prepared well, the conditions were not absolutely perfect – the weather has been unsettled of late – and for such a delicate phenomenon as that which she intends to bring forth, all external factors must be favourable. Earlier today I overheard the baker's boy, Sam, telling Betsy that he expects the weather to improve tomorrow and he is rarely wrong on such matters. In the meantime I must try to calm my nerves and be patient. It will not be long now. All my hope and trust is in Madeleine. She will not let me down.

MARGARITA MORRIS

PART ONE
FRIDAY 13 JULY

1

"What's the matter? You're not scared are you?"

Lauren didn't answer.

She stood gazing out of her bedroom window at the street below, twirling a loose strand of hair between finger and thumb.

Five o'clock on a hot Friday in mid July: the evening rush hour; drivers with their shirt sleeves rolled up and their car windows wound down inching their way up and down Highgate Hill. Snatches of Capital FM and the rhythmic thump of car subwoofers. The throb of engines. Motorbikes weaving their way in between the cars; the Finchley bus, a red double-decker advertising *The London Dungeon*, pulled into the bus stop on the other side of the road. The end of the week. The start of the summer holidays. Time to relax. Be happy.

And then in amongst the cars, bikes and buses transporting the living home to their Friday dinners and fun-filled weekends, a sealed black hearse appeared, like a skeleton at the feast.

Black and shiny, the hearse looked like an overdressed gentleman, suited and buttoned up to the neck, at a party where the dress code was "casual." It bore a wooden coffin with shiny brass handles that glinted in the sun. On top of the coffin lay a bouquet of white lilies.

Lauren leaned her forehead against the glass, unable to look away. She felt she ought to do something, show her respects in some way, but she didn't know how.

Should I say a prayer? Make the sign of the cross?

In the end she just watched the hearse as it climbed up Highgate Hill in first gear, maintaining a stately five miles an hour and creating an even bigger traffic jam than usual in its wake.

Following the coffin was a cortège of two black limos, their darkened windows shut tight against the glare of the evening sun.

A strange time of day for a funeral, thought Lauren, the middle of rush hour.

"Well then?" The voice more insistent this time.

Lauren turned away from the window. "Sorry. There was a coffin. I..." She trailed off. The blank look on her friends' faces told her that neither of them was the least bit interested in a funeral procession. "What did you say?"

"I said, you're not scared are you?"

"No. Should I be?" It came out sharper than she'd intended. Maybe she *was* scared. She was certainly uncomfortable about the idea.

Megan and Chloe were sitting on Lauren's bedroom floor, Megan lounging on her side propped up on one elbow, Chloe sitting cross-legged. Between them lay a wooden board.

When school had broken up for the summer earlier that afternoon they'd hung out in Waterlow Park eating ice-creams and then Megan said she had something she absolutely had to show them, but they needed to be somewhere quiet, not in the middle of the park. So they went to Lauren's house because that was the nearest and that was when Megan produced the wooden board from her bag.

Typical of Megan to suggest something like this. Brave, confident Megan who would dare to do anything.

Megan was always compelling them to do things, always wanting to push the boundaries. Like that time last summer when they'd dolled themselves up to the eyeballs and sweet-talked their way into a nightclub for over-twenty-ones even though they were only fifteen. Megan had done all the talking, assisted by a top that plunged so low Lauren wouldn't have dared wear it.

And now this.

Megan and Chloe were both looking up at her, waiting for an answer. It was Megan, of course, who had asked the question.

Lauren wondered what Chloe thought of Megan's latest hare-brained idea but Chloe was too pliable and always willing to go along with whatever Megan suggested. Chloe looked down and started fiddling with a piece of loose skin on the edge of her fingernail.

Lauren cleared her throat and tried to sound relaxed. "No, of course I'm not scared, I just think these things can be a bit…" she searched for the right word to use. *Dangerous* sounded melodramatic. *Spooky* made her sound like a frightened six-year old on Halloween. In the end she plumped for, "…weird."

"Oh, that's all right then," said Chloe looking up from her fingernail with a nervous giggle. "I thought you were going to say you thought it was dangerous or spooky."

Lauren felt herself reddening. *I didn't speak those words out loud, did I?* She put a hand to her cheek, feeling its warmth. She didn't believe in telepathy. It was all a load of nonsense.

"You OK?" asked Chloe.

"Yeah. Sure."

Calm down. Chloe just happened to be thinking what I was thinking but she's given the game away by saying the words out loud. She's just as nervous as I am.

"I'll take that as a 'no' then," said Megan. "Come on, let's get on with it. We haven't got all day." She sat up, shaking out her hair which today was dyed black with a single peroxide streak down one side.

Still not entirely convinced but feeling less of a fool now she knew Chloe was also jittery, Lauren sat down on the floor. The opening line of Macbeth, which they had been studying in school, drifted into her mind – *When shall we three meet again* – but she pushed the thought away. They weren't witches after all. This wasn't magic.

They were sitting around a battered old Ouija board. Megan proudly told them how she spied it at Portobello market and bought it for a couple of quid after haggling with the stallholder to reduce his price by fifty percent. *Wicked*, she called it when she pulled it out of her school bag, holding it up proudly like a work of art.

Lauren had immediately felt uncomfortable. She distrusted anything to do with the occult and wished that Megan hadn't brought it round. But here they were preparing to *contact the other side* as Megan laughingly put it. Megan had got her way, as usual.

The rectangular wooden board measured about eighteen inches by twelve, its surface worn smooth through years of use. The letters A to M were engraved in an old fashioned script in an arc in the top half of the board and the letters N to Z in an arc in the bottom half. In a row between the two arcs of letters were the ten digits 0 to 9. The words *Yes, No, Hello* and *Goodbye* were engraved in the four corners of the board. Intertwining vines decorated the border and the words *Magical Talking Board* were carved along the bottom. In the centre of the board lay the planchette; a flat heart-shaped piece of wood with a small star engraved on the top. Neither Lauren nor Chloe had yet dared touch it.

"Will this work in daylight?" asked Chloe. "I thought séances were normally done in the dark."

"Not this sort of séance," said Megan. "It only needs to be dark if you're trying to make a spirit materialize." Lauren couldn't tell if Megan was being serious or sarcastic.

"Besides," continued Megan, "if we wait 'til it's dark we won't be able to see the letters on the board."

"Fair enough," conceded Chloe. "But should we hold hands? Or sing a song? You know, like a hymn?"

Megan frowned. "That's just mumbo-jumbo. Look, it's simple. Put your right index finger on the planchette and see what happens." Megan thrust her finger forward and rested it on the planchette as if to demonstrate. She looked up at the others. "Go on then." First Chloe and then Lauren placed the tips of their right index fingers on the planchette. They waited.

Nothing happened.

"We need to ask a question," said Megan. She turned to Lauren. "Since we're doing this in your house, you can ask the first question."

Oh great!

Being a passive participant was one thing, but being responsible for asking the first question made Lauren feel like she was being picked on in class. She tried to think of something original and witty to ask. Something that would make them laugh. This was all too serious. But her mind was a blank. She closed her eyes and tried to think.

Nothing.

She was about to tell Megan to think of a question herself since it had been *her* idea, when a question popped into her head.

That's a total cliché, you can't ask that. Think of something else for goodness' sake.

But she couldn't think of anything else and the question wouldn't go away. It was the only question they could ask.

She wanted to say she thought the whole idea was beyond stupid and she wasn't going to participate any more but instead she heard herself saying, "Is there anybody there?"

Silence.

Then, a frisson of movement in her right index finger.

Lauren opened her eyes in astonishment as the planchette started to glide across the board.

2

Tom was struggling to breathe.

He told himself it was the heat but knew it was more to do with the lump in his throat and the pain in his heart. He ran a finger under his too-tight shirt collar, prising it away from his neck which prickled with sweat, and tried to focus his attention on the Vicar of St. Michael's.

He must be melting under that full-length cassock.

Tom imagined the Reverend Martin Andrews reduced to nothing but a black puddle. The vicar's bald head glistened with perspiration and his silver-rimmed reading glasses had slipped down his nose and appeared to be in danger of falling off. He was intoning the words of the Anglican funeral service from the Book of Common Prayer.

Tom tried to tune in to the rise and fall of his voice, but the words coming from the vicar's mouth might as well have been Mandarin Chinese for all Tom was able to make sense of them.

"We shall not all sleep, but we shall all be changed in the twinkling of an eye…"

What on earth did that mean?

There was only one thing that Tom understood.

His dad was dead and was lying, this very minute, in an oak coffin with shiny brass handles, resting on wooden slats above an open grave in Highgate Cemetery.

Tom stared at the coffin, half expecting the lid to

spring open any minute and for his dad to sit up and say, "Fooled you." He remembered his dad telling him about Victorians who were so terrified of being buried alive they had bells placed in their coffins so they could summon assistance if they "woke up." Tom had laughed at their fears and their foolishness. But now, at the sight of his dad's coffin and the thought of the black, airless space inside it, his chest heaved and he gasped for air.

Just hold it together a bit longer, he told himself. He clenched his fists, the nails digging into his palms. He closed his eyes for a moment and tried to distract himself by replaying the events of the day in his mind's eye.

The thud as a pile of sympathy cards hit the doormat; putting on the dark grey polyester suit and black tie his mother had bought from Marks and Spencer two days ago; the arrival sometime in the afternoon of Uncle Bill and his wife Brenda with their five year old twins Patsy and Daisy all the way from Newcastle (was that why the funeral had been arranged so late in the day?); the usual platitudes – *how was the journey? Was the traffic bad on the M1? I'll put the kettle on* – from his mother. Tom couldn't remember if he'd eaten anything for lunch or not. He wasn't hungry now, just thirsty. It was too hot to be wearing a polyester suit.

Then, at five o'clock, the hearse had pulled up outside the house in Cromwell Avenue, the coffin lying in the back adorned with a huge bouquet of lilies. The hearse was accompanied by two black limousines. As they walked down the path to the waiting cars Tom was aware of the neighbours' curtains twitching. A funeral, it seemed, was as entertaining as a wedding. Tom and his mother climbed into the first limo, Uncle Bill and his family into the second.

Tom had always wanted to travel in one of those white stretch limos like a movie star on the way to the Oscars. He had pictured himself stretched out in the back with a glass of champagne in one hand and a remote control for the DVD player in the other. But his first ride in a limousine had been in a black one on the way to his dad's funeral and the idea of a white limo and champagne now seemed shamefully trivial, almost obscene.

The drive up Highgate Hill had been excruciatingly slow and Tom was all too aware of the huge traffic jam they had caused, at rush hour of all times, the hearse bearing his dad's coffin keeping to an unflinching five miles an hour. They might as well have opted for a horse drawn carriage like the Victorians did. *Dad would have liked that.* The thought almost made Tom smile.

During the funeral service in the church, Tom had wondered on more than one occasion if the vicar had muddled his dad up with some other deceased person. Tom simply didn't recognise the man the vicar talked about as his dad. The scholarly academic the vicar described sounded dull and pedantic and wasn't the dad Tom remembered – the fun-loving, outdoorsy person who liked to go mountain biking with his son or boating on the Serpentine in Hyde Park. Where had the vicar got this description from? His mother?

The church service had finished with endless hand-shaking and condolences from people Tom had never met before and then the undertaker, an unobtrusive man who looked like he wore black every day of his life, had ushered them back into the limousines for the short drive down Swain's Lane to the cemetery gates.

The cars glided through the Victorian gothic entrance and came to rest in front of a semi-circular colonnade of arches. The undertakers slid the coffin out of the hearse and the funeral party proceeded on foot up a flight of stone steps into a world of twisted, old trees, dappled sunlight and stone angels. Either side of the path, ivy-clad gravestones vied for space with one another and top-heavy urns threatened to topple from crumbling pedestals. A real Victorian Valhalla. It was easy to believe that ghosts roamed here at night.

Tom opened his eyes and scanned the faces of the mourners gathered around the graveside. Uncle Bill, his father's younger brother, stood at the foot of the grave, shoulders back and chin thrust out, staring straight ahead. There were other members of the extended family that Tom barely recognised, a great aunt, a second cousin, whatever – it made Tom's head hurt to try and remember who they all were. His dad's best mates from the local Highgate cricket club, John and Mike, looked stricken. One of them, Tom could never remember which, had been best man at his parents' wedding.

Then there were his dad's work colleagues. Alan Nesbit, Professor of History at University College London where his dad worked (*had worked*, Tom reminded himself) was a pale, gaunt-faced man in his late fifties. He stood slightly apart from the main group, gazing down on the open grave with deep-set, hooded eyes as if he was an impartial observer of the scene being enacted in front of him, and not one of the chief mourners. Tom had met Alan Nesbit on a couple of occasions when his dad had taken him into the department but he wasn't someone you warmed to. His dad had hoped to become Professor when Nesbit retired but of course that wouldn't happen now.

Richard Newgate, the college principal, was a much jollier looking chap and, judging from his stout figure and florid complexion, enjoyed a pint or two. Then there was a younger woman, probably in her mid-thirties, with a ginger bob who had introduced herself as Nancy Letts, the department secretary. For a moment, at the entrance to the church, it seemed as if Nancy was about to throw her arms around Tom in an outburst of sympathy but then suddenly, without warning, she burst into tears causing her mascara to smudge. Much to Tom's relief Richard Newgate had escorted her away to the pews without another word.

To Tom's right his mother stood bolt upright, dressed in a tailored black suit, her face partially obscured by the black lace veil which hung like a spider's web from the brim of her hat. She clasped a black Chanel bag in both hands. Tom supposed she was putting a brave face on things, but, to be honest, he didn't really know.

The fact was, he had been much closer to his dad than he was to his mother. It was Dad who really mattered in his life, Dad who had taught him how to do all the important things like ride a bike, swim a length, make a successful rugby tackle. It was Dad who had helped him with his homework, explained algebra to him, chemistry formulae, Newton's laws of motion and the history of the Second World War. His mother was a somewhat distant figure, always busy with the fashion boutique she ran on Highgate High Street. They had a succession of au pairs to do the housework but the current one had returned to Poland for her sister's wedding and was not due back until the end of the summer. Tom glanced across at his mother's immobile face and tried to imagine how they were going to get along without his dad. He couldn't do it. He and his mother were too much like strangers who happened to live in the same house.

The vicar stopped speaking and lowered the prayer book. The silence startled Tom and made him look up. *What now?* Beside him his mother clutched her handbag even closer to her body, the knuckles of her hands turning white. Richard Newgate adjusted his stance, cleared his throat and clasped his hands behind his back as if bracing himself for the next part of the ceremony. Nancy Letts made discreet sniffing noises and dabbed at her eyes with a tissue. Only Alan Nesbit stood as rigid as one of the stone angels that adorned the cemetery.

Tom wished the vicar would resume his reading or say a prayer, anything to fill the uncomfortable silence that had descended on the party of mourners. But instead he inclined his head towards the undertaker who had been waiting, forgotten, in the background.

With practised ease, the pallbearers, looking strangely

old-fashioned in their black frock coats and top hats, stepped forward and took their places around the coffin, two on either side. They stood precariously close to the open ground, the tips of their black, polished shoes jutting over the edge. Then they lifted the coffin by the straps that were slotted through the handles and held it aloft whilst the undertaker and his assistant removed the wooden slats that had lain across the hole in the ground. Then the pallbearers started to lower the coffin, inch by inch, into the grave.

For a moment Tom was mesmerised by this well-practised performance that proceeded wordlessly, but then, as the top of the coffin started to disappear from view he felt his heart start to thump as if it were trying to break out of his ribcage and he realised he'd never expected things to go this far.

He looked around the group of mourners, desperate to catch someone's eye. But everyone was staring at the ground. No one had noticed the panic in his face.

Tom wanted to shout, *Stop, we can't bury him yet. This is all wrong. We still don't know how he died. We think we do but we don't. The police were wrong. I'll prove it.*

But his tongue was stuck to the roof of his mouth and his throat was so constricted he could hardly breathe. He tried to raise a hand but his limbs felt heavy and lifeless, like in a dream when you want to run or shout but can't move. Yet this wasn't a dream. It was all too real. A living nightmare.

The pallbearers continued lowering the coffin, gliding the straps through their hands.

How deep is it, for crying out loud? Surely they've reached the bottom by now?

The vicar resumed his reading. "We therefore commit his body to the ground; earth to earth, ashes to ashes, dust to dust." It was too late now for Tom to say or do anything. The coffin had vanished from view. The pallbearers stepped away, melting back into the cemetery landscape.

His mother unclasped her handbag and took out a single white rose. She kissed it once then threw it into the grave. Tom hadn't known she was going to do that.

Uncle Bill took the spade that the undertaker held out to him and, with a shake of his head, threw the first clod of earth onto the coffin. He handed the spade back and turned away, wiping his eyes with the back of his hand.

This is it then, thought Tom. *Goodbye Dad.*

As tears started to blur his vision Tom turned away.

A movement in the distance caught his eye. He thought he saw a figure in black, flitting between the trees, but he couldn't be sure. He wiped his eyes, but when he looked again whatever it was had gone.

A blue butterfly fluttered into his line of vision. He watched its beating wings as it circled over the grave, then came to rest on the edge, like a tiny guardian angel.

3

Reflections of Will Bucket, Gravedigger, In the Year of Our Lord 1870.

It's dirty work and backbreaking. But as I always says at least it's what you'd call *regular.* Couldn't fault it on that score. We might get a dozen burials a day and when the weather's real bad that can go up to twenty, even thirty, or more. A winter cold enough to freeze the balls off a donkey and they're dropping like flies. Then me and Big Bert has to work extra hard digging fresh graves or lifting the stone slabs on family tombs so as the next dead relative can go in on top. We'll never be out of work here at Highgate Cemetery, you mark my word.

But it ain't all mud and digging and dead bodies. Oh, no. It ain't just dead'uns what come here. There's plenty of living folk too and working here gives me chance to have a good gawp at all sorts of people. Don't get me wrong. I don't mean to be disrespectful, like. I just think people are interesting. As me old man says, *Will*, he says, *there's nowt so queer as folk*.

So when me and Big Bert have dug our share of graves for the day I likes to stand by one of them trees close to the path that leads from the Dissenters down to the main courtyard. From there you don't half get a splendid view of the funeral cortèges as they come in through the cemetery gates from Swain's Lane. And there ain't nuffink like a funeral cortège for a bit of pomp and ceremony - plumes of black ostrich feathers on the horses' heads; them deaf mutes with their wands; the coffin on display in its glass-sided carriage; the mourning carriages with the next-o'-kin and then, more mourners on foot. Some cortèges are so huge it's a right palaver getting all them horses and carriages in and turned around. The mourners are all togged up in black silk trimmed with crêpe and they gather under the arches of the colonnade at the back of the courtyard before they follow the coffin up the steps into the cemetery proper.

When you get a *Lord So-And-So* or a *Lady This-Or-That* being buried then there's a right old crush of horses, carriages and whatnot and the mourners, especially the women, are dressed to the nines in enough silk and crêpe to clothe a family of twelve.

But we do get more modest funerals of course. Families who cling to each other for support. Young widows. Young widowers come to that. I always gets the feeling their sorrow is more genuine than the fancy displays put on for the benefit of some dead big-wig whose relatives are likely as not going to start arguing over the contents of the will before the day is out.

But it's the kiddies what gets me.

I wouldn't say I was a softie – can't afford to be doing this job - but still the sight of them tiny coffins is enough to break a lad's heart.

And then there was that lady.

Not much younger than me I reckon, about nineteen.

15

She weren't dead, of course. Though she were none too perky, come to that.

There I am watching the funeral cortège of a gentleman who's made his fortune importing tea from China and is off to spend the rest of his days in a catacomb in the Egyptian Avenue when I sees this young lady hovering nearby on the path.

I doffs me cap to her, thinking she must be one of the mourners at the funeral of the rich gentleman but then she takes a step towards me and looks at me with such sad eyes that I looks at her and says as politely as I can, "May I be of assistance, Miss?"

"I think you can," was all she says.

Well, I waits for her to speak, thinking now that she ain't with the funeral party after all and maybe she wants directions to a particular grave or catacomb. I knows this place like the back of me hand and I would've been delighted to escort such a pretty young lady anywhere she wanted to go – the Egyptian Avenue, the Circle of Lebanon, the Dissenters' section (some people are a bit funny about that but I ain't got nuffink against them) – but she don't ask me for directions.

Instead she takes a step closer and whispers so as I hardly hears her.

"Can you meet me here this evening? At dusk?"

Well, I don't know what to say to *that*. She don't look like no strumpet. It's obvious from her plain but nice clothes and well-spoken voice that she's well bred – not like them lassies up at the penitentiary what used to flog their wares down the West End, if you get me meaning.

"Bring your spade, please," she adds softly before turning away and walking down the hill towards the main gate.

I wants to call after her to ask what she means, but she's gone and I don't want to disturb the mourners climbing down from their carriages in the courtyard.

Me spade? What does she want I asks myself? Some

digging by the sound of it.

Well, that was a week ago now and I still ain't sure if I done right or wrong. I lies awake at night sometimes thinking about it.

She didn't want me to dig nuffink up, thank goodness, 'cause if she had I'd've had to say *No* and I don't like saying *No* to a lady. No, turned out she had sumfink she wanted buried. A tiny bundle, no bigger than a bunch of rags. And I thinks to myself, this ain't right, this ain't proper and I starts to protest but she lays a hand on me arm, and there is such a look of sadness in them eyes of hers that me heart goes out to her and I says, "Follow me, Miss."

I takes her down to a real quiet spot on the edge of the cemetery, a long way from the main gate. It's one of me favourite spots, by the statue of the sleeping angel. I gets to work and I digs a hole real quick, right next to the angel. Then she lays this bundle of rags in the hole, says a quick prayer, and she tells me to fill it in, which I do.

Then I escorts her back to the gate 'cause you wouldn't want to get locked in the cemetery after dark. We gets there just in time before the gates are locked for the night. She turns to me and presses a sovereign into me palm. I tries to say I don't want no money 'cause I gets paid for the work I do by the London Cemetery Company but she turns and runs down Swain's Lane and I can't run after her without Mr Hills, the superintendent, asking awkward questions 'cause he's standing by the gate talking to a gentleman.

I haven't spent the money. It don't seem right. I'll look out for her and if I see her I'll give it back or tell her to give it to charity.

Now, when I gets a minute I go over to the sleeping angel and makes sure the spot is kept nice'n tidy. There ain't no cross or nuffink to mark whatever's buried down there but the sleeping angel will keep it safe.

I think the lady must've been back to visit though

'cause the other day I found a small bunch of primroses laid there.

If anyone asks, I'll have to say I don't know nuffink.

4

"Who the hell is Isabelle Hart?" asked Lauren, snatching her finger away from the planchette as if it was burning her. Her heart was thumping like crazy and she felt seriously freaked out. She hadn't expected the planchette to move at all, had rather hoped the séance would fail so they could put the Ouija board away and do something normal instead like listen to some music and gossip about their classmates.

But the planchette had glided effortlessly across the Ouija board spelling out the name of someone called *Isabelle Hart* and then, on reaching the final "t" had stopped abruptly, its energy spent.

Megan was grinning insanely. "That was amazing. This thing really works. Did you see how it moved so definitely, spelling out every letter? Cool."

Lauren stared at her. How could Megan be so unfazed by this eerie event? Unless…

"Oh, OK," said Lauren. "I get it. You've set us up haven't you Megan? You had me fooled for a while there." She tried to laugh, but it sounded forced.

Megan glared at her. "What are you saying? That I cheated? That I moved the planchette deliberately?" Megan looked really angry.

"No, no, I'm sorry," said Lauren, backing down. "I didn't mean to say you were cheating." She sighed. "Look, this has freaked me out, that's all, and I'm just trying to find an explanation for what happened." She glanced at Chloe who looked pale and wide-eyed.

"OK," said Lauren, taking a deep breath. "Let's think about this logically. Maybe one of us has read about or heard of someone called Isabelle Hart? Maybe one of us was sub-consciously guiding the planchette? Like, we made it work because we wanted it to work, if you see what I mean."

"Bollocks," said Megan.

Lauren ignored her and turned to Chloe. "What do you think?"

Chloe shook her head. "Sorry, I've never heard of her. That was well weird though."

Understatement of the year.

Lauren stood up and went back to the window.

The funeral cortège was long gone but the traffic was still crawling slower than a tortoise rally. A blue butterfly landed on the window sill. Lauren watched it, noticing the pale ivory dots on its wings, and tried to think. Had she heard the name *Isabelle Hart* before? She didn't think so, and yet already the name was sounding familiar, like a case of delayed déjà vu.

"Are you OK Lauren?" The concern in Chloe's voice made Lauren pull herself together.

"Yeah, sure."

Megan looked at her watch. "Let's ask one more question. I've got ten minutes before I start work at the café."

"Go on then," said Chloe, who seemed to have recovered from her initial state of shock. "Just one more."

With a heavy heart Lauren took her place beside the others. It was obvious what the next question should be and Chloe asked it as soon as they had all laid their fingers on the planchette.

"What do you want?"

The answer was quick and clear. The planchette moved across the board spelling out a single word.

Justice.

5

It was already late by the time the funeral guests arrived at the house in Cromwell Avenue.

Tom's mother had pulled out all the stops, arranging for the local delicatessen to lay on a magnificent spread including smoked salmon, roasted peppers, stuffed olives, Cajun chicken and five different flavours of ciabatta. Bottles of wine and beer adorned the sideboard. Tom thought the quantity of food and drink more appropriate for a birthday celebration than a funeral wake but he kept his thoughts to himself.

He played the part of a dutiful waiter, wandering around the room with a blank expression, offering platters of food to the guests and eavesdropping on fragments of conversation. With a drop or two of alcohol inside them most people had cheered up considerably.

Good sport was Jack...Remember that time he dressed up in a lion's costume and ran the London Marathon...We'll miss him on the cricket team...Must have been a dreadful shock for the family...Do you think Deborah will sell the house? It's a bit big for just her and Tom.

This last comment was spoken by one of the distant relatives to one of the other distant relatives in a hushed, confidential tone. Tom pretended not to hear and moved on with his platter of king prawns before the relatives started trying to guess the value of the property or speculate as to the contents of his dad's will.

His mother was pouring herself another glass of wine. How many had she had? Too many judging by the way she was laughing at something Richard Newgate had said.

Nancy Letts, mascara restored, was nibbling a chocolate cupcake and regaling the next door neighbours, Sheila and Tony, with an anecdote about how Jack had lost his lecture notes on a conference in Rome and had phoned her in a panic five minutes before he was due to give the inaugural lecture, asking her to fax him through his notes on Disraeli's life and career. But it had been a bad line and she'd sent him something on Raleigh instead. That was in the days before smart phones and email.

Only Professor Nesbit remained as dour and taciturn as he had been at the graveside. He stood in the corner of the room, a solitary figure, methodically picking up and examining each book on the bookcase in turn. Tom offered him a smoked salmon sandwich which he declined without so much as a "No thank you."

Tom didn't eat a thing. He wondered how much longer the wake was going to go on.

Then, as if an unseen hand were ringing a bell, people started looking at their watches and saying, "Goodness me, is that the time?" There was a collective gathering up of coats and bags and shuffling of feet towards the front door. Then more handshaking and kind words.

You'll have to take his place on the cricket team (Mike and John)...*My door is always open to you* (Richard Newgate)...*Must get together more often, not just at christenings and funerals* (distant relatives.) A suffocating hug from Nancy Letts and a formal handshake and nod of the head from Professor Nesbit.

Then they were gone.

Silence descended on the house like a shroud.

His mother closed the front door and made her way back into the dining room, swaying slightly from side to side. For the first time in hours it was just the two of them. She was obviously drunk. Tom shifted from one foot to another and bent down to pick up a prawn that someone had dropped. Dirty plates and wine glasses littered the room.

Tom watched as his mother walked past him, seemingly oblivious to his presence, reached for her wine glass which she had left on the mantelpiece and poured the remains of a bottle of red into it. Wasn't she going to say anything? Anything at all?

He wanted her to look at him, listen to what he had to

say. There were things he'd kept bottled inside but which were now threatening to explode in a torrent. But she did not look at him. In the end he spoke to her back.

"I think the police got it wrong." His voice sounded too loud in the silent house, but now that he'd started he had to go on. "I don't believe Dad's death was an accident and it certainly wasn't suicide. DCI McNally didn't do a thorough job. We should go back to the police and demand they re-examine the evidence."

His mother downed the wine in one gulp and set the glass down on the sideboard, knocking over a batch of sympathy cards. "Not now, Tom." Her voice sounded brittle. She held up a hand. "I'm tired. I'm going to bed." And before he could say another word she turned and walked out of the room.

Damn! If not now, then when?

Why didn't she want to talk about his dad's death? She had accepted the police explanation all too easily as far as Tom was concerned. If you could even call it an explanation, which Tom seriously doubted. Tom certainly didn't accept it. Something about the whole affair wasn't right and the thought kept gnawing at him, kept him awake at night.

He pulled out a chair and sat down. He needed to think. *What would Dad do?*

The answer rose to his mind as clear as if his dad was in the room talking to him.

Go and investigate.

Yes, that's what his dad would do. As a historian it was his job to investigate the past. His dad had always been rummaging around in the archives at the British Library. But, Tom knew, the further back in the past something was, the harder it was to investigate it. So there was no better time to start than the present. Right now in fact.

Tom stood up, knocking over an empty wine glass. He picked it up and placed it on the table. The room was strewn with dirty dishes. Well that wasn't his problem. The washing up could wait until the morning. Tom had more important matters to be dealing with. Like solving the mystery of his dad's death.

But where to start?

Again, the answer rose unbidden to his mind.

Dad's study.

But I haven't been in there since before…

His dad used the converted loft room at the top of the house as a study. It was so full of reminders of his dad that he hadn't been able to face going in there yet. Was he ready to do it now? He wasn't sure, but then he thought of the coffin being lowered into the ground and he made up his mind.

He walked out of the dining room and along the hallway to the foot of the stairs, pausing for a moment by the newel post. The house was silent. Maybe his mother really had gone to bed. He hoped she had because he didn't want to be disturbed.

He didn't bother with the light, but crept up the stairs, tip-toed across the landing, and continued up the spiral staircase that led to his dad's study. The door was closed. He took a deep breath, turned the handle, pushed open the door and stepped quickly inside.

A crowd of memories rushed to greet him, almost knocking him off his feet. Dad sitting at his desk by the window tapping on the computer keyboard; or reading a book in the room's one comfy armchair; or running his finger along the spines of the many volumes that lined the walls from floor to ceiling. A half-drunk mug of coffee sat on the floor by the comfy chair. A faint odour of his dad's aftershave lingered in the air.

Much as he would have liked to, Tom resisted the urge to curl up in the armchair and wallow in memories. Instead he walked over to the desk, a slightly battered but still beautiful mahogany bureau from a local antique shop, and sat down in the leather swivel chair. Centre-stage was an old desktop computer. To one side was a three-tier in-tray piled high with papers. He pulled the tray forwards and started leafing through the contents, even though he had no idea what he was looking for. But he remembered his dad saying it was important, in research, to always keep an open mind. The top level of the tray contained a pile of admin stuff from the university – minutes of faculty meetings (they didn't look like a bundle of laughs), lengthy examination procedures (clearly written by someone with a broom up their backside), and a memo about the funding for the new student cafeteria. The middle and bottom layers contained stacks of marked and unmarked student essays. He pushed the tray back into its place.

He toyed with the idea of booting up the computer and having a look at his dad's email but something held him back. It seemed a bit too intrusive on the day of the funeral. Maybe later. He picked up a memory stick that was lying on the desk, holding it between his thumb and forefinger. Was it likely to contain any relevant information? It was probably just a back-up of the computer's hard-drive. He put it back down and made a mental note to come back to it tomorrow.

Then he noticed an envelope poking out from under the keyboard. Tom pulled it out. Crisp, white paper, not your usual flimsy junk mail. It was stamped with the initials "UCL" in bold type. University College, London. Tom peeled back the seal and pulled out the card that was inside. It was an invitation. To a dinner.

Professor Barlow
Invites
Dr Jack Kelsey
To his retirement dinner
Friday 22nd June 2012, 8pm
University College, London.
Dress is Black Tie
RSVP by Friday 8th June 2012

Tom stared at the card as if it was a death warrant, which in a way it had been. Attending this dinner was the last thing his dad had done. His last supper. Like a condemned man. Although, of course, neither Tom nor his dad had known that at the time.

Tom thought back to that evening. His dad had popped his head around the living room door in the middle of Top Gear, looking like a middle-aged James Bond in his dinner jacket and black bow tie – *I'll be off now. Don't wait up. See you in the morning.* At the time Tom had been paying more attention to Jeremy Clarkson, something which he deeply regretted now. *OK, Dad. See you.* Then he'd gone. Forever.

Tom stood up as tears started to blur his vision. This investigation was going to be hard. He pocketed the invitation, then went and sat in the comfy chair to give himself a moment to recover. Some reading glasses were perched at a precarious angle on top of two books on the small round table by the side of the chair. Tom folded the glasses and laid them to one side, then picked up the top book. *Death and Burials in Victorian London* by Mark N. Knight. He glanced at the blurb on the back cover – *In this book Mark N. Knight explores Victorian attitudes to death and burial* - not exactly a page-turner by the look of it. He opened it up and saw that it had been borrowed from the local public library which was a bit odd since his dad had access to thousands of books at the university. He checked the date the book was due back.

Fourteenth of July. Tomorrow.

No problem. He could take it back in the morning. It would be good to have a reason to get out of the house.

He picked up the second book in case that too was a library book that needed returning.

It wasn't.

It was something altogether quite different. It was old. Very old by the look of it. It was bound in soft black leather and had no writing on the cover and when he opened it up it smelled musty as if it had been kept too long in a cellar. It wasn't a printed book but was handwritten in a florid, old-fashioned script that Tom struggled to read. The ink had faded to a dull brown, like an old sepia photograph and in places was smudged. The entries were all dated 1870.

A diary.

Tom turned to the flyleaf at the front of the book. Someone, presumably the writer of the diary, had written their name. The first letter was a funny shape, more like a "J" but Tom guessed it had to be an "I" for the word to make sense. It looked like *Isabelle Hart*.

PART TWO
SATURDAY 14 JULY

6

A dense forest of tall, thin trees towered into the sky, their canopies shrouding the path, blocking out what remained of the fading daylight. Soon it would be dark as the grave. A fox scurried in the undergrowth, rustling dead leaves. Bats flitted overhead like miniature cloaked vampires. Somewhere an owl hooted.

Lauren inched forward, her skin prickling. She stubbed her toes on gnarled roots that rose out of the ground like giant skeletal fingers. Brambles snagged at her clothes, impeding her progress. Thorns scratched her bare legs.

She was searching for a way out of the forest. She was lost.

With a mounting sense of panic she turned around and started at the sight of a skull. Carved onto a stone. A tombstone.

This wasn't a forest, then, but a graveyard.

She had to escape. She tried to run. But now the trees

were metamorphosing into stone columns, bushes were solidifying into urns. Stone angels with unseeing eyes loomed out of the shadows, pointing with petrified fingers towards Heaven.

Lauren stumbled forwards.

Then stopped.

She had come to a clearing where the moonlight shone on a stone angel lying asleep on her side. In front of the angel, a figure was kneeling. A woman. The woman must have sensed Lauren's presence because she stood up and turned around.

She was young with a pale face, skin like ivory. Her long, dark hair fell over her shoulders in loose curls. She wore a floor-length black dress that trailed on the ground.

The woman stepped forwards and clasped Lauren's hand in hers. They were stone cold. She spoke in a whisper. "I'm glad you've come. I've been waiting for you. Let me tell you my story…"

Lauren looked into the woman's dark eyes and waited for her to speak.

A rapping sound made her jump.

"Are you awake yet?" Her mum's sing-song voice outside the bedroom door intruded into Lauren's dream. The woman with the pale skin, the angels and the tombstones, all dissolved into a myriad of tiny fragments and blew away.

Lauren groaned and opened her eyes. She hated being woken in the middle of a dream, even a scary one, because she always wanted to know how it would end. It was like someone turning off the television just as the murderer was about to be revealed. Had this dream been scary? The trees and tombstones had made her skin crawl, but the woman's presence had comforted her and Lauren had wanted to know what she was going to say. She felt bereft, as if something of real significance had just been snatched from her grasp. She couldn't shake the feeling that she had been on the verge of learning something important and now it was gone forever.

Never mind, it was only a dream.

She rolled over. The day was already bright. "What time is it?" she called.

"Nine o'clock." Wendy sounded brisk and chirpy, using her *don't-you-think-it's-time-you-got-out-of-bed* voice. "What do you want for breakfast? I can do you an egg."

"Don't worry. Cereal's fine."

Why is she offering to make breakfast? What's going on?

"I'll have it on the table in fifteen minutes. Then we can make a start on the attic."

Ah. The attic.

Lauren had completely forgotten about the attic. Wendy had caught her off guard weeks ago when she was getting ready to go out and was already late. She'd all but erased the conversation from her memory but it came back to her now:

"Will you help me clear the attic in the holidays?"

"What?" (Where did I put my phone?)

"I want to clear the attic so we can turn it into a proper spare room with en-suite. It'll be more convenient for when Gran comes to stay."

(There's the phone under the bed — what's it doing there?) *"Yeah, fine, no problem, sorry, must dash."*

It was the first full day of the summer holidays and, true to form, her mum was wasting no time - the day of the great attic clear-out had arrived.

The attic makeover was just the next in a line of projects Wendy had planned, *to give them a fresh start.* She had already redecorated every room downstairs. Next would come a redesign of the garden, Lauren was sure.

Lauren had agreed to help clear out the attic but she intended to keep well out of the way once the builders started work. She had no intention of making endless cups of tea – *milk, two sugars love* – all summer.

Lauren swung her legs out of bed and stood up. She felt disoriented after the abrupt end to her rather weird dream. In a fug of sleepiness she made her way to the bathroom, slipped off her pyjamas and stepped into the shower. Ten minutes later, feeling more awake, she re-emerged wrapped in a fluffy towel, returned to her bedroom and yanked open the wardrobe door.

No point wearing anything nice today, it'll be filthy up there in the attic. Better not be too many spiders.

She pulled an old pair of cropped jeans off their hanger. As she did so, a silk shirt on the neighbouring hanger slipped down and fell to the wardrobe floor. She bent down to pick it up and saw the Ouija board lying at the bottom of the wardrobe, looking up at her, accusing her of tossing it away like some unwanted piece of junk.

How could she have forgotten? Her dream had been so vivid, it had obliterated all thoughts of yesterday evening. Megan, Chloe, the séance. *Isabelle Hart.*

She knelt down and picked up the board, almost afraid to touch it. Megan had left it behind when she dashed off to go and do her shift at the local café.

Typical Megan – always desperate to try the next new thing and then dropping it half an hour later.

Lauren had thrown the board into the wardrobe, not wanting to look at it and knowing that her mum wouldn't approve of messing around with things like Ouija boards, dabbling with the occult.

No wonder she'd had such a weird dream after her experience with that board though. *Isabelle Hart.* She said the name to herself. Even though the whole thing had freaked her out, Lauren had to admit that Isabelle Hart was a nice name. It suggested someone who was intelligent and kind. It sounded like a character from a nineteenth century novel. Like the woman in her dream.

But still, it was a load of nonsense wasn't it? How could the planchette have spelled out that name? Lauren was still half tempted to believe it was just Megan playing a trick on them. But Megan had denied it so vehemently. Chloe then. Chloe wouldn't have done it deliberately, but she could have subconsciously guided the planchette around the board. Or was there such a thing as group consciousness? Maybe they were all to blame. And *justice?* Where had that come from? They'd probably been watching too many costume dramas and detective series.

She cast her eyes over the board and suddenly she couldn't stop herself picking out the letters of Isabelle's name – I, S, A, B – it was as if the letters were leaping out at her, demanding to be noticed.

She pushed the board to the back of the wardrobe and shut the door with more force than was necessary. She was shaking.

She took a couple of deep breaths and told herself to calm down.

Stop it. It's just a wooden board with the alphabet on it. It doesn't have any special powers. It can't hurt you. Give it back to Megan later today and tell her not to bring it round again.

Maybe a morning clearing out the attic was just what she needed to bring her back to the world of reality. She pulled on the jeans and grabbed an old T-shirt from the chest of drawers before heading downstairs for breakfast. She would put the events of yesterday behind her and move on.

7

Tom blinked open his eyes and stared at the ceiling as he had done every day for the last three weeks. Ever since his dad died he'd woken to a feeling of shock followed by empty numbness. Today, the day after the funeral, was no different. If he could have done, he would have fallen back into the oblivion of sleep, but a fly was buzzing around the room, periodically crashing into the window.

Stupid creature.

Bzzzz. Crash. Bzzzz. Crash.

Tom tried to ignore it but the demented insect was hurling itself at the glass like it was on steroids. He was going to have to open the window and let it out.

He rolled out of bed and kicked over the two books he'd found in his dad's study – the library book and Isabelle Hart's diary. He'd left them on the floor by his bed so he wouldn't forget about them in the morning. Which he had.

He stumbled over to the window and lifted the box sash so the fly could find its way out if it had any sense. Then he sat back down on the edge of his bed and picked up the two books, turning them over in his hands.

The diary intrigued him but he was too tired to read any of it last night and in any case, he wasn't sure he had the patience to decipher the handwriting. As for the library book, he knew the library shut on Saturday afternoons so he'd have to take it back this morning. That was probably a good thing. Doing a normal activity like returning a library book might make him feel more human, instead of like a zombie.

He took a quick shower, pulled on a pair of jeans and a blue T-shirt, and ran his fingers through his blond hair that was getting long and starting to fall in front of his eyes. Then he crept past his mother's closed door, hoping she wasn't awake. He wasn't in the mood for another strained conversation.

He pushed open the door to the dining room and reeled at the stench of yesterday's buffet. Stale beer, sour wine, overripe blue cheese, garlic. Tom took a deep breath and walked over to the table, wondering if he could salvage some sort of breakfast from the decomposing remains of the feast.

The cream cheese dips had congealed and the dainty triangular sandwiches had dried and curled at the edges. He suspected the prawns would give him food poisoning. Flies were crawling over the single remaining chicken drumstick.

He helped himself to a handful of cheese biscuits that looked to be the safest things on offer. They were already going soft, but he ate them anyway. Then he went into the kitchen to look for some milk. There was half a pint left in the fridge door. Tom unscrewed the lid and gasped at the sour smell that pierced his nostrils. His mum hadn't been shopping for days. He hurriedly poured the ruined milk down the sink and rinsed it away. Then he filled a glass with tap water and glugged it down. It was too warm because he hadn't let the water run.

So much for a healthy start to the day. He felt sick.

Best to just get outside. His dad had liked to go for a walk when he needed to think and Tom could understand why. Fresh air and open space was what he needed. His mother still hadn't appeared. He wanted to leave before she did.

He ran back up to his room, pulled a backpack out of his wardrobe and put the library book and the diary inside. Then he grabbed his keys and his phone and left the house, slamming the door shut behind him.

8

The attic was just as filthy as Lauren had feared. And stifling.

Wendy had opened the one small window, which overlooked Highgate Hill, but it was going to be another hot day and there was no breeze.

A film of grey dust covered all the boxes, and thick sticky cobwebs clung to the corners where the ceiling sloped down to meet the walls. A small tarnished mirror with a gilt frame hung on one wall. A single bare bulb dangled from the central ceiling rafter which looked as if it was rotting away.

Since they had moved in, the room had only been used for storing junk and Lauren was struggling to see how it could be transformed into a guest suite where someone would actually want to stay. But the builder, Neil, had persuaded Wendy he could do a good job – *no problem, love, bit of plumbing and a bit of plaster board and I'll 'ave this place transformed in a jiff. You see if I don't.*

Wendy was pulling old curtains out of a trunk and stuffing them into black bin liners. "Ah, there you are," she said, as Lauren stepped around piles of boxes. "I've made a start because I've only got the morning free. I'm on duty at the cemetery at twelve." When her mum wasn't working as a NHS manager at the local Whittington hospital she worked as a volunteer for the charity that ran Highgate Cemetery, the Friends of Highgate Cemetery as they were called. As well as organising new burials, they also saw to the restoration and maintenance of the existing graves and monuments, and conducted guided tours to members of the public.

"We're incredibly busy at the cemetery at the moment," said Wendy, rolling up the curtains that Lauren had had in her room as a baby and adding them to the nearest plastic bag. "There seem to be more visitors than ever wanting to go on the guided tours. I'm helping Alice create a computer database of all the burial plots so we know exactly who's where and now we've got a broken railing on Swain's Lane that needs fixing." She turned back to the trunk and pulled out a moth eaten blanket made of knitted squares. "Oh dear, that was your gran's. Oh well, never mind." She added it to the bag and bent down to retrieve the next forgotten object.

Lauren hoped her mum wasn't overdoing things. She'd always been a workaholic but it had only got worse since Dad had left six months ago to go and live in France with his new partner.

Lauren looked around at the piles of boxes and old furniture and felt her heart sink. *Why do we still have all this junk? Why didn't we dump it when we moved here ten years ago?*

"Where do you want me to start?" she asked trying to sound more enthusiastic than she felt.

"How about those boxes over there?" Wendy pointed to a pile of eight large cardboard boxes stacked in one corner. They were stamped with the name of the removal firm they'd used when they moved here. Never unpacked.

Right here goes.

Lauren tore the tape off the first box, pulled back the flaps and delved inside. It contained embarrassingly frilly dresses from when she was a little girl and T-shirts with pink hearts or cuddly animals on the front.

Did I wear this stuff?

She rammed the clothes into a bin bag and moved onto the next box.

This one was even worse. Baby clothes, for goodness' sake - romper suits, bootees and bibs. Lauren was mystified. Why keep all this? Lauren opened her mouth to ask Wendy why she hadn't thrown these things out years ago, then stopped herself. It was obvious, really. Her mum must have been hoping for another baby one day but that day had never come. Lauren was an only child. The realisation made her pause. She felt a pang of sympathy for her mum. It would have been nice to have had a brother or a sister. And now, of course it was out of the question with Dad gone. Lauren didn't want to think about him. She hadn't seen or heard from him in six months and she and Wendy were getting on just fine on their own, thank you very much. She pulled open another plastic bin bag and started filling it with the romper suits and bibs. She'd take the bags to Oxfam later.

Lauren put the two bin bags full of her old clothes out on the landing and folded the empty boxes flat so they could be put into the recycling.

Now there was more floor space it would be easier to sort through the remaining boxes. She stepped into the newly created empty space and was suddenly thrown off balance as the floor gave way beneath her.

Crash.

She fell into a box overflowing with Christmas decorations – silver tinsel, shiny red baubles, a tangle of Christmas lights.

"You OK?" asked Wendy, jumping to her feet.

"Er, yes, I think so," said Lauren pushing herself up out of the box.

What on earth happened there?

She looked at the spot where she had stepped and saw that one of the old floorboards had shifted a couple of inches. The wood was blackened and rotted with age. She bent down and pushed the loose floorboard with her fingers. It rocked up and down like a see-saw.

Something stirred at the back of her mind. A memory. Probably something she'd read in a children's book a long time ago. She glanced at Wendy who had returned to sorting through the trunk and was kneeling with her back to her.

Lauren examined the floorboard more closely. It was short, only about two feet long. She pressed one end and the opposite end lifted about six inches. It was pivoting in the middle on the underlying floor joist, but that didn't mean it was attached to the joist.

Lauren slipped her fingertips in at either end of the board. There was just enough space for her to get a grip on the wood. Then she started to lift the board up, praying that she wouldn't dislodge an extended family of spiders living underneath.

There was nothing there. Just the wooden beam of the joist supporting the floorboards and a quantity of dust and dead insects.

Disappointed that she hadn't discovered a bundle of Victorian love letters or a bag of gold, Lauren was about to replace the board when she noticed something pushed just beyond the gap left by the loose floorboard.

She put the floorboard to one side and lowered her face to the floor to get a better look. There was something there after all.

A box.

It was hidden in the space between the ceiling of the room below and the joist supporting the attic floor. It looked like it had been there for a very long time.

With a beating heart Lauren reached down and very carefully lifted it out.

9

Tom crossed over Highgate Hill and entered Waterlow Park. The shouts and laughter of children's voices reached him and he was reminded of how his dad used to bring him here as a small child to play on the swings. The memory brought a lump to his throat and he hurried past the kiddies' playground, keeping his head down.

He exited the park on Swain's Lane and found himself opposite the grand Victorian entrance to Highgate Cemetery.

Why had he come this way? It was hard to imagine that only yesterday he'd swept through those same gates in the back of a black limousine following the hearse bearing his father's coffin.

The mood outside the cemetery was quite different now. Tourists in jeans and T-shirts, cameras at the ready, were already gathering for the first of the hourly tours that ran at the weekends. Strange, in a way, that the cemetery should be so popular, that people should want to walk amongst old gravestones and crumbling monuments.

Tom thought of his dad lying six feet under on the other side of the wall. The grave would be completely filled in by now, the pile of fresh earth the only clue that here was a new body, come to join the thousands of others buried here. It was absurd, he knew, but Tom hoped that the existing residents would welcome the new arrival. Make him feel at home.

Tom moved on, keen now to get away from the tourists. As grave owners, he and his mother were entitled to enter the cemetery at any time during the hours of daylight. But Tom didn't want to go back yet. It was too soon. The memory too raw.

He walked down Swain's Lane, alongside the railings that marked the boundary of the East Cemetery. Karl Marx was in there. He imagined his dad conducting a ghostly debate with Marx on the effects of Communism in Eastern Europe. Or maybe he'd be discussing advances in science with Michael Faraday who was buried in the Dissenters' section of the West Cemetery.

At the southern edge of the cemetery, where Swain's Lane met Chester Road, he stopped for a moment. It wasn't as if he was in any hurry to go to the library and back home. What would he do at home all morning? The washing up? Argue with his mother? Avoid her? He checked his watch. It was still only ten o'clock and the library would be open until twelve. On an impulse he turned right instead of left and headed in the direction of Hampstead Heath.

He'd avoided the Heath for the last three weeks, had even thought that he might never go there again, but now he felt drawn to it. He took it as a good sign. It must mean he was ready.

He took the path through the Heath, gazing out on the acres of grass that stretched as far as he could see. This was the place where he and his dad had kicked a ball around at the weekends and where his dad had taught him to ride his bike without stabilizers and where his dad…he pushed the thought from his mind as he doggedly put one foot in front of the other, following the path to the ponds, the six lakes along the western edge of the park.

He continued until he came to the largest of the ponds, the model boating pond. Then he found a quiet spot on the bank and sat down on the grass.

The water sparkled silver in the morning sun; the screech and cackle of geese split the air; a flock of gulls swooped low over the water. Dog owners were out walking their pets; young mums with pushchairs were guiding toddlers along the path around the water's edge; a runner carrying a plastic water bottle and wired up to his iPod jogged past. Normal, everyday activities.

No sign of the tragedy that had occurred here three weeks ago.

But what exactly had happened? Tom replayed in his mind the facts as he understood them.

At approximately seven o'clock on the morning of Saturday the twenty-third of June, according to the police report, an early morning jogger by the name of Mr. Edward Burrows had spotted the roof of a blue Vauxhall Astra, just visible above the surface of the water. He couldn't see if there was anyone in the car, but like a responsible citizen he had dialled 999 on his mobile and requested police and ambulance.

The police and ambulance were there in minutes but there was little they could do. Within half an hour a police diver swam out to the car and discovered the body of a man in his mid-to-late forties. It was too late to save him and he was pronounced dead at the scene. He was identified as Dr. Jack Kelsey from his driving licence which was in his wallet.

The police report noted that Dr. Kelsey was in the driver's seat, still wearing his seatbelt. The driver's window was wound down a few inches, which wasn't considered strange because the weather had been so warm and the nights were muggy. Water had flooded into the car through the open window, drowning the occupant. No suicide note was found and there was no sign of a struggle having taken place so the coroner had returned a verdict of accidental death.

Tom didn't believe a word of it.

He accepted that the car had been found in the pond and his dad had drowned. That much was non-negotiable. But an accident? How could something like this be an accident for God's sake? And why would he have been driving around Hampstead Heath of all places? And in the middle of the night?

It was a complete fluke that the gate at the bottom of

Merton Lane had even been open (the council had hired a team of tree surgeons to carry out work on some ancient oaks and the contractors had opened the gate in order to gain vehicular access.) A huge row had ensued about whose fault it was that the gate had not been secured at night – the council's or the contractors'. No one was prepared to accept responsibility and in the furore that followed the fact that his dad's car had ended up in the water came to be seen as nothing more than a regrettable incident.

When Tom and his mother had gone to the police station to formally identify the body, Tom had tried talking to the Inspector in charge, but that had been a waste of time. DCI McNally was overworked and overweight and looked like he might have a cardiac arrest any minute. He had too much to do, he complained, hunting down the knife-carrying hooligans of London and wasn't prepared to consider there might be anything suspicious about the circumstances of Tom's dad's death. As far as DCI McNally was concerned the case was closed. Finito.

Tom tried to think back before the events of his dad's death. He'd been busy at school himself then, sitting his GCSEs, but, still, he'd noticed his dad working extra hard on something. Jack hadn't been around as much at weekends as he normally was. He'd spent even more time than usual cooped up in his study at the top of the house and had seemed preoccupied with something. Then on Friday the twenty-second of June he'd gone to Professor Barlow's retirement dinner and the rest, as they say, was history.

The retirement dinner. It was obvious that something must have happened at that dinner. Something bad. Before the dinner everything had been fine. After it, his dad had wound up in Highgate Ponds. The dinner was central to everything. And what made Tom even more cross was the fact that his dad normally avoided those kinds of events, preferring to be at home. He always complained about college dinners, saying they were full of academics trying to justify their existence by claiming they'd done more research than their colleagues when usually they were just rehashing the same old arguments and hadn't had an original thought in thirty years.

Well, if the police weren't prepared to help then Tom would have to do his own investigations. And the first question was, who had been at the dinner? Maybe Nancy Letts, the department secretary, could help him out there. He made a mental note to get in touch with her, maybe after he'd been to the library.

And here was another strange thing. Why was his dad borrowing books from the local public library when he had the university library at his disposal? He pulled the library book out of his backpack and idly turned to the table of contents. There was a chapter entitled *The Magnificent Seven*. That sounded intriguing. Like a bunch of superheroes. He turned to the relevant page and started reading.

Between 1833 and 1841 The London Cemetery Company opened seven new cemeteries around the outskirts of London - Kensal Green, West Norwood, Highgate, Abney Park, Brompton, Nunhead and Tower Hamlets. They became known as the Magnificent Seven.

Not superheroes then.

Before the opening of the new cemeteries, burial conditions in London's churchyards were in a dire situation. The small City churchyards were overcrowded and unable to cope with the huge rise in population in London in the early nineteenth century brought about by the Industrial Revolution.

Tom yawned. He skipped a couple of paragraphs then turned the page and flicked his eyes over the words, picking up the gist of what the author was saying.

Before the cemeteries were built...bones sticking out of the ground...disease-ridden churchyards...body snatchers who made a living from digging up fresh corpses and selling them to the medical schools...

Tom closed the book and put it back in the backpack, unable to read any more. Ordinarily, such gory details as bones sticking out of the ground and the antics of grave robbers would have amused him. But not now. Not now his own dad was lying in a freshly dug grave. Now the idea of grave robbers sickened him.

He took the diary out of his bag instead. The soft leather felt warm and comforting in his hands. Where had this book come from? He examined the inside front pages, but there were no stamps on it so it didn't belong to the university. Tom turned to the first entry. It was dated January 1870. He tried to decipher the florid handwriting.

I... have... taken... lodgings... in... a house... on Highgate Hill...Athelston Lodge.

He gave up and closed the book. The handwriting was too much effort to read and he didn't have the patience to persist with it.

But Athelston Lodge. Where had he seen that name before? Then he remembered. It was the house on Highgate Hill just round the corner from Cromwell Avenue where he lived. So he and Isabelle Hart were neighbours of a sort. Just separated by 140 years or more. Funny that.

He put the diary back in his bag and checked his watch. It was already eleven o'clock. He'd need to get a move on if he was going to get to the library before it closed at twelve.

10

Lauren scrambled to her feet, clutching the object she had found, her heart beating with excitement. It was a wooden box, about nine inches by six inches and three inches deep. It was coated in a thick layer of dust and sticky cobwebs.

"Mum, look at this." She held the box out with both hands. "It was hidden under that loose floorboard. It looks like a jewellery box. It's filthy though."

"How fascinating," said Wendy coming over to see. She passed Lauren a yellow duster. "Here, wipe it with this."

Lauren wiped away the dust to reveal a dark, polished wood with an inlaid mother-of-pearl flower design that glimmered in the sunlight. Lauren thought it was beautiful.

"Go on then, open it." Wendy sounded as excited as Lauren felt.

Lauren knelt down, resting the box on a pile of old encyclopaedias and carefully lifted the lid. Thankfully, there was no lock. Inside was a piece of cream coloured cloth, folded so that it would fit neatly inside the box. It looked as if it had been there a long time. Lauren wiped her grubby fingers on her jeans and then lifted the cloth with her fingertips and opened it out.

It was about the size of a large handkerchief and was embroidered with tiny stitches that must have taken hours and hours of work. Around the edge of the cloth was an intricate patten of ivy sewn in dark green silk. Blue butterflies flew in and out of the ivy. In the middle of the cloth was a verse. Lauren read the words out loud, a chill running down her spine.

A baby's cradle with no baby in it,
A baby's grave where autumn leaves drop sere;
The sweet soul gathered home to Paradise,
The body waiting here.

Along the bottom of the cloth was the name *Emily* and a date, 1870.

"It's a sampler," said Wendy. "It looks Victorian to me. I think that verse is by Christina Rossetti, you know, the sister of the Pre-Raphaelite painter, Dante Gabriel Rossetti?"

"What's a sampler?" asked Lauren.

"It's what they call this type of embroidery work. Girls did them in the nineteenth century to show how proficient they were with different stitches. It was a way of practising sewing and making something beautiful at the same time. From the verse and the name at the bottom, I'd say this was a mourning sampler."

"What, in memory of someone who died?"

"Exactly."

Lauren re-read the verse to herself and looked more closely at the ivy, butterflies and flowers.

"It's beautiful," she said. "It must have taken hours of work to produce those tiny stitches. Do you think it's worth anything?"

"I shouldn't think so. These things were ten a penny back in the nineteenth century. But if you want to keep it I'll get it framed for you. You could hang it on your wall."

"All right," said Lauren. It wasn't the sort of thing she would normally hang on her wall, but it didn't seem right to keep it in a box, hidden from the light of day. Surely Emily, whoever she was, deserved to be remembered.

Wendy looked at her watch. "Right, I need to get cleaned up so I can go to the cemetery. Thanks for your help this morning."

"No problem. I'll just finish off here and then I'll take the bags of old clothes to Oxfam."

"Thanks love."

Lauren smiled to herself. She had to admit, clearing out the attic hadn't been as dull as she'd feared and discovering the wooden box with the sampler inside had been a real find, like discovering long lost treasure.

She bent down to put the sampler back in the box for safe keeping and noticed a piece of black card lying at the bottom of the box which she hadn't spotted before.

Lauren laid the sampler to one side and lifted out the card. It was folded over like a birthday card. Inside was an old brown-toned sepia photograph of a young woman mounted in an oval frame. The woman in the photograph looked familiar but Lauren couldn't place her. She was wearing a full-skirted, off-the-shoulder gown with a string of pearls around her neck and was seated in front of a ruched curtain, beside a potted palm tree. Her dark hair had been curled into ringlets that tumbled gently over her shoulders and she was staring straight at the camera with a soft, clear gaze.

The cardboard mount had the name of the photographer embossed on the back – Carter and Son, but there was no clue as to the identity of the sitter. Lauren eased the photograph out of its mount to see if there was a name on the back, although she had a feeling she already knew what she was going to find.

Breathing steadily to calm her nerves Lauren turned the photograph over and read the name written in an old-fashioned script on the back. *Isabelle Hart, 1869.*

11

Tom ran up the steps of the library. It was an old Edwardian building on Chester Road opposite the southern edge of the cemetery. When he was little his dad used to bring him here most Saturdays. They must have worked their way through most of the children's non-fiction section, borrowing books on astronomy, trains, World War II and insects. Tom had outgrown the children's section years ago and hadn't been to the library much in recent years, but as soon as he walked inside and inhaled the familiar smell of paper and dust, it was as if he was seven years old again, returning a book about spaceships and asking if he could borrow one on battleships.

He stopped by the community notice board near the entrance, pretending to read the posters advertising yoga classes and Music for Toddlers whilst he waited for the memories to settle and his pulse to return to normal. Was this going to happen every time he went somewhere that reminded him of his dad? Probably. He might as well get used to it.

He took a deep breath, pulled the library book out of his backpack and walked up to the Returns desk. For a moment he didn't want to let it go and thought about renewing it. But then he remembered he didn't have his dad's library card with him and, anyway, it was probably illegal to use a dead person's library card. Might count as fraud.

The librarian smiled at him as he handed her the book. She scanned the spine and placed the book on a trolley of recently returned items ready to go back to the shelves.

"Can I help you with anything else?" she asked, taking off her reading glasses which hung around her neck on a beaded chain.

"Actually there is something," said Tom, reaching into the backpack. He hadn't planned to do this, but the librarian looked like a kind lady and there was no one else waiting at the desk. He pulled out the diary.

"Is that another book to return?" she asked, holding out her hand.

"No, it's not a library book."

"Oh?" She sounded intrigued.

"It's a diary. It turned up when we were clearing out the house." The little lie seemed harmless enough. He wasn't about to go into personal details with a complete stranger. "It's very old."

"I can see that," said the librarian. "May I?"

Tom nodded and passed her the book. She opened the book carefully, taking care not to bend the spine. "What beautiful handwriting."

"Yes," agreed Tom, "although I find it quite hard to read. But the thing is, it's written by someone called Isabelle Hart and at the moment all I know about her is that she lodged at Athelston Lodge on Highgate Hill. Do you know if there's a way to find out who she was?"

"She's not a relative then?" asked the librarian.

"I don't think so." His mother's maiden name had been Dawson. There were no Harts in the family as far as he knew.

The librarian looked at the name and date inside the front cover. "It's dated 1870 and there was a national census in 1871. You could try looking at the census records on line to see who was living at that address back then. It should give the names of all the occupants of the house and their relation to each other. It won't tell you much but it's a start."

"That sounds great. How do I...?"

"Come with me." The librarian led him to a bank of computers and clicked on an icon that opened up a website about the 1871 Census.

"Thanks," said Tom. He entered the details into the search box and hit return.

12

The plastic bags containing Lauren's childhood clothes were bulky and difficult to carry. They bumped against her legs as she walked down Highgate Hill and slipped in her sweaty palms in the heat of the late morning sun.

Bother.

She put the bags down for a moment and wiped her hands on her jeans. Then she twisted the end of each bag around one hand and slung the bags over her shoulder. That was better. Now she could walk and think at the same time.

The thing that puzzled her was, why wasn't she more

freaked out by the discovery of the box and the photograph with Isabelle's name on it? She should be, she knew. Something weird was going on. She hadn't wanted to participate in the séance yesterday evening and when the planchette had spelled out Isabelle's name she had found the experience disturbing, like they were interfering with things best forgotten. Who knew what the consequences might be?

But the box was real, not just a figment of her subconscious mind, and that somehow made her feel better. It gave her something tangible to focus on.

Lauren had never considered whether she believed in ghosts. At least not since she'd outgrown her childhood night-time fears of monsters in the cupboard. It wasn't that she was fearless like Megan (reckless some would say) and she wasn't a daydreamer like Chloe. She was the practical one of the group, the one who made sure they didn't miss the last bus home, that sort of thing. Bit boring, you might say. Still, being practical and clear-headed had its uses. It helped you to think things through and the only logical conclusion that Lauren could come to was that Isabelle Hart, or someone connected to her, must have lived at Athelston Lodge, where Lauren and her mum now lived.

The photograph was dated 1869 and the sampler 1870. Late Victorian then. But who was Emily? If her mum was right about it being a mourning sampler then Emily must have died in 1870. Were Isabelle and Emily related? And who were they anyway?

Lauren pondered all these thoughts as she made her way to Oxfam. She pushed open the door with her shoulder and joined the back of the queue.

She dumped the bags at her feet and continued to think whilst a guy with a ponytail served an old lady stocking up on fair trade chocolates and a young mum with a wailing toddler in a pushchair paid for a stack of second hand books. An idea was taking shape in her mind. She checked her watch. Eleven thirty. There was no need to hurry home – Wendy would be at the cemetery by now and Lauren had the day to herself. There should be just enough time if she was quick.

"Can I help you?"

Lauren looked up, startled. She hadn't noticed that the old lady and the mother with the wailing child had gone.

"Can I donate these?" She lifted the bags onto the counter, keen now to be out of the shop as quickly as possible.

"Thank you so much, that's fantastic, we're so grateful for all donations no matter how big or small, we…" The assistant seemed inclined to chat but Lauren really didn't have time.

"No problem," said Lauren moving towards the door. She felt rude cutting him off – he seemed nice – but she'd be there all morning if she didn't make a move.

Once out of the shop she headed off in the direction of Chester Road. She knew the library had access to a subscription-only website where you could look up people based on old census records. A few years ago Lauren had tagged along whilst her mum was researching the family tree. They hadn't unearthed any connections to the aristocracy or any convicts in the family, but one branch had emigrated to Canada back in the nineteenth century. There was just time for her to do a quick search on Isabelle Hart before the library shut at twelve.

She dashed up the steps of the library two at a time and collided, head on, with a fair-haired boy, about her own age, who was coming out.

"Sorry," she said, but the boy pushed past her with his head down and didn't even look at her.

Oh, whatever.

She might have been in a hurry but he clearly wasn't looking where he was going. *Idiot.*

She told herself to calm down and walked into the library's cool, air-conditioned interior. Right, where were the computers?

Lauren found the bank of computers and sat down at the end one. The seat was still warm as if someone had just been sitting there. What's more, the screen was already displaying the website she needed.

Bizarre.

Still, tracing family trees was all the rage now wasn't it? Like the whole country had suddenly become obsessed with getting in touch with its roots. Lauren typed Isabelle's name and her own address into the Advanced Search screen and clicked *Search*.

The librarian was logging off the other computers. "We're closing in ten minutes, dear." She must have seen what Lauren had typed on the screen because she said, "Oh, Isabelle Hart. That's a coincidence. You're the second person today searching for information on her."

"Really?" Lauren was baffled. Who would do that? Surely not Megan who never set foot inside the library, probably didn't even know where it was. Chloe then. But why would Chloe do that without inviting Lauren along? After all, the séance had taken place at her house. She couldn't help feeling that gave her a special claim to Isabelle.

"Yes," continued the librarian not appearing to notice the confusion on Lauren's face. "A young lad was in here not long ago looking up Isabelle Hart. He rushed out just now. Seemed a bit upset," she added in a confidential whisper.

Lauren remembered the boy she'd collided with on the library steps.

"What did he look like?" she asked, her curiosity growing by the second.

"About your age, dear, fair hair. He was wearing a blue T-shirt and jeans. I'm quite perceptive you know – I have a good eye for details like that." The librarian gave a little laugh.

"Thank you," said Lauren, standing up. "You've been

very helpful."

"You're welcome."

Lauren hurried out of the library. She had just enough of a mental image of the boy she'd collided with to recognise him if she saw him again. She had no idea who he was but she knew she wanted to find him. It was just too much of a coincidence that he, too, had been looking for information on someone called Isabelle Hart. It had to be her Isabelle.

Back outside the midday sun was hotter than ever. She couldn't run very far in this heat. She looked up and down Chester Road but the boy was nowhere to be seen.

13

Athelston Lodge. Tom stood on the pavement and looked up at the house. He must have passed it dozens of times and had never given it a second thought. Why would he? Like its neighbours it was a four-storey Victorian terrace with a kitchen in the basement, box-sash windows on the ground and first floors, and a poky attic window in the roof. The house was set back from the road by a paved front garden. A flight of half a dozen stone steps led up to the front door. But now the house held a strange fascination for him.

After his embarrassingly quick exit from the library, which he didn't want to think about right now, he'd found himself walking up to the house for no other reason than the fact that Isabelle wrote about it in the first line of her diary - *I have taken lodgings in a house on Highgate Hill, Athelston Lodge* - and he was curious to see it.

As it happened, Athelston Lodge was just around the corner from his own house on Cromwell Avenue, but he had no idea who lived here. London was like that – you were lucky if you knew the people living next door to you never mind someone round the corner. And whoever lived here now had most likely never heard of Isabelle Hart.

The front door was painted pillar-box red and sported a brass knocker in the shape of a lion's head. He was tempted to knock, but at the same time had no idea what he would say if someone actually answered.

Whilst he stood dithering on the pavement, a girl with Cruella Deville hair came striding down the Hill, looked at him with one raised eyebrow, then turned into the front garden, ran up the steps and rapped loudly on the door.

Well, that decided things for the moment. He couldn't knock on the door whilst she was there, but if he hung around he might get a glimpse of whoever lived there now.

The girl stood on the doorstep, watching him. Tom didn't think he was acting suspiciously, but he turned away. He wasn't having much luck in his encounters with girls today. First there was the one he'd bumped into at the library, and now this one was staring at him as if standing on the pavement was a crime.

Tom thrust his hands into his jeans' pockets and watched the traffic. He wasn't going to be frightened off by this girl, even if he did find her intimidating with her ghoulish black and white hair.

He pulled his phone out of his pocket and pretended to dial a number, all the time listening in case the front door should open.

Two buses trundled past, one going up the hill towards Highgate Village and the other going down the hill towards Kentish Town. They reminded him of yesterday's journey up the hill in the limousine following the hearse. He wished whoever lived in the house would hurry up and open the door. He couldn't stand here much longer faking a phone call. If he really was phoning a friend they would have answered by now or it would have gone through to voicemail. He cancelled the fake call, made a point of looking at his watch as if he was expecting someone who was late and started thumbing through some old texts. He could feel the girl's eyes boring into the back of his head.

She knocked loudly one more time. When there was

still no answer she gave a grunt of frustration and walked down the steps, back onto the pavement.

Tom glanced at her out of the corner of his eye. She glared at him, as if it was his fault the occupants of the house were not at home. Then she turned and continued on her way down the hill.

Tom breathed a sigh of relief. At least he'd established one thing. There was no one at home so there was no point hanging around anymore. The question now was, should he go home to face piles of washing up and his mother or should he go to the park which was just over the road? It wasn't the hardest decision he'd ever had to make. As soon as there was a break in the traffic Tom darted across the road and through the gates back into Waterlow Park.

14

Lauren trudged back up Highgate Hill. There was no sign of the boy from the library. She kept an eye out for him amongst the passers-by but didn't see him. He could be anywhere by now and there was no point going on a wild goose chase. She scanned the faces of the people waiting at the bus stop – the old woman from Oxfam, a man in a suit, a young lad in a baseball cap playing with his iPhone. She might as well give up.

"Hey, Lauren!"

She looked up. Megan was striding down the hill, waving at her.

"Where've you been? I was just knocking on your door."

"Oh, I had some stuff to take to Oxfam and then you'll never guess…"

"Right, never mind, listen, you and Chloe have just got to come out tonight. *Saints and Sinners* are doing a gig at the Club. Everyone's going. It's going to be awesome." Megan always got straight to the point. She ran her hand through her hair and grinned, waiting for an answer.

"Well…" Lauren wished she had a good excuse but couldn't think of one right at that moment. Megan's brother, Matt, was the lead singer of *Saints and Sinners*, a retro-rock band that tried to recreate the hard rock culture of the Seventies although Lauren knew Megan's interest was more focused on Rick the drummer than love of the music or loyalty to her brother.

"Are you coming or not?"

"Oh, all right then," said Lauren, trying to sound enthusiastic. It wasn't like she had any other plans for the evening. "What time is it?"

"Starts at eight. I'll call by and get you," she added as if she suspected Lauren might not get there under her own steam.

"Don't worry. I'll see you there."

Megan looked at her watch. "Gotta go. I'm doing extra hours at the café." She turned to leave, then stopped. "Oh, by the way, I was at your house just now and there was this boy hanging around on the pavement. He was watching your house. He tried to pretend he wasn't but he didn't fool me."

Lauren felt her stomach do a somersault. "What did he look like?" she asked trying to sound unconcerned. Megan gave her a quizzical look.

"Fair hair, blue T-shirt, jeans, boring really."

Lauren ignored the last comment. Just because Megan was mad about Rick's gothic look with dyed black hair, black T-shirts and ripped jeans, any other boy was boring in her book. But Megan's description matched the librarian's so it was almost certainly the boy she'd bumped into outside the library, the one who had been researching Isabelle Hart – but why was he standing outside her house?

"Did you see where he went?"

Megan raised her right eyebrow and tilted her head to one side. "Is there something you haven't told me, Lauren?

Like you've got a secret boyfriend?"

She was teasing, but Lauren blushed as if she'd been accused of hiding state secrets. "No, of course not."

"So who is he?"

"I don't know."

"Yeah, right. Surely you don't expect me to believe…"

"Look it's complicated," Lauren interrupted. "If he's who I think he is, I ran into him this morning and…" she trailed off. Where to begin? It was a long story and she hardly understood it herself.

"OK," said Megan, smiling, "I haven't got time to hear about your secret love life right now. I've got to go or I'll get the sack, but I shall want to hear all the details tonight." She winked at Lauren then turned to go.

"But I haven't got a secret love life," Lauren called after her. It was no use. Megan wasn't listening.

Blast! She couldn't believe it. The boy she'd been looking for had actually been right outside her house and Megan had seen him. Knowing Megan she'd have given him one of her *who-the-hell-do-you-think-you-are* looks and frightened him off. Lauren ran the rest of the way home, but by the time she got to her house, hot and out of breath, the boy was nowhere to be seen.

15

Tom flopped down on a park bench by the lake and watched as a family of ducks swam past. What a morning.

The trip to Highgate Ponds hadn't revealed any new information about his dad's death, which he realised now was what he had been hoping for. And as for the trip to the library, he should have just returned the library book and got out of there as quickly as possible. It had been a huge mistake to spend more than a few minutes in a place that held so many memories.

He blushed, even now, to think how he had broken down in front of the librarian. What a dolt. He'd heard that grief could hit you suddenly out of the blue but if he was going to keep cracking up like that in public then he'd have to spend the whole of the summer holidays at home in his room.

He'd been fine in the library until a young boy had come in with his dad and they'd gone to the section on trains and planes, the boy keen to borrow a book about fighter jets and his dad promising him an ice-cream later. Tom had been that young boy once with a dad just like that. Then the librarian had come over to see how he was getting on with his research and he'd burst into tears and had run from the building, colliding with that girl who must think he was an idiot.

And what in God's name had possessed him to go and hang around outside some stranger's house on Highgate Hill? Just because it was mentioned in a diary written over a hundred and forty years ago by some woman he'd never heard of until last night. And that girl with the black and white hair had looked at him as if he was a right weirdo, although when he thought about it he could see she had a point.

No, it hadn't been a good morning.

He rested his forearms on his knees and let his head hang down, staring at the cigarette butts that littered the ground under the bench. Maybe he should just go home and ease his conscience by helping to clear away the dishes, but he really didn't feel like it. It was easier to sit here and let time drift past.

He tried to think about the future but found that anything beyond the present moment was just a blur. He was supposed to be starting his A-level courses in September. English, History and Geography. He'd discussed it with his dad and those three subjects had seemed like a good combination since he wanted to go to University and study archaeology. He had always wanted to go to Greece or Egypt and work on a dig, unearthing buried treasure. Now everything was a mess and Tom didn't know if he had the will to go back to school.

He rubbed his eyes. They still felt red. He made a mental note to always carry a pair of sunglasses with him whenever he went out. Just in case.

The bench shifted. He kept his head down but turned his eyes to see who had sat down.

Oh shite.

Just when he thought things couldn't get any worse. It was the girl he'd bumped into outside the library. She was holding a baguette, a bag of crisps and a bottle of coke, and she was staring straight at him.

16

"Hi there." Lauren laid the baguette down on the bench and broke open the bag of crisps. Barbecue flavour. She held the bag out. "Would you like one?" She tried to keep her voice steady but inside she was buzzing with excitement. She couldn't believe her luck in actually finding the boy she'd been looking for, just sitting here in the park like he was waiting for her to show up. Although she had to admit, he didn't look exactly thrilled to see her.

After the disappointment of finding he was no longer waiting outside her house (well why would he be?), she'd realised that the morning's exertions had left her ravenously hungry. But the idea of grabbing a slice of toast on her own in the empty house wasn't very appealing, so she'd gone and bought herself a ham and cheese baguette from the local deli and taken it into Waterlow Park. She'd walked over to her favourite spot by the lake and was just about to sit down on the grass when she'd spotted him. Sitting on the bench. Alone.

Introducing herself to a total stranger, particularly of the opposite sex, wasn't really Lauren's thing – that was more Megan's style. But this boy fascinated her. Why had he been looking up Isabelle Hart in the library? What did he know about her? And, this was the weird thing, why had he been hanging around outside her house? Something strange was going on and Lauren was going to get to the bottom of it.

The librarian had told her he'd seemed a bit upset about something and, as he pushed his floppy fair hair off his forehead and looked at her, she could see his eyes were red-rimmed and puffy. They were still nice eyes though, dark brown and framed by thick lashes. As he looked at her, Lauren felt the heat rising to her face and tried to draw attention away from herself by giving the bag of crisps a little shake. She was glad now she'd bought a bag of crisps as an afterthought. Sharing food was such a good ice-breaker. She held the bag out a bit further.

"Please, take one."

He didn't take a crisp.

Instead he stared at her with a look she found hard to read.

He thinks I'm trying to chat him up.

Her heart thudded inside her ribcage. She had to admit, he was very good looking. Not at all boring like Megan had said. But Lauren didn't go around chatting up boys. She didn't have the nerve. She was only talking to him, she reminded herself, because of her interest in Isabelle Hart. She thrust her hand into the crisp packet in an effort to hide her embarrassment.

"I bumped into you just now outside the library," she said munching on a crisp. It sounded pathetic. Like something from a slushy romantic comedy. Why could she never think of anything interesting to say?

"It was my fault. I wasn't looking where I was going."

"No, it was my fault. I was in a hurry to get into the library before it closed."

"Whatever."

He turned back to look at the lake.

Lauren felt her confidence take a nosedive. The wheels of conversation had ground to a halt before they'd even taxied to the runway. She cursed herself for being so dull.

She was going to have to do a whole lot better if this conversation was ever going to get off the ground, let alone stay airborne. She nibbled the corner of another crisp and sipped some coke before trying a different tack.

"I went to the library to see if I could find out anything about someone called Isabelle Hart."

That did the trick. He sat up straight and turned to face her.

"What did you say?"

"Isabelle Hart. I've come across the name recently but don't know who she is. The thing is, yesterday evening…"

He cut her off. "And who are you?"

"Lauren Matthews."

"And do you live at Athelston Lodge on Highgate Hill?"

"Yes, but, how did you know that's where I live when you don't even know who I am?"

He didn't answer her question but instead reached into his backpack and pulled out a book bound in black leather. "Take a look at this."

"What is it?"

"A diary."

Lauren expected him to say more but he obviously wasn't going to. She hurriedly licked her fingers clean and wiped them on her jeans, regretting her decision to buy crisps after all. She didn't want to leave greasy fingerprints on the beautiful black leather. She took hold of the book, laying it carefully on her lap. It was clearly very old and fragile.

As Lauren turned the front cover she felt the hairs on the back of her neck standing on end. She had a feeling she knew whose diary this was. She wasn't wrong. The name Isabelle Hart was written in a curling script on the inside of the front cover. She turned to the first entry.

Thursday, 20th January 1870
I have taken lodgings in a house on Highgate Hill, Athelston

Lodge.

So that was it. Isabelle had lodged in her house, over one hundred and forty years ago.

Brimming with excitement, she looked at the boy. "It all makes sense now."

"What does?" he asked frowning.

Lauren took a deep breath. "Well you see it's like this. Yesterday evening my friend Megan came round to my house, I think you met her just now by the way, and she had this Ouija board she'd picked up at the market. Anyway, she insisted we give it a go and I didn't really want to but Megan can be very persuasive when she wants to be and Chloe, that's my other friend, she was up for it, so we sat around the Ouija board and I asked the question, 'Is there anybody there?' and the planchette spelt out the name *Isabelle Hart.*"

She sat back with a smile on her face and waited for him to say something. She knew she'd been gabbling and hoped he'd followed what she said. But it was so exciting how things were slotting into place. Last night she would have been the first to admit that she thought Ouija boards were a load of hocus pocus, but now the pieces of the jigsaw were fitting together. Isabelle Hart had lived at Athelston Lodge and it must be that, somehow, her spirit still lingered there. She waited for the boy to tell her how he'd come by the diary and then everything would make sense and maybe, just maybe, they could start getting to know each other better. She wondered if she had the courage to ask him to come and hear *Saints and Sinners* this evening. She imagined her friends' faces if she turned up with him.

Her smile faded when she saw the look on his face. It was a mixture of anger and incredulity in almost equal measures.

"Come off it. What do you take me for?" he almost shouted. "Some kind of gullible half-wit? You don't really expect me to believe all that nonsense about a Ouija board do you?"

Lauren was stunned. She felt her excitement turning into anger. She didn't like being accused of lying. "Look, I didn't want to believe it either. I didn't even want to participate in the stupid séance. I thought it was a really bad idea, if you must know. But I did join in and I'm just telling you what happened, that's all. The least you could do is give me a bit of credit. After all, you were researching Isabelle Hart at the library before I was and you were the one hanging around outside my house this morning."

He flinched at her words. "All right, keep your hair on."

She hadn't meant to sound so aggressive and now she regretted her reaction. "I'm sorry," she said, biting her lip.

"No, I'm sorry," he said rubbing his forehead, "I shouldn't have shouted at you like that. But you have to admit, your story does sound a bit weird."

She nodded. "You're not kidding. And there's something else."

"Go on."

"I was helping Mum clear out the attic this morning and I found an old Victorian photograph of a young woman. It was in a box hidden under a loose floorboard. I took the photograph out of its mount and on the back was the name…"

He held up a hand. "Don't tell me. I can guess."

"So do you believe me now?"

He sighed. "I guess so." He took back the diary, opened the front cover and ran his finger over the name of its owner. "But who is she?"

Lauren shrugged. "That's what I'd love to find out. Where did you get this diary from?" She was relaxing again now that the argument had blown over.

"I found it last night in my dad's study." He looked away and blinked as if he had something in his eye.

"Oh, well that makes life easier then. Why don't we just

ask your dad who Isabelle Hart is?"

He stuffed the diary back into his backpack and stood up.

"Where are you going?"

He fiddled with the straps on his backpack, not looking at her. "I have to go." There was a crack in his voice. He started to walk away.

Lauren jumped up and ran after him. "What's the matter? Did I say something wrong?" Tears were streaming down his cheeks but she couldn't understand what had caused this sudden turn of events.

He faced her, not bothering to hide his tears. "My dad's dead. We buried him yesterday. I can't talk to you right now." He turned and walked away.

Lauren was too stunned to move. She watched his retreating back, waves of guilt washing over her.

"I'll come back tomorrow," she called after him. "Same time, same place." She knew it sounded ridiculous but she couldn't think of anything else to say. He showed no sign of having heard her.

Lauren returned to the bench and sat down, deflated. She picked up the remains of the bag of crisps and scrunched it in her hands. She was a dolt. It was obvious he'd been upset about something when she bumped into him outside the library. Even the librarian had mentioned it. And his eyes were still red when she'd joined him on the bench. *My dad's dead. We buried him yesterday.* No wonder he hadn't been in the mood to listen to her rambling on about her experiences with the Ouija board and contacting the other side.

She tore off a piece of bread from her baguette and threw it to the ducks. A family of mallards swam over in a line. Like a procession. It reminded her of something.

Of course. The funeral cortège.

That must have been his dad in that coffin, and he must have been in one of the limousines. How awful.

All she could hope for was that he would come back

tomorrow so she could apologise to him and they could restart their failed conversation. Then she realised, she hadn't even asked him his name. She had no idea who he was.

17

The Trials and Tribulations of a Household Maid in the Year of Our Lord 1870.

Rats.

Not again, I said to myself. They're a bleedin' nuisance, they are. They've only gone and gnawed through a sack of potatoes in the pantry. Now I'll have to sort through all the spuds and find the ones what aren't spoilt.

Daisy, the scullery maid, should've gone and got more rat poison from the chemist but she's worse than useless is that girl, I don't know why Mrs Payne keeps 'er on. It's not like I've got time to be fetching rat poison when there's all the cooking and cleaning to do. I had to ask Sam, the baker's boy, to pick up some poison when he's on his rounds – I don't know what I'd do without him. "Don't you worry, Betsy," he said to me. "We'll 'ave them little buggers catched in no time."

As if I didn't have enough to do without catching vermin. Ever since Mrs Payne's old man kicked the bucket and she started taking in lodgers it's like I'm waiting hand and foot on bloomin' everyone. It's *Betsy, do this* and *Betsy, do that*. There's that Madeleine Fox for a start with her endless stream of visitors and now there's a new lodger come and taken the attic room. I didn't catch her name but I caught a glimpse of her when she arrived. Pale she were, like she hadn't eaten properly in a month of Sundays. Lord, I thought to myself, don't say we've got a consumptive on our hands. We don't need that kind of thing here, thank you very much. I watched her follow Mrs Payne up the stairs, then I went back down to the kitchen and that's when I spotted the rat droppings in the pantry.

You wouldn't think there'd be so many rats out here. It's not like we live in the slums or anything. Out here in Highgate we're practically in the country. Me, I blame that cemetery. You don't know what's lurking in a place like that. Will, bless him, says it's a lovely place, but I ain't so sure.

Oh, here's Sam back already with a bottle of white powder.

"Here you go," he says. "Sprinkle that on some cheese and the rats'll be dead before you can say Jack Robinson."

PART THREE
SATURDAY 14 JULY

18

Tom pushed open the front door and stepped inside, blinking as his eyes adjusted to the gloom of the Victorian hallway after the bright sunshine outside. The brisk walk back from Waterlow Park had calmed him down and now he regretted leaving the girl, Lauren, in such a hurry. She'd seemed nice. It was just that he didn't want her to see him crying. He wouldn't have dreamt of crying in front of his mates and certainly not in front of a girl he'd only just met. What would she think of him?

He dumped his backpack at the foot of the stairs and went through to the dining room. His Aunt was attacking the carpet with the Dyson whilst Uncle Bill was fixing the loose cupboard door on the sideboard – Tom's dad had rarely got round to DIY jobs. The remains of yesterday's buffet had gone and the dirty plates and glasses had all been cleared away. Now he felt guilty for not having helped. The twins were sitting on the sofa, leafing through a picture book. They stared at him as if to say, who are you? He ignored them and went through to the kitchen where his mother was removing clean plates from the dishwasher and stacking them on the worktop. She didn't look up when he came in.

"Anything I can do?" asked Tom feeling redundant.

His mother straightened up, a pile of dessert bowls in her hands. She didn't ask him where he'd been. "No. We're fine here."

"Right then." Tom shifted from one foot to the other. "Well, in that case…"

He wasn't going to hang around where he wasn't needed, or wanted it seemed.

He hurried out of the kitchen, through the dining room, picked up his bag from where he'd dumped it in the hallway and ran up the stairs to his dad's study.

He pushed open the door and went in.

His nose twitched. Something was different. A smell. What was it? Mothballs? He'd smelt something like it before. At his Gran's. In Yorkshire.

Maybe he was imagining it. He opened the window to clear the air and sat down at the desk. This time he didn't hesitate but booted up the computer. He wanted to try and find out what his dad had been working on before he died. He had an idea it might just help him get to the bottom of his dad's death.

As the screen flickered into life he looked at the stuff on the desk. The pile of boring memos was still there. He could probably bin most of this stuff. But there was something missing, he was sure of it. He ran his hand over the front of the desk trying to think. Then he remembered.

The memory stick.

He'd left it in front of the keyboard but now it wasn't there. He lifted the keyboard to look underneath. Nothing.

He pulled open the drawer in the desk. Highlighter pens, biros, a couple of broken pencils, a stapler, a glue stick – it looked like his desk at school. But no memory stick.

Suddenly, he was no longer interested in the computer. Someone had been in here and had taken the memory stick. Tom didn't even know if it contained anything important or not. That wasn't the point. Someone had interfered with his dad's stuff and they had no right to.

He closed the drawer and went back downstairs to the kitchen. His mother had finished unloading the dishwasher and was arranging the wine glasses in a glass-fronted cabinet. She didn't turn round when he came in, was maybe unaware he was even there.

"Has someone been in Dad's study today?" He tried to keep his voice neutral but he knew it had an accusatory tone to it.

His mother turned round slowly, wine glass in hand. "Why?" She sounded totally uninterested in his question.

"There was a memory stick on his desk yesterday. Now it's gone."

She turned back to the cupboard and reached up to put the glass on the top shelf. "Oh, that must have been what he was looking for."

"Who was looking for it?" Tom wished she'd stop putting the stupid glasses away for a moment and look at him.

"Oh, you know," waving her hand vaguely in the air. "What's his name? Your father's colleague - Professor Nesbit."

Professor Nesbit?

Tom suddenly had a vivid mental image of him at the funeral, standing apart from everyone else, and then at the wake, not joining in the conversations, but browsing the bookcase. Bit of a cold fish, Tom had thought. It hadn't bothered him yesterday. He hadn't been in the mood for making small talk either.

But why would Professor Nesbit come to the house? And why would he remove stuff from his dad's study?

His mother finished putting the wine glasses away and

moved onto the cutlery, dropping knives and forks into the drawer so that they clattered like a piece of modern percussion music.

"What was he doing here?" Tom spoke to his mother's back.

"How should I know?" she said shrugging her shoulders. "He called round this morning, said there was something he needed to collect. It was important for the work they're doing in the faculty apparently. Really, Tom, does it matter? I've got other things to worry about without your father's work. I told Professor Nesbit he was welcome to look around the study and take whatever he needed."

"But *Mu-um*, he could have taken anything. It might have been important. He had no right." What he wanted to say was, *you had no right to let him*, but he didn't want to get into a slanging match so held his tongue.

His mother shrugged again infuriatingly. "All I know is that I've got to sort out life assurance policies and mortgage payments and the last thing I need is to have to deal with your father's work matters as well. If his colleagues are happy to come and sort out that side of things then that's fine by me."

"But we should have seen what was on that memory stick before we let Professor Nesbit take it away." He was almost shouting now. The vacuum cleaner had been turned off in the dining room and his voice sounded uncomfortably loud.

Uncle Bill appeared in the doorway. He was a large man and in his lumberjack shirt looked like the town sheriff come to sort out a tiff in the local bar. "Tom. You're mother's tired. Leave it. Like she said, Professor Nesbit is a colleague of your father's. I'm sure your mother did what she thought was best."

Tom knew he'd lost. There was no point arguing. "Excuse me," he said, trying to squeeze past Uncle Bill in the doorway.

"Where are you going?"
"Out."

19

Professor Alan Nesbit stood by the first-floor window of his office at University College London looking down onto Gower Street. As he watched the cars and buses and passers-by, his mouth curled into a thin smile and he allowed himself a moment of self-congratulation.

The morning had been more successful than he could have hoped. Yesterday, the day of the funeral, he'd achieved nothing. Of course, it had been necessary to show his face, appear mournful and express his condolences to the widow and the boy. But really, it had been a monumental waste of time, first the church service and then the burial (how he loathed vicars with their pious words) and then the interminable wake at the house with the mountain of unnecessary food and the inane conversations. Nancy Letts had infuriated him with her incessant chatter about how wonderful Jack had been. No, compared to yesterday, today was already a significant improvement. He was moving forwards again. Making progress.

And the spoils of his morning's work? Such a small thing but potentially of enormous significance. He reached into his pocket and pulled out a small plastic stick. It was blue in colour and measured roughly three centimetres by one centimetre. The memory stick from Jack's home computer.

He twiddled the stick between his fingers and laughed out loud. He couldn't believe how easy it had been. The woman had practically told him to take what he liked; even seemed relieved that he was offering to sort out her husband's work so she wouldn't have to bother. He could have cleared out the entire study if he'd had a van with him. He'd taken his time examining the books but, disappointingly, there was nothing he didn't already have or couldn't have borrowed from the university library.

The one book he was interested in was nowhere to be seen, so he'd turned his attention to the desk and computer. He couldn't very well walk off with the computer, a bulky, old-fashioned desktop, but then he'd seen the memory stick and knew that it would contain everything of significance. Jack had always been fastidious about backing up his work.

Poor old Jack. His colleague. Late colleague, he reminded himself and he laughed again. That had been easy too, getting rid of Jack.

He hadn't planned it, of course. Well, not in advance. He wasn't a psychopathic killer. Not a deranged lunatic like the sort of people who made the headlines and were locked up in high-security prisons. But the night of the college dinner he had become convinced that Jack was standing in the way of his lifetime's ambition. He had become convinced that Jack had to go.

It might not have been necessary to eliminate him if Jack had been willing to talk. Jack had said something to Richard Newgate over dessert about a Victorian diary and the sleeping angel in Highgate Cemetery. Alan had overheard this snippet of conversation which didn't lead anywhere and afterwards he had invited Jack back to his room in an attempt to obtain more information. Because Alan knew there was a secret connected with the sleeping angel. He'd experienced it himself all those years ago. It had marked him for life and determined his destiny.

But he might as well have conversed with the marble statues in the cemetery, for all the information he was able to prise out of his colleague. When Alan asked him specifically about the diary Jack became defensive, saying that it wasn't his to pass around. He refused Alan's offer of a brandy, saying he was driving and really must be getting back. Alan persuaded him to at least stay for a coffee. Jack relented, saying he'd just go to the toilet whilst

Alan put the kettle on.

It was then that Alan had acted.

He reasoned to himself that maybe the drug would help loosen Jack's tongue. Wasn't it what young men gave to women when they wanted them to lose their inhibitions? The infamous date-rape drug? Alan had found a couple of the pills in his room after a tutorial. They had probably fallen out of a student's pocket. He ground one of them now with the back of a spoon and poured the white powder into Jack's coffee. He was just adding milk and stirring the hot liquid when Jack returned from the bathroom.

Jack sat back in one of the old college armchairs and sipped his coffee. Alan waited. Jack crossed his feet one over the other and yawned. Alan could see him relaxing. Jack finished his coffee, rubbed his hands over his eyes, and fell asleep.

Alan had tried to rouse him and the best he managed was a semi-conscious state in which Jack didn't seem to know where he was or who he was with. Alan had practically had to carry him to his car and then drive the car himself all the way to Highgate. Jack remained comatose in the passenger seat.

But he hadn't taken Jack home.

He parked the car in Swain's Lane, beside the Victorian gateway to the cemetery. It was two o'clock in the morning. Then what? Alan wasn't exactly sure. Maybe it was being near the cemetery that did it, but he was overcome with a conviction that he should be doing the work that Jack was now engaged in and the only solution was for Jack to disappear.

He drove the short distance to Hampstead Heath with no clear idea of what he was going to do, but then, miraculously, the gate onto the heath was standing wide open.

It was clearly a sign. An invitation to drive the car up to the pond.

After that he acted on auto-pilot. He hoisted Jack into the driver's seat, fastened the seat belt, opened the driver's window, released the hand brake and jumped out just as the car started to roll down the bank towards the water.

Alan watched, unmoved, as the car tipped into the water and sank. It didn't go right under, but was submerged sufficiently for the water to pour in and drown the occupant.

As he walked away his thoughts drifted back to the night of Friday the thirteenth of March 1970 when it had all started. It wouldn't be long now, he was sure of it. Soon he would solve the mystery that had plagued him most of his life.

The phone rang snapping him out of his reverie.

"Yes, who is it?"

"Reception. You've got a visitor."

"I wasn't expecting anyone today."

"It's Tom Kelsey. Jack's son."

This was unexpected. What could the boy possibly want?

"What shall I tell him?" asked the receptionist.

Alan thought quickly. He hadn't been able to obtain the information he wanted from Jack, and there was still the question of the missing diary. Maybe the kid would be more compliant than his foolish father. It was worth a try. He slipped the memory stick back into his trouser pocket and smiled to himself. "Tell him to come up."

20

The receptionist, a young woman with her hair in braids, put the phone down and gave Tom a sympathetic smile. "You can go up. Professor Nesbit is in his office. Do you know the way? Up the stairs to the first floor, turn right, along the corridor, last door on the left."

"Thanks."

Tom headed off in the direction the receptionist had

indicated, pausing for a moment to look at the bizarre figure of Jeremy Bentham in his glass case. His dad had called it an auto-icon, and it never failed to attract Tom's attention.

Jeremy Bentham was a nineteenth century philosopher who had specified in his will that his body should be dissected in a public lecture on anatomy and then preserved for posterity. After dissection the skeleton was stuffed with straw, dressed in a white frill shirt, a black jacket, brown trousers and wide-brimmed hat and now sat in a glass-fronted cabinet as if he was about to have his passport photo taken.

Jack had first shown him this curious object years ago, explaining to a fascinated young Tom that the head was made of wax because, apparently, the real mummified head had been too gruesome to keep on public display. It was certainly a novel way to spend the rest of eternity.

Tom dragged himself away from the figure of Jeremy Bentham and headed for the stairs. He knew he was playing for time because, now that he was here, he didn't really know what he was going to say to Professor Nesbit. *I think you've got something of my father's that doesn't belong to you* sounded a bit aggressive, as if he was accusing the professor of stealing. That was how Tom saw it, but still. There was nothing to be gained by alienating the one person who might be able to help. As he climbed the stairs he decided he'd be better off asking about the night his dad died. The Professor must have been at the dinner as well, Tom assumed. Would he know anything? It was worth a try.

At the top of the stairs he turned right and all but collided with Nancy Letts, the department secretary. She was carrying a big pile of papers which, Tom noticed with relief, prevented her from giving him a hug. Still, it was reassuring to meet a friendly face.

"Talk of the devil," she said, giving him a big smile. "I was just thinking about you."

"Oh?"

"I've been sorting out your dad's stuff here in college."
She looked up and down the corridor before continuing in
a low voice. "That nosey old so-and-so Professor Nesbit
couldn't keep his hands off your dad's papers, but I
shooed him away saying it was my job as department
secretary to sort out Jack's stuff and I'd make sure
everything was delivered to your house. The boxes are at
reception now. I'll arrange to have everything sent up to
Highgate later today."

"Thanks," said Tom. He hadn't thought about all the
stuff his dad must have had here at the university. There
was so much to sort out when someone died. "I'm going
to see Professor Nesbit now, actually."

Nancy pulled a face and leaned close, speaking in a
confidential whisper. "He's a weird one that Professor
Nesbit. Not like your dad who was so easy to get on with.
Watch what you tell him. He's sticking his nose into
everything at the moment. Gives me the creeps."

"Right. Thanks for the warning." Tom was surprised at
her frankness.

"You're welcome. If you need anything, you know
where I am," and she gave him a smile and a wink before
heading off down the stairs.

Tom didn't like what he'd just heard. *Nosey old so-and-so
- Gives me the creeps.* Well, what did they say? *Forewarned is
forearmed?* He'd have it out with the Professor and then
leave as quickly as possible.

Tom found the door marked *Professor Alan Nesbit* and
knocked.

21

Lauren turned her key in the lock, opened the door and
slipped inside. Wendy would still be at the cemetery, so
Lauren had the house to herself. And yet she didn't feel
entirely alone. Not anymore.

Now she knew, for certain, that Isabelle Hart had lived here, she fancied she could sense her presence, almost hear the rustle of silk skirts. She imagined Isabelle entering through the front door as she, Lauren, had just done. What had the hallway looked like then? Probably darker, with only candles or maybe gaslights to light the way.

Lauren kicked off her sandals and stepped onto the floor tiles, enjoying their coolness under her throbbing feet. They were the original Victorian tiles, laid out in a mosaic of diamonds, squares and triangles in terracotta, black and cream and were one of Wendy's favourite features about the house. She followed the intricate pattern of the tiles, as if seeing their detail properly for the first time.

Isabelle walked over these tiles. Did she study their pattern as I'm doing now?

She walked through to the kitchen at the back of the house and helped herself to a juice from the fridge. She'd spent the last hour wandering aimlessly around Waterlow Park, the events of the last twenty-four hours playing in her head on an endless loop – the séance, the box in the attic, meeting that boy. God, how she wished she'd asked him his name.

And the diary.

She'd only held it for a moment, but she'd give anything to be able to take a proper look at it. Her only hope was that he'd go back to the park tomorrow at the same time.

But was that likely? Christ, his dad had just died. He must be going through a hell of a time right now.

I wonder how he died?

A memory stirred at the back of Lauren's mind. She left the coke in the kitchen and went back into the hallway, opening the door to the cupboard under the stairs. It was where they kept their recycling boxes, one for glass, one for metals and one for paper.

Lauren pulled out the box for paper and started

rummaging through it. Because the council only collected the recycling on alternate weeks, it was overflowing with junk mail, catalogues, fliers and old newspapers. She pulled out everything in the top half of the box and laid it to one side. What she was looking for, if they still had it, would be near the bottom.

She tossed aside advertisements for pizza delivery companies and the new tandoori restaurant until she found what she was looking for – the local newspaper, *The Ham & High,* from two weeks ago.

She perched on the bottom stair and shook out the crumpled newspaper. She was sure she had the right edition because she remembered now seeing it on the breakfast table when she'd come down for school one morning. She hadn't paid much attention because she'd been in a hurry, as usual. Getting up in the morning wasn't her strong point. At the time she'd turned the pages, idly, whilst eating a bowl of cereal.

She turned them more deliberately now, scanning each page. She found what she was looking for on page five. *Drowned Man in Car in Pond* ran the headline. The accompanying photo showed the roof of a blue car just visible on the surface of the water and two policemen and a police diver standing on the bank. Lauren re-read the article, more slowly this time.

Dr Jack Kelsey, lecturer in history at University College London, was found drowned in his car at Highgate Ponds early on Saturday 23rd June. A passing jogger, Mr Edward Burrows, raised the alarm when he saw the car floating in the water. Dr Kelsey was pronounced dead at the scene. DCI McNally, in charge of the investigation, was not available for comment. Investigations are focusing on why the gate at the end of Merton Lane had been left open after council contractors had been working on the heath. A council spokesman told this newspaper they were unavailable for comment. Dr Kelsey leaves behind a wife and son.

Of course, there was no reason to assume that the boy she'd just met was the *son* referred to in the article. But if it was him, then there was something very strange about the manner of his dad's death.

And what about the boy himself? Lauren realised, with a smile, it wasn't just the diary she was interested in. She really hoped she'd see him again.

22

"Do come in, Tom. What a pleasant surprise."

Tom was thrown off guard. He wasn't expecting such a warm welcome from the dour and taciturn man of yesterday. But pre-warned by Nancy to be on his guard, Tom thought he detected something not quite sincere in the professor's tone of voice.

Professor Nesbit held the door open and gestured with a sweep of his arm that Tom should enter. Gone was the evasive, skulking figure of yesterday and in his place the professor seemed to have put on a new demeanour that didn't quite suit him.

Tom hesitated for a second, then crossed the threshold into the professor's office. It was too late to change his mind now. Professor Nesbit closed the door with a decisive click and then strode into the middle of the room, rubbing his hands.

Tom watched him closely, trying to decide what was making him feel so on edge. The professor's mouth twitched upwards at the corners and his eyes gleamed, then narrowed slightly. Too keen. That was it. The professor was too eager, like a child who has been told to stand still for ten minutes before opening his Christmas presents. It was as if the professor had been hoping he would visit and was now relishing every moment. Tom couldn't shake the feeling that he'd walked straight into the lion's den.

And there was something about the room that wasn't

right, but Tom couldn't put his finger on it. He glanced across at the desk, hoping to see the memory stick the professor had taken from his dad's study, but all he could see were untidy piles of papers which, judging from their yellowed edges, looked as if they had been there for decades.

"Cup of tea, Tom?"

Professor Nesbit had moved over to a plastic jug kettle perched on top of a small round table. Next to the kettle were two dirty mugs, a box of teabags and a carton of milk that couldn't possibly be fresh in this heat.

"No thanks."

The professor hovered for a moment by the kettle, then gestured to a couple of armchairs badly in need of re-upholstering that faced each other across a small coffee table.

"Do sit down, Tom."

Tom took the nearest chair and perched on the edge of the seat. He realised now what it was he didn't like about the room. His dad had occupied a similar room down the corridor but his dad's room was a home from home. It had pictures on the wall and photos on the bookcases of Tom at different ages – riding his bike aged five, paddling in the sea aged seven, standing on top of Scarfell Pike aged fifteen. Professor Nesbit's room had nothing like that. Not a single picture. Not a single photo. It was full of books and papers but it was unreadable – it told Tom nothing about the man he'd come to see other than that he probably didn't have any family or outside interests.

Professor Nesbit sat down opposite him. "So what was it you wanted to see me about, Tom?"

Tom didn't like the way the professor kept using his name every time he spoke to him. Like he was being too pally, trying too hard to win him over. He decided to get straight to the point. The sooner he got this over with the sooner he could get out.

"The night Dad died…"

"Terrible tragedy. Terrible tragedy." The professor seemed to be staring at something behind Tom's right shoulder and wouldn't meet his eye.

"The night he died," Tom persisted, "he'd been to a college dinner."

"Yes, Tom, that's right. Venison. Followed by crème brûlée. The starter was smoked salmon I think."

Tom fidgeted in his seat and mentally rolled his eyes at the ceiling. "What I mean is, was there anything unusual about him that night? Did he seem in any way different to you? Who else was at the dinner? Did you talk to him? What did you talk about?"

A thin smile spread across Professor Nesbit's mouth and he looked straight at Tom.

"Goodness me, questions, questions. Of course you want answers, Tom. Of course you do." Professor Nesbit stood up and walked over to the window so that Tom was forced to turn around in his seat to look at him. "We all want answers to questions don't we?"

"Well, right now all I want to know is…"

The professor cut him off. "For example, the work your father was doing just before he died. Did he talk to you about it?"

"Not really, I mean, why would he?" Tom was confused at the direction the conversation was taking.

The professor moved to stand behind Tom's chair. "Oh, come on, I bet the two of you were as thick as thieves." Professor Nesbit was obviously trying for a jolly tone of voice, but it struck Tom as false. "Didn't he talk to you about his work at the weekends when he took you out to football matches, you know, father and son – a bit of, what do they call it – bonding?"

The professor moved round to the side of the chair, keeping one hand on the back, and leaned towards Tom. Tom shrank backwards. Professor Nesbit's attempt to be pally repulsed him. He reminded Tom of a snake – slippery and deadly at the same time. The idea of this childless bachelor pretending to know anything about a father and son relationship was absurd. And anyway, what he and his dad had talked about was none of this creep's business. He'd come here to ask questions but somehow the tables had been turned and he was the one being interrogated.

To Tom's relief the professor moved back to the other armchair and sat down.

"Your father came into possession of some papers a couple of months ago. I know that much for certain."

Tom listened, trying to keep his face neutral, giving nothing away. He might learn something here after all. Professor Nesbit seemed to think his dad's work was significant.

"Those papers had something to do with Highgate Cemetery. Were you aware of him visiting the cemetery?"

Tom had, in fact, known about his dad's visits to Highgate Cemetery but he hadn't thought anything of them at the time. His dad had even invited him along once but he'd wanted to stay in and watch the football. Now he regretted his decision. What might he have learned if he'd gone along?

"He might have gone to the cemetery once or twice," he said in response to the professor's question. *He's there right now in fact.*

Professor Nesbit hit the arm of his chair with his fist, making Tom jump.

"Your father should have come to me. He had no right. I'm the expert on the cemetery." All the fake jollity had gone from the professor's voice.

Tom didn't know what to say. He hadn't expected that little outburst and felt he was beginning to lose the plot.

"I could have done the work better than him."

Tom didn't know what work the Professor was talking about but he felt an instinctive surge of anger at this slight to his dad's abilities. "You've got no right to criticise him like that."

The Professor held up his hand. His voice was icy. "You have to understand Tom that some people see things that others cannot."

What?

The words sounded strange in Professor Nesbit's mouth as if they weren't his own but he'd pinched them from someone else. If it was a quote, Tom couldn't place it.

"I'm sorry, I don't understand."

"It is the fault of our science that it wants to explain all; and if it explain not, then it says there is nothing to explain."

"What on earth are you talking about?" Tom shifted in his seat. The professor was starting to sound like a madman.

And this lunatic was Dad's colleague. How did Dad put up with him?

Tom looked closely at the professor. His eyes had taken on a fevered look and drops of perspiration were appearing on his brow.

Despite the heat of the day and the stuffiness of the room, Tom shivered. A tiny germ of understanding had taken root in his brain. It was as if he'd just glimpsed the truth and it horrified him.

It can't be true.

Tom gripped the arms of the chair. His ears were buzzing and he thought he might be sick. He tried to tell himself it was just a suspicion, that he had no evidence, but he couldn't shake the conviction that he was sitting in the presence of his dad's murderer.

"I have to go," said Tom jumping to his feet and heading towards the door.

"Stop." The voice was commanding and surprisingly loud.

Tom froze.

"Do you know of any papers, letters, journals that your father may have hidden somewhere? It's important. I need to see them."

The diary. He wants to see Isabelle's diary.

Tom stared straight into the professor's eyes, trying to hold his voice steady. "Nope. Sorry. Can't help you there."

He bounded for the door and left without another word.

23

Alan Nesbit stood at the door to his office and listened to the sound of Tom's footsteps hurrying down the corridor. Like the boy couldn't get out of there fast enough.

It was obvious Tom knew more than he was letting on. Alan had seen a flicker of understanding in his eyes at the mention of the word *journal* and the boy's denial had been unconvincing – too forced.

Alan had an urge to chase after him and demand that Tom tell him the truth but he was no longer a young man and by now Tom would be out on the street, lost in the London crowds. Besides, it would look suspicious to go running after him. No, he needed to stay calm and bide his time.

Far better to work on the widow. She wasn't wary of him and he could easily manipulate her with offers of sympathy and support. He was confident that he would get what he wanted eventually if he made himself a welcome guest in the house. He could be ingratiating if he needed to. For now, though, he had other things to think about.

He closed his office door and sat down at his desk where he pulled open the top drawer, and took out a small key. Then he unlocked the large bottom drawer in the desk and used both hands to pull out a sturdy cardboard box of the sort used by removal firms.

He placed the box on the desk and lifted the flaps. On the top was an old A4 cardboard wallet which he removed and laid on the desk. Next came a parcel wrapped loosely in newspaper. He unfolded the newspaper to check that he had sufficient supplies. Good. Everything was in order.

He re-wrapped the newspaper parcel then lifted it out and placed it in a black leather holdall that he kept under his desk. Then he retrieved his tools from the box and put them into the bag as well. He put the A4 wallet back into the box, returned the box to the bottom drawer of the desk, locked it and dropped the key into the top drawer. He was ready.

He stepped out into the corridor, glancing to left and right. The corridor was empty. He locked his door, picked up the black holdall and strode out of the building in the direction of Euston from where he would be able to catch a northbound Northern Line train to Highgate. Then all he had to do was go to the cemetery and request to visit his parents' grave like any other dutiful son. He smiled to himself as he dodged the cars and buses on Euston Road. He was close to fulfilling his mission, he was sure of it. It wouldn't be long now.

24

The heat and noise hit Lauren like a tsunami. Bodies were packed, cheek by jowl, in the dimly lit space. Already regretting her decision to come, Lauren took a gulp of air and plunged into the sea of Saturday night revellers thronging the underground cellar that constituted Highgate's trendiest venue for live music.

She was late. It was already nine-thirty and Megan had said to meet at eight. But after dinner she'd spent another hour helping Wendy clear the attic because the builder had called to say he would start on Monday. And then she'd needed a shower to remove the dust that clung to her hair and skin. Megan, of course, would assume she'd been on a date with her *secret boyfriend* and would no doubt give her the third degree later on. That's if Lauren ever found Megan and Chloe in this crowd.

She spent about ten minutes squeezing her way around sweaty bodies and was tempted to just give up and go home when she spied her two friends tucked into a corner by the side of the stage. They were standing next to a monster amplifier that was blasting them with decibels. Lauren thought they were mad for choosing such a spot until she realised it was the closest Megan could get to Rick who was perched behind his drum kit, no more than three feet away. Lauren inched her way around the stage, until she reached her friends, mouthing *Hi* at them.

Chloe smiled and waved but Megan pointed at her watch and raised her eyebrows as if to say, *where have you been?* Lauren ignored her. It was too loud to talk so she turned to watch the band.

Megan's brother Matt was striding around the stage, microphone in his right hand, punching the air with his left fist and screeching out the lyrics to their latest song. Lauren didn't know the bass player who was new and seemed to be concentrating hard on playing the right notes. She recognised the keyboard player – he'd been the best pianist at school a few years back and was the real musical talent behind the group. But the only band member that Megan ever talked about was Rick, the drummer. With his pale face, thin mouth, black hair and black eyes, he had a haunted look which made Lauren's skin crawl.

Not like the boy she'd met this afternoon.

She closed her eyes and tried to picture him. Floppy blond hair, brown eyes.

I hope I see him again.

An elbow jabbed her in the back and she turned her head to see what was going on. More people than ever were crowding into the underground space and she was being squashed against the stage. This wasn't Lauren's idea of fun. She looked towards the exit but it was too far away. She'd never be able to push past all those people. Besides, Megan would never be persuaded to leave until the end.

Lauren tried to enjoy the music and ignore the fact that she was constantly being elbowed and shoved. The song was rising to a crescendo. Rick was hammering wildly on the drums, strands of long black hair whipping around his face. The bass player was tossing his head up and down to the beat and Matt was standing centre stage, eyes tight shut and mouth wide open on a long, high note.

Then everything stopped.

In an instant the cellar was plunged into pitch blackness and the amplifiers went dead. For a second there was nothing. Then someone screamed. Then the shouting started.

What the hell's going on?
Turn the lights back on!
Out of the way, moron!

Panic swooped down on the crowd like the moment in a disaster movie when everything suddenly goes wrong.

Lauren wished for all the world that she hadn't come. She could have just said *no* to Megan. She didn't always have to do what Megan wanted.

She tried to move but she was trapped by the mass of people surrounding her, and besides it was as dark as a black hole. She wouldn't be able to find the exit if she tried. Someone shoved her and breathed the sickly, sweet smell of beer into her face. She turned away, gagging, and reached for the edge of the stage, every muscle in her body taut as she braced herself in an effort to stay on her feet and not be pushed over by these idiots. If she was knocked down in this crowd she could be trampled to death. Someone large and heavy fell on top of her from behind, knocking the breath out of her as her ribcage pressed into the hot metal of one of the spotlights.

You have to get up onto the stage before you're crushed to death.

She placed her palms flat onto the stage and tried to haul herself up but she was jammed in too tight.

A blinding white light suddenly flooded the cellar accompanied by an ear-splitting screech from the amplifier. Lauren winced and jammed her fingers in her ears.

The power was back on.

But by now a full-scale riot had erupted. Fuelled by alcohol and fear, fists flew through the air. A man standing next to Lauren staggered backwards with a bloodied nose. Someone swung a bottle through the air like a baseball bat. And the amplifier continued to screech like a bat out of hell.

Lauren looked around for Megan and Chloe. Megan had managed to climb onto the stage and was hauling a tearful Chloe up by the arms. Lauren called out to them to help her but her voice was lost in the din of amplifier feedback and shouting.

Then someone pulled the plug on the amplifier and that was when she heard shouts of *Police*. She felt dizzy and black dots danced in front of her eyes. If she didn't escape this crush soon she would pass out.

Suddenly she felt strong hands grab hold of her upper arms and she was being hauled out of the crowd, up onto the stage. Matt and Rick had hold of her and were dragging her upwards. For a few excruciating seconds it felt as though her shoulders were going to be ripped from their sockets, but then she felt her lower body break free of the crush and she toppled forward onto the stage.

Relief flooded through her. For a moment she knelt on all fours trying to get her breath back. Then she became aware of Megan and Chloe pulling her to her feet.

"Go that way," Matt shouted to them. He was pointing at a fire door at the back of the stage. They ran for it.

Megan threw herself against the horizontal barrier on the door and they stumbled out into a dark, stinking yard filled with rubbish bins and smelling of vomit and urine.

"Oh my God, what happened in there?" said Lauren, gasping at the foul smell but relieved to be outside.

"Drugs raid," said Megan.

"You are kidding!" Lauren was horrified. She never wanted to be involved in anything like that ever again.

"Come on, let's get out of here," said Megan who was

already heading towards a flight of stone steps at the far end of the yard. Lauren and Chloe followed her up the steps which emerged in a narrow back alley.

"This way," said Megan, who was the only one who seemed to know where they were.

They walked quickly away and, for a while, no one spoke. Lauren's ears were still buzzing from the ferocious pounding they'd been subjected to and she was shaking from the shock of the blackout and the subsequent fighting that had broken out. What would have happened to them if they hadn't escaped?

They came to the main road and Lauren had never been happier to see streetlights, cars and ordinary people enjoying the warm summer evening. They passed an Italian restaurant with half a dozen tables outside under the red, white and green awning. People were eating pizza and pasta and drinking glasses of wine. Lauren inhaled the aroma of garlic, basil and oregano and began to feel more like herself.

"You all right?" Chloe asked her.

Lauren nodded. "And you?"

"I'm OK now," said Chloe, "but that was scary."

Lauren looked across at Megan. She was the only one of them who didn't look relieved. In fact she looked pissed off.

She's probably cross that we had to leave early and she didn't get to talk to Rick.

Chloe turned to Megan and said in a bright, cheery tone, "Rick couldn't take his eyes off you."

"Couldn't he?" said Megan trying to sound cool about it but obviously pleased with the comment.

"Maybe you two will get together over the summer," said Chloe.

"Perhaps," said Megan. "But I'm not the one with a secret love life right now," she added in a mysterious tone of voice.

"Oh?" asked Chloe, standing still and looking amazed.

Here we go, thought Lauren.

Megan was striding ahead and already turning into Swain's Lane.

It was not the route Lauren would have chosen late at night but Chloe was running to catch up with her and Lauren had no choice but to follow.

"Who's got a secret love life?" asked Chloe.

"Lauren has," said Megan.

"Lauren, you never said. Who is it?"

It was the moment Lauren had been dreading. "I haven't got a secret boyfriend," she said, trying to make her voice sound convincing.

"Don't listen to her," said Megan. "This boy was hanging around outside her house this morning and when I told her I'd seen him she practically bit my head off wanting to know where he'd gone."

"Ooh, how exciting," said Chloe. "Who is he? Anyone we know?"

"OK, OK," said Lauren, sighing. "If you let me explain I'll tell you what happened."

She told them about finding the box with the sampler and photo in the attic, how she'd gone to the library, bumped into this boy, discovered that he too was researching Isabelle Hart and how, when she'd tracked him down, he actually had a diary belonging to Isabelle, the girl whose name had been conjured up last night by the Ouija board.

"Wicked," said Megan, laughing. "I told you that Ouija board was the real McCoy. Aren't you glad now I brought it round? It's helped you to find romance."

"I haven't found romance. There's nothing going on." Lauren was starting to feel cross and was glad they couldn't see her blushing in the dark.

"So what's his name?" asked Chloe. "Will you be seeing him again?"

"I don't know his name," Lauren admitted. "I forgot to ask."

"You don't know his name?" asked Megan in disbelief. "Really, Lauren, what are you like?"

Both Megan and Chloe burst out laughing. Lauren did her best to join in although she didn't think it was very funny.

By now they had reached the railings that ran along the edge of the cemetery. Lauren remembered what Wendy had said about the broken fence and sure enough, there in front of them, in the five foot high row of metal railings, was a gap about eighteen inches wide. Lauren wasn't going to mention it, but then Megan spotted it.

"Hey," she said. "Look at that." She stuck her head through the gap and peered into the blackness of the cemetery beyond. "Who's up for a ghost walk?" she asked turning to grin at Lauren and Chloe.

"Don't be stupid," said Lauren. "We can't go in there."

"Why not? Who says we can't?"

"We'd be trespassing."

"Who's going to find out? The residents won't complain. They're all dead."

Lauren thought that was downright disrespectful, but she let it go. "Can't we just go home?"

"For God's sake, don't be so boring, Lauren. We won't do any harm and it'll be fun. I'm going in. Coming Chloe?"

Chloe giggled. Lauren couldn't tell if she was scared or actually thought it would be fun like Megan said.

"Please," said Lauren. But Megan had already climbed through the gap and Lauren felt a horrible sinking feeling as Chloe followed her. She didn't want to go into the cemetery but neither did she want to be left on her own in Swain's Lane in the dark.

Megan turned to look at her from the other side of the railings. "Are you coming or not?"

Lauren glanced around, worried that someone might see them breaking into the cemetery, but Swain's Lane was deserted.

"OK," she sighed. "But promise me we'll be out of

here in ten minutes at the most."

"Sure," said Megan waving a hand in the air. "Whatever you say."

Feeling a mixture of nerves and guilt, Lauren squeezed through the gap and joined her friends on the other side. Wendy would kill her if she knew what she was doing. She pushed the thought from her mind.

"Come on," said Megan. "Time for a spot of ghost hunting." She made a howling noise, then laughed and headed off into the dark. Lauren and Chloe followed behind, trying to keep up.

They were in an area of long grass spiked with thistles that scratched at Lauren's bare legs. With only the moon to guide them, it was hard to see the gravestones which protruded from the ground in unexpected places, often at lopsided angles. There was no regular layout to the graves which lay dotted in all directions, often close to one another as if for company. Picking a path through them was like navigating a Halloween obstacle course. Lauren knew the cemetery well from years accompanying Wendy on tours, but entering as it were by the back door, a long way from the main path, meant she was hopelessly lost. Megan was already a long way in front, disappearing into the darkness.

"What's that?" whispered Chloe grabbing Lauren by the arm and pointing at two pinpricks of light visible in the undergrowth.

"A fox, I think," said Lauren. As they approached there was a rustling of leaves and the animal disappeared.

"I hope there aren't any bats in the cemetery," said Chloe.

"Probably are," said Lauren. She felt Chloe's grip on her arm tighten.

"Where's Megan got to? I can't see her."

"I think she went that way."

"Ouch!"

"What's the matter?"

"I bashed my knee on a gravestone. I can't see where we're going."

"We need to find Megan," said Lauren, "and then I think we should get out of here."

"I agree," said Chloe. "You were right. We shouldn't have come in here. It was a stupid idea."

They stumbled on through the long grass until they felt the ground under their feet become hard and stony.

"We've reached the path," said Lauren. "But where on earth has Megan got to?"

They peered into the darkness, seeing nothing.

A light appeared on the path no more than ten yards ahead of them. Lauren held her breath and felt Chloe's hand on her arm.

"Where did you two get to?" At the sound of the familiar voice, Lauren breathed out and Chloe dropped her hand. It was Megan using the light from her phone as a torch.

"Megan, thank goodness it's you," said Lauren.

"Who else did you think it would be? A psycho? What's the matter with you two? Anyone would think you'd just met Dracula."

"Don't be silly," said Lauren. "We just got a bit spooked, that's all. Can we go now?"

"Not until you've seen this," said Megan.

"What?"

"Come this way and I'll show you," said Megan mysteriously.

Cursing under her breath, Lauren followed, trying not to lose sight of Megan this time. Chloe linked arms with her, holding her close, and Lauren could feel her warm breath against her cheek.

The path sloped uphill and brought them to a row of stone catacombs, each one about the size of a beach hut but built to house lead-lined coffins rather than deckchairs.

"Look," said Megan, pointing at the ground in front of one of the catacombs. Lauren and Chloe stepped closer and peered at the ground. At first Lauren couldn't see anything but then Megan shone the light from her phone onto the ground and Lauren saw a row of garlic bulbs lying in front of the door to the catacomb. She counted twenty bulbs lined up two inches apart. Someone had put them there deliberately. Lauren felt the hairs on the back of her neck stand on end. Chloe put out a hand to pick one up.

"Be careful," said Lauren.

Chloe pulled her hand back as if she'd been burned. "But what are they doing there?" she asked.

"Obvious, isn't it?" said Megan. "Garlic keeps vampires away."

Chloe stood up, laughing. "That's ridiculous. There's no such thing as vampires."

"Well someone obviously thinks there's one in here," said Megan.

"*Shhh*," said Lauren grabbing Megan by the arm, "I think there's someone coming."

"Get off," hissed Megan, "you're hurting me."

"Sorry," whispered Lauren letting go of her.

They stood in silence and listened. Lauren could hear the blood pumping inside her head. Despite the mildness of the night she shivered. An owl hooted overhead making her jump.

"I can't hear anything," said Megan.

"*Shhh*, there's definitely something…"

A twig snapped. Stomping in the undergrowth. And then a dark figure appeared on the path no more than twenty feet away from them. Megan switched off her phone. No one moved.

"Who goes there?" shouted an angry male voice. The man took a step towards them. Something flashed in the moonlight. Lauren couldn't see the man's face but she glimpsed the blade of an axe held high as if about to strike them dead.

They turned and ran.

25

Reflections of Will Bucket, Gravedigger, In the Year of Our Lord 1870, continued…

Now I don't mind burying 'em – it's what I does for a living an' all and, like I says, the work's regular so you just get on with it and don't make a fuss. But sometimes you get asked to dig 'em up and that don't half give me the willies.

We had one last year what caused a right old palaver. In fact, she were one of the first I buried when I come here as a young 'prentice and there we were, seven years later, digging her up again. It were enough to make all the other bodies turn in their graves.

Lizzie her name was. Lizzie Siddal. I heard from Josiah Heap, the senior grave digger, that she were only 'bout thirty or so when she died. She'd copped it from an overdose of laudanum. Now, I ain't one to judge, but I heard too she was married to some fella who was a painter and a poet with some fancy name – Rossetti (I ask you) – and it struck me at the time that a young missus like her (I'd heard she used to work in a hat shop) would've been better off with a nice young cobbler or butcher or baker. What did she want to go running off with a poet for? From what I've heard they're all a bit queer in the head. No wonder she went a bit loopy, poor thing.

So anyway, there she was, dead as a doornail and sealed up in her coffin. We buried her in the Rossetti family tomb and I thought no more 'bout it.

But last year, seven years after we put her under, we gets a special request. It turns out this poet's got an agent (scoundrel if you ask me) by the name of Charles Howell and this agent fella wants us to dig her up 'cause the poet (sentimental old git) only went and put a copy of his poems into her coffin before it was sealed and now he wants 'em back. Did he think she was gonna read 'em or what? I tell you, you couldn't make this stuff up.

'Course, we couldn't go digging her up in the middle of the day. We have burials here all the time and lots of people come to pay their respects to their relatives. They wouldn't have been none too happy if they'd seen us digging her up when they'd come to spend a few quiet moments admiring the family memorial (some people gets a bit competitive over the size of their urns or the gracefulness of their angels, but that's another story.) No, we have to dig her up at night when the cemetery is closed and all God-fearing people are at home in their beds.

So there we are, in the dark. We have to light a bonfire to see by. Mr Hills, the cemetery superintendent is there with the agent, Mr Howell. Her husband, the poet, don't show up. Just as well otherwise I might not have been able to stop myself from telling him to go and get a proper job. Josiah Heap is there to oversee the digging but me and Big Bert have to do all the hard work.

We work around the slab with a crowbar each so we can lever it up and lift it out. It's slow work and hard to see properly in the dark – the bonfire don't give off that much light. After about an hour we've loosened the slab and we slides it out to reveal the grave. It's deep 'cause they're planning to bury a whole load of Rossettis in it eventually. Big Bert and me jump down into the hole and start shovelling earth off the top of the coffin. Lucky she was the last person to be buried in here so she's on the top of the pile, even if she's still 'bout eight feet down.

When we've cleared the earth off the coffin Josiah Heap throws down some ropes which we ties to the handles. Then we climbs back out using a ladder and we helps Josiah Heap and Mr Hills pull the coffin up by the ropes. It's heavy and I nearly loses me footing at one point on the muddy ground. "Whoa," I shouts. Everyone stops pulling 'cause no one wants anyone to fall in. "All right lad?" asks Josiah Heap. "Right as rain," I says and we carries on. I've never known Josiah Heap be so concerned. Maybe he don't like this neither.

So we gets the coffin out and lays it down on the ground. Now this agent chap is so excited he can't control himself and he shouts, "Lift the lid! Lift the lid!" It's like he's got some kinda urge to look at dead bodies. He gives me the willies, for sure.

Big Bert and me work around the coffin lid, unscrewing all the screws and putting each one carefully in our pockets 'cause we've gotta put 'em all back again when we've finished.

When we've got all the screws out we stands back. I know Big Bert's thinking the same as me – we don't want to be the ones who lift the lid. Mr Hills steps in and takes charge which is the only useful thing he's done so far. The agent is hopping around like he's 'bout to burst. We ignores him as best we can.

"Will and Bert, you take the bottom of the lid," says Mr Hills, "and Josiah and I will lift the top." In the light of the bonfire I sees Mr Hills looks a bit queasy which ain't surprising.

We lifts the lid and, despite myself, I can't help looking inside the coffin. I'm curious. What does a seven year old dead body look like?

Like an angel.

She's beautiful. She's lying there with her hands crossed over her chest and this amazing long red hair flowing all around her like silk.

The agent dives in and starts rummaging around in her hair. I want to tell him to stop but me tongue is glued to the roof of me mouth.

The agent jumps up clutching something in his hand. "Got it." It's the book of poems. He stuffs it inside his coat pocket grinning like he's just found the crown jewels.

"Right, let's get the lid back on," says Mr Hills.

I takes one last look at this angel before the lid goes back on and me and Big Bert start putting all the screws back.

"Rest in peace," I says to her, but real quiet, like, so no

one else can hear.

PART FOUR
SUNDAY 15 JULY

26

Lauren bought the same baguette as yesterday, another packet of barbecue flavoured crisps and a bottle of coke. Wendy was doing another stint at the cemetery so Lauren could please herself for lunch. She took the food into Waterlow Park and headed over to the same bench as yesterday. It was empty. The boy was nowhere to be seen.

If she was honest, she hadn't really expected him to be here. The boy, whatever his name was, had enough on his plate without listening to the ravings of strange girls who prattled on about Ouija boards and unknown Victorian ladies and then upset him by tactlessly mentioning his dead father. She couldn't blame him if he didn't want to see her again. She'd have no doubt felt the same in his shoes. Still, she couldn't help feeling disappointed.

She sat down, put her lunch to one side and rubbed her eyes. She felt awful. She hadn't slept well and knew she looked a fright. Not surprising really after everything that had happened last night – the crush and noise in the Club, the fighting that had broken out, their lucky escape and then, just to round things off, that encounter with the mad axe-man in the cemetery. She'd had no more than a fleeting glance of that blade, but the memory of it made her stomach turn over.

Who goes there? Lauren was sure she'd recognise that voice if she heard it again – hard and callous with no hint of humanity. He'd sounded like a deranged landowner who wouldn't hesitate to shoot anything or anybody who trespassed on his property. For one heart-stopping moment she'd really thought she was about to meet her maker. It was a miracle they'd managed to run back to the gap in the railings so quickly without getting lost or falling over a gravestone and breaking a leg. What had they been thinking of? Lauren had been furious with Megan for making them do something so stupid and she'd told her so. But secretly she was even more furious with herself for going along with it in the first place. In future she'd tell Megan where to stick her crazy suggestions.

At breakfast this morning, when Wendy asked her if she'd had a nice time, she almost blurted out the story of the garlic bulbs and the man with the axe but had then thought better of it. She couldn't ever tell her mum what she'd seen because that would mean admitting to trespassing in the cemetery in the middle of the night. If Wendy knew what she'd done, she'd be grounded. Instead she just nodded and said, yes the band was great. If word got out about the police raid at the gig then she'd have to say they left early because it was so crowded.

And then she'd had that weird dream again last night – the forest and the trees turning into stone columns and angels, the woman in black who held out her hand, still stone-cold. She'd heard the sound of angels singing. Then the singing had turned into a scream and she'd woken up, the duvet tangled around her legs.

She stretched her legs out and turned her face up

towards the hot sun, closing her eyes. Maybe she should just sit here all day.

A shadow fell across her.

Startled, she blinked her eyes open.

"Hi there."

It was the boy from yesterday. Standing in front of her. Blond hair falling in front of his eyes. His eyes really were very nice now they weren't all red and bloodshot.

"Is it OK if I join you?" he asked. "You did say you were going to be here today." He didn't sound confident that he was welcome.

"Yes, sorry, I was miles away." She sat up, flustered, and moved the food out of the way. He sat down, dropping his backpack on the bench between them.

Lauren studied his face, trying to gauge his mood. She didn't want to say the wrong thing again. In the end she said, "I wasn't expecting to see you."

He frowned and she bit her lip. That hadn't come out right. It sounded like she didn't want to see him. She tried again, "I mean, I'd have understood if you didn't want to meet me again. You must have thought I was a bit weird yesterday, going on about a séance and I'm really sorry about your dad…" She was rambling, trying to fill the silence.

Shut up or he'll do another runner.

"It's OK. You weren't to know." He gave her a small smile.

"Thanks." It looked like she was forgiven.

"I don't know your name," she said. If she didn't ask now Megan and Chloe would have every right to laugh at her and call her a hopeless case.

"It's Tom," he said. "Tom Kelsey."

"Pleased to meet you, Tom," said Lauren extending her right hand.

He took her hand and, in his strong, firm grip, Lauren felt all the tension of the night before melt away from her. Maybe they could become friends after all, and then who knew what might happen. She wanted to keep holding his hand, but Tom had already let go and was starting to undo the flaps on his backpack.

"Listen," he said, "I had an idea. I don't know if you've got time to do this, or even if you'd want to but I think somebody should and I'm not sure I've got the patience."

"Sure. What is it?"

He opened the backpack and pulled out the black leather diary he'd shown her yesterday. "I thought you might like to have a go at reading Isabelle's diary. I know you're interested in her and, well, I've tried deciphering the handwriting but it's a real slog and there are other things I need to be getting on with right now." He held the diary out to her. "Would you like to read it?"

She stared at him open-mouthed. She couldn't believe he was willing to trust her with something so precious when they hardly knew each other.

He must have taken her silence for reluctance because he said, "Of course, if you don't want to I'd understand, and I know I only met you yesterday but I feel I can trust you and…"

"No, no," she said. "I was just surprised, that's all. I'd love to read it for you. I really would." She took the book in her hands and held it as if he'd just given her the original Dead Sea Scrolls.

"But are you sure you don't mind me taking this home?"

"Quite sure. In fact, it would be safer with you right now than with me."

That's an odd thing to say, she thought. But she wasn't going to argue. He must have his reasons. And besides, she'd like nothing better than to read this diary. She couldn't believe her luck.

She turned to a page at random, squinting in the bright sunshine. He was right about the handwriting. Although it had a beauty of its own, it was difficult to read because of all the loops and scrolls; the capital letters in particular were much more elaborate than their modern-day printed counterparts. She flicked over a couple of pages. Sometimes the handwriting was firm and well rounded, at other times it leaned heavily to the right or the letters became jagged and uneven as if the writer had been in a hurry or had not been in a calm state of mind when she wrote. Lauren tried reading a page towards the end:

Saturday, 19th March 1870, 11 o'clock in the evening.
It is late but I am wound up like a spring and know it would be hopeless to attempt sleep at the moment. This evening we did not achieve the hoped-for results but it will happen tomorrow – I am sure of it.

She would happily have dived straight in and started reading from the beginning – Megan often teased her for being a bookworm - but now was not the time. She closed the diary and rested her hands on the soft black leather. It would take time to get used to the handwriting. She'd have to be patient.

"You're right, it is a bit of a slog to read but I'm sure I'll get the hang of it. I could re-type it on the computer if you like."

"That would be great. Thanks."

"But can I ask one thing?"

"Sure."

"Why do you want to know what's in this diary?"

Tom looked straight at her with his clear brown eyes. He took a deep breath, then said, "I think Dad was murdered and I think it had something to do with this diary."

A cloud drifted in front of the sun and the sudden shift in air temperature set up a breeze. A newspaper scudded along the ground at their feet. Lauren shivered, but it was less from the sudden shade than from what Tom had just told her. She wished she'd misheard him, but she knew she hadn't.

"Murdered?" she managed to croak. There had been nothing about suspicious circumstances in the article in the *Ham & High*. "Are you sure?"

"All I know," said Tom, "is that Dad didn't drive his car into Highgate Ponds on his own. It's absurd."

She nodded, trying to understand. "But why aren't the police treating his death as murder?"

"Because they're idiots, that's why." There was no hiding the contempt in his voice.

"But haven't you told them about your suspicions?"

"They don't want to listen. I need to get some hard evidence first. That's why I was hoping you'd read the diary for me, so I can get on with checking out my dad's computer and going through his emails."

He was already doing up his backpack, preparing to leave.

"Hang on," said Lauren. "At least give me your phone number so I can get in touch with you."

"Sure." They swapped numbers then Tom stood up. "I need to be off now, but I'll be in touch."

"I'll look forward to it." Lauren watched him as he walked back up the path. She had no idea if he found her remotely attractive or just thought she was someone he could trust to read Isabelle's diary. She sighed. Still, at least she had the diary. She tucked it under her arm then picked up her uneaten lunch and headed for home.

27

Tom could have kicked himself. Instead he kicked a stone that was lying in his path. Why had he dashed off like that? Why hadn't he stayed and chatted to Lauren for a bit? He told himself it was because he had a lot on his mind and he needed to pursue the investigation into his dad's death, both of which were true, but he also knew it was because he found it difficult to talk to girls. They never seemed to want to talk to him. When he'd shaken hands with Lauren just now he'd experienced a sudden urge to keep hold of her hand and pull her towards him, but that was the kind of risk he would never dare take, so instead he'd dropped her hand and taken refuge in opening his backpack and retrieving Isabelle's diary.

It was funny how the discovery of the diary had led to him meeting Lauren. He'd had the idea of giving her the diary last night after his disastrous meeting with Professor Nesbit. The professor obviously wanted to get his hands on the diary but if Tom's suspicions about Nesbit were correct, there was no way he was letting him anywhere near it. That's why he'd said the diary would be safer with Lauren, and he meant it. Plus, he thought to himself with a smile, it would give him an excuse to see her again. But right now he was determined to make a start on solving the mystery of his dad's death.

He pushed open the front door of the house on Cromwell Avenue and stepped inside, listening.

Silence.

His aunt and uncle had gone back to Newcastle yesterday evening. His mother was probably in her room. Things still hadn't improved between them. He'd almost told her about his visit to Professor Nesbit, but then decided against it. What was the point? She'd be on the Professor's side and would tell him to give Nesbit whatever he wanted.

He went through to the kitchen, made himself a large mug of strong, black coffee and took it upstairs to his dad's study. Then he sat down at the desk and pressed the power button on the computer. The time for discretion was over. He was going to read through his dad's emails before Professor Nesbit interfered with anything else.

The thought of Professor Nesbit made his skin crawl. It hadn't taken much for the professor's welcoming façade to crumble to dust, revealing the manipulative individual underneath. Tom recalled that brief moment of – what was it? – intuition? - when he'd had the feeling he was in the presence of his dad's murderer. Could it possibly be true? And what was all that nonsense about seeing things that others could not? Did he know something or was he just a delusional nutcase? Maybe he should just go straight to the police but then again, maybe not. At least not for the time being. All he had at the moment was a hunch and DCI McNally would want something firmer to go on. Like a taped confession.

A picture of Tom on the beach, aged twelve, appeared on the computer screen - his dad always used holiday shots for things like screensavers. But there was no time to be getting sentimental. He needed to start investigating.

He opened up Outlook and waited as a stream of new emails poured into the Inbox. Seventy-two in all. And how many old ones? The scroll bar on the right hand side had shrunk to a thin horizontal line. *Did Dad never delete anything?* He scrolled up and down – there were literally hundreds, if not thousands, of emails. If he was going to make sense of this lot, he would have to do some organising. He created three new folders called *UCL*, *Personal* and, after a moment's thought, *Isabelle*. Then he started sifting through the emails, starting with the most recent.

Most emails he just deleted. Begging letters from impoverished Nigerian princes, adverts from Amazon and spam from dodgy-looking drug companies. There were dozens of emails from Nancy Letts, obviously sent before Jack died, to do with student grants or conferences in Cambridge and Harvard. Tom filed these under *UCL*. Emails from Mike and John at the cricket club inviting Jack out for a drink went into *Personal*. So far he'd found nothing of any relevance but it felt good to be doing something positive. Keeping busy was the one thing that stopped him being swallowed up by grief.

He drank a mouthful of coffee and ploughed on – Amazon, Nancy, more Amazon, another Nigerian prince – *hang on a minute, what's that?*

He'd just spotted an email from someone called Peter Hart.

Hart.

The same surname as Isabelle. Of course, it could just be a coincidence – Hart wasn't such an uncommon name. But still, it was the most promising thing he'd come across so far. Trying not to get too excited, he double-clicked on the email and started to read. It was quite formal for an email, more like an old-fashioned letter.

Dear Dr Kelsey,

It was a pleasure to meet you yesterday evening at UCL. Following on from our conversation, I'd very much like to show you my great great grandfather's paintings and notes. Nathaniel Hart was a remarkable Victorian lepidopterist. His water-colour illustrations are exquisite and this fine book deserves to be displayed where it can be enjoyed by as many people as possible. Therefore I intend to donate it to the British Museum but before I do that I would like you to have the pleasure of seeing this wonderful collection.

Tom's heart sank. Lepidopterist? He had a vague idea that was someone who studied moths and butterflies. Maybe this email from Peter Hart was nothing after all. He drank another mouthful of coffee and read on.

When we met I also told you about a diary I had found when I cleared out the attic in my late father's house.

Tom breathed in sharply. This had to be it after all.

I would like to lend Isabelle's diary to you to use in your current researches which you told me about. Please do get in touch. My number is 020 4685 56785. I look forward to meeting you again.

Yours sincerely,
Peter Hart.

So that was it. Someone called Peter Hart had met Jack at an event at UCL and they'd got talking. Peter had then loaned him the diary to use in his research. Had his dad told any of this to Professor Nesbit?

Tom clicked on the *Sent* folder to see if there was a reply from his dad to Peter. There wasn't. Jack must have telephoned Peter Hart to arrange their meeting.

Tom knew he had to see Peter Hart, whoever he was. Did Peter even know that Jack was dead? Possibly not. Without giving it a second thought, Tom picked up the telephone and dialled the number at the bottom of Peter's email.

28

Lauren had the house to herself. Wendy was still at the cemetery and wouldn't be back until after five o'clock. That gave Lauren nearly three hours to start reading and transcribing the diary. She made herself a peppermint tea then sat down at the dining room table with the laptop she shared with Wendy. Whilst she waited for the computer to boot up she opened the diary and turned to the first entry.

Thursday, 20th January 1870

I have taken lodgings in a house on Highgate Hill, Athelston Lodge. It is a modest room and I think it will suit my current circumstances very well. I know that I can never return home and do not wish for my family to find me. In time I may look out for a governess's position but for now I wish to be left alone to mourn in peace.

The room was advertised in the newspaper – Respectable male or female lodger sought. Five shillings a week. All meals included. I made myself as respectable as I could in a plain black dress, bonnet and shawl, and, not without some hesitation, presented myself at the house.

The maid answered the door. She is a ruddy-faced girl of about twenty. I fear I may have disturbed her in the middle of some household chores because she stood there with her sleeves rolled up and her hands on her hips looking me up and down as if to say, who are you and what do you want?

When I explained to her that I had come about the room she muttered something about there being no peace for the wicked and told me to wait in the hallway whilst she went to fetch the mistress. I am sure the maid is not a bad sort and would have been more congenial if I had not interrupted her work.

I waited in the hallway as she had bid me do. I was shaking, whether from the cold or nerves, it was impossible to tell. To steady myself I concentrated on following the intricate pattern of the floor tiles with my eyes, picking out the diamonds and triangles in terracotta, cream and brown. A mahogany clock on a side-table ticked loudly.

I looked up at the sound of footsteps and the swish of silk against the tiled floor. The mistress had appeared at the foot of the stairs although I hadn't noticed where she had come from. She was wearing the crêpe-trimmed black silk of full mourning with a black lace cap over her silver-grey hair. I guessed her to be about sixty although she could have been older. Her cheeks were hollow and her white skin had the appearance of marble against the black of her dress. She looked like someone who no longer took any interest in the affairs of the world.

She introduced herself as Mrs Payne and told me she had started taking in lodgers five years ago when her husband died. I was surprised to hear he had died so long ago. From her clothes I had assumed her to be relatively recently bereaved, say in the last six months. But then who am I to judge? Our dear Queen has been in mourning for the last nine years and shows no sign of ever coming out of it.

At the mention of her husband Mrs Payne gazed absently past my right shoulder as if he might walk through the door at any moment. The sound of the clock chiming the half hour brought her back to herself. She shook her head and returned her attention to me. For a moment I thought she had forgotten why I was there but then she recollected herself and said, yes the room was still available if I wanted it. She did not ask me where I was from or why I required a room in her house. She saw that I had money to pay her and that was enough, I suppose, to satisfy her. She merely asked me my name and I told her.

"Miss or Mrs?" she wanted to know.

"Miss."

She nodded.

I looked down, fearing that she would guess my story. I trembled in case she should say that "my sort" were not welcome in her house but she merely fetched a door key from a cupboard of keys she keeps in the hallway and beckoned me to follow her up the dark stairs.

"There is one other lodger in the house at present," she said as we reached the first floor landing. She indicated a room at the front of the house but declined to say who resided there. I did not ask. No doubt I shall become acquainted with the other lodger in due course. She continued up the stairs to the next floor and I followed her.

In my weakened condition I found the stairs steep and tiring. I paused a moment, holding onto the banister, to catch my breath. She watched me with one eyebrow raised as if I had just confirmed her suspicions. I told her I was tired, recovering from a recent illness.

"Of course," she replied. I took a deep breath and followed her.

She led me to the attic room at the top of the house, unlocked the door and stood aside for me to enter. She informed me that meals are served downstairs in the dining room at twelve o'clock and six o'clock. I thanked her and she nodded briefly before leaving me on my own. I sank down on the bed and gazed about the room.

It is a plain but large enough room at the front of the house, overlooking Highgate Hill. It is sparsely furnished with an iron bedstead covered in a quilt and woollen blanket, a wooden chest of drawers, a wardrobe, a washstand with a china bowl and jug, a desk and chair by the window and a chamber pot decorated with roses under the bed. I need nothing more.

When I had recovered a little of my strength I unpacked my few meagre belongings from the bag I had brought with me. A spare dress, my box, my Bible and my diary. Then I sat down at the table in front of the window where I find myself now.

The window is small and high up but if I stand on tiptoe I can peer down onto the street below and in the distance I can see the green spaces of the cemetery.

I thank God for the dear, kind gravedigger I found there who did what I asked of him without question. I feel sure he will not betray me.

Lauren saved the document she had been typing, sat back and stretched. At first she had found Isabelle's handwriting tricky to decipher, but now she was confident she had got the hang of it. The peppermint tea she had made earlier had gone cold, she had been so engrossed in reading the diary. She went to the kitchen and made herself a fresh cup. Then she continued reading.

Thursday, 20th January 1870 - evening

I have attended my first evening meal in Mrs Payne's house. I would rather have remained in my room and worked on the sampler I am sewing, but I must maintain at least an outward appearance of normality.

The dining room is at the back of the house. The oil lamps which were burning on the sideboard revealed William Morris wallpaper on the walls and a portrait of Queen Victoria as a young woman above the fireplace. A large mahogany table fills most of the space. Mrs Payne and a young woman were already seated at the table when I arrived. Mrs Payne introduced us. Her name is Miss Fox. She is the other lodger and I am ashamed to say that she unnerved me a little.

I can't say exactly why, but there was something not quite ordinary in her manner. She looked to be roughly the same age as myself, about twenty. She has coppery red hair and piercing green eyes and when she looked at me I felt, for a moment, as if she could see into my soul.

But then the maid who had answered the door to me earlier in the day arrived with the food on a tray and the spell was broken. Mrs Payne addressed the maid as Betsy. Her mood had not improved from earlier. As she slopped the food onto our plates she complained about rats in the larder ruining the potatoes. Apparently Daisy, the scullery maid, should have gone to buy more rat poison the other week but that girl, as Betsy called her, was a good-for-nothing layabout.

I wondered at Mrs Payne allowing her servant to speak in such a manner whilst serving at the dinner table but Mrs Payne had a faraway look in her eyes and did not seem to register what Betsy was saying. Miss Fox watched Betsy moving around the room, her mouth twitching with unconcealed amusement. I feel it will take me a little while to become accustomed to life in this house.

Later, whilst Betsy was clearing away the main course, I caught her eyeing me with suspicion as she had done earlier. I understand that it's wise to be on the right side of the servants, especially in a strange house, so I complimented her on the food even though the beef stew she had cooked contained hardly any meat and what little there was, was grisly and difficult to chew. She stood up straighter and patted down her apron which was spotted with grease. I could see that my words had pleased her.

At the end of the meal Mrs Payne retired to the front parlour and I climbed the stairs with Miss Fox. When we reached the first floor landing she turned to me and, laying her hand on mine, said, "Goodnight, Miss Hart. I hope we shall be friends."

"Please," I said. "Call me Isabelle."

Her eyes twinkled in the flame of the candle she was holding. "In that case, you must call me Madeleine. Goodnight, Isabelle."

She disappeared into her room and I was left alone in this strange house.

29

Alan Nesbit turned the key in his office door at University College, locking it on the inside, and sat down at his desk. He didn't want to be disturbed and especially not by that foolish department secretary Nancy Letts who had been treating him like an unwelcome guest in his own department ever since she had found him browsing the files in Jack's old office down the corridor. Just now she'd brought him his post and had lingered in the room longer than was strictly necessary, her nose twitching, as if she detected a bad smell. If she continued to be a nuisance he might have to arrange a little accident for her; something that would keep her out of the way for a while.

He was not in the best of moods anyway. Those girls in the cemetery last night, intruders as he thought of them, were lucky to have escaped. Didn't they know what dangers lurked in that place? Dangers that he was determined to defeat.

He reached into his pocket, took out the memory stick that he'd taken from Jack's home study and plugged it into a USB port on his computer. Windows Explorer popped up and Alan Nesbit silently thanked his dead colleague for being so organised.

The memory stick appeared to contain a copy of all the folders and files from Jack's home computer. And since Jack had been so keen on working from home, spending time with that drip of a son of his, then it was likely he would find something of significance here.

He could see from the dates on the files that the backup was recent, the last copy taken the day before Jack died. He ran the mouse pointer down the list of folders. Most of them were of no relevance whatsoever - *Christmas Letters, Family Photos, Mortgage Details* and the like were of no interest to a man who didn't celebrate Christmas, had no family, never went on holiday and didn't own his own house. At the bottom of the list was a folder called *Work*. This was more like it.

He double-clicked.

More folders – *Lectures, Tutorials, Undergraduates* (in Alan's opinion all tedious distractions in the life of an academic) – and one called *Research*.

Double-click.

The screen filled with a list of dozens of Word documents in alphabetical order – *Ascension of Queen Victoria, Asylums, Bazalgette and London Sewers, Bedlam, Christian Institutions* – the list went on and on. Alan clicked the Date Modified button twice so that the most recently changed files were at the top. Now he could see what Jack had been working on just before he died. There were two files both dated the day before he died.

One was called *Isabelle Hart – notes*.

The other was called *Highgate Vampire*.

He knew it. Jack had been meddling in things that didn't concern him and Alan had been right to get him out of the way. He double-clicked the *Highgate Vampire* file and cast his eyes down the page – just the bare facts of what had happened on Friday 13 March 1970 and the following weeks and months, most of it cut and pasted from Wikipedia. There was nothing there that Alan didn't already know.

He did a search for his own name in the file but it didn't come up. Good.

He closed the *Highgate Vampire* file and turned his attention to *Isabelle Hart*. Now he might learn something useful.

30

Monday, 24th January 1870

I must have an occupation whilst I am living in Highgate. I do not mean that I need to earn money. I am fortunate that my grandmother bequeathed an income to me before she died. What I mean is that I need to have something with which to fill my time, otherwise I think I may go mad from grief and idleness and then I should have to be locked up in a lunatic asylum.

I remembered that a friend of my mother's, a Lady Morecambe, spoke once of the St Mary Magdalene Penitentiary in Highgate. It was during one of Mother's At Homes, when Lady Morecambe raised, in between sips of Darjeeling, the subject of the great social evil and of the fallen women who were housed in the penitentiary. Mother, of course, had been scandalised that such a thing should be discussed in polite society. I was not expected to understand the term fallen women and at the time had wondered what was meant by such a singular turn of phrase. Now I know only too well.

Anyway, since I am now resident in Highgate, it seemed fitting that I should offer my services at the St Mary Magdalene Penitentiary. Although what I might offer these women, God only knows. Maybe it is my own salvation I seek.

I went to Park House this morning, where the Penitentiary is to be found. I was met by Sister Burns, the Lady Principal, to whom I offered my services, if she would have me.

Sister Burns led me into her office, a sparsely furnished room on the ground floor with a painting of Christ on the cross above the fireplace. She wore a plain black dress and a string of black beads and a crucifix around her neck. Her manner was straightforward and business-like. She didn't waste time on formalities, for which I was grateful, but got straight to the point. From what she said it appeared that one of the Sisters who usually works there has been called away on urgent family matters and therefore she had a vacancy that needed filling. I do not know if I would have been her first choice, but she was in need of extra assistance and I was willing and available, so she agreed I could start tomorrow on a trial basis. I thanked her warmly.

"Before you leave today I'll ask one of the other Sisters to show you around," she said.

She stepped out into the corridor and called, "Sister Christina, could you come here please?"

Sister Christina entered the office. She too wore a black dress with a string of black beads and a crucifix around her neck. Her brown hair was tied back under a muslin cap and her large, dark eyes set in a long, pale face were like calm pools. I liked her at once. Sister Burns spoke quickly to Sister Christina.

"This is Miss Isabelle Hart. She has volunteered her services to the penitentiary and will be starting tomorrow. Could you show her around please?"

Sister Christina bowed her head to Sister Burns and beckoned me to follow her.

As we walked, I wondered if she would ask me any questions about myself and I tried to think what I would say. But Sister Christina showed no curiosity and I was grateful to her for being so reserved.

She took me first to the chapel which was a simple room with wooden pews and a carving of Christ on the cross above the altar. "The women meet here several times a day for prayers," she explained. "Religious teaching is at the heart of all we do. You should understand that the women here have lost their way and we seek, above all, to bring them back into the fold. Some of them have never received proper instruction in the teachings of the Bible so we try to rectify what has been neglected in their lives to date."

I nodded to show that I understood and hoped that Sister Christina would not notice my discomfort which, I was sure, must be written plainly on my face. Where, I wondered, had I lost my way?

Next she took me to the laundry, a large, steam-filled room where a group of women, under the supervision of another Sister, were hard at work. The women all wore blue gingham dresses and white caps which made them look like schoolgirls although I guessed their ages to be anything from sixteen to twenty-five.

Some of the women were stirring laundry in large tubs using long wooden poles with handles at the top and a circular base with short legs sticking out of the bottom. These wooden contraptions looked cumbersome and heavy to use and water slopped over the edge of the tubs so that their dresses were soaked around the bottom.

One woman was heaving wet sheets through a mangle whilst her companion used both hands to crank the massive handle that turned the rollers. Water poured off the sheets into a metal tub on the floor. Linen, petticoats and dresses that had already been through the mangle were hanging from wooden beams that could be lowered and then raised above head height.

The remaining women were pressing sheets and clothes using heavy irons heated on the fire. They all worked in silence and every one of them was red in the face from the heat of the room and the efforts of their labours.

"It is here, and in the kitchens, that the women learn habits of obedience and industry," said Sister Christina. "If we are to prevent these women from returning to a life of prostitution they must be able to gain employment when they leave the penitentiary. We teach them to launder and cook so they can find jobs in domestic service."

I was standing close to one of the wash tubs and the woman stirring the contents looked up and caught my eye. Beads of sweat *glistened on her forehead. A curl of red hair had escaped from her cap and was sticking to her skin. She paused in her work for a moment whilst she tried in vain to tuck the stray curl back under her cap.*

"Keep stirring the laundry," said the Sister in charge of this room. She spoke firmly although not unkindly. "Remember, Ellen, you are here to learn habits of discipline which have been sadly lacking in your life thus far. There is no place in the Kingdom of Heaven for idleness."

A frown flickered across Ellen's forehead and her mouth puckered into a pout. She hung her head and resumed the stirring but in a manner that suggested to me she was weary in the extreme.

I stepped forward, wanting to say, "Let me stir the laundry for you whilst you sort out your hair," but Sister Christina had already turned to leave and I was obliged to follow her. I smiled at Ellen as we left but she just stared at me with sullen, grey eyes.

After we had visited the laundry, Sister Christina showed me the kitchens where yet more women in the regulation blue gingham dresses were preparing a midday meal of broth in a large pot over an open fire.

Finally, as the day was a mild one for the time of year, Sister Christina led me outside to view the gardens. They have many apple trees growing in the grounds of Park House but Sister Christina informed me that the women are forbidden from picking the fruit. Learning to control their temptations is clearly one of the lessons they are expected to learn.

Tuesday, 1st February 1870

I have been busy at the penitentiary all week and have not had the opportunity, until now, to write in my diary. Sister Burns arranged for me to spend time in both the laundry and the kitchens so that I could learn the ways of the house. I have also accompanied the women to their prayers in the chapel where the Warden, the Reverend John Renshaw, leads the prayers and delivers a daily sermon, usually on the subject of repentance. He is a well meaning man but I wonder how much of these women's lives he really understands.

Today I was left in charge of the laundry for the first time, the Sister who usually supervises there being called away on some other duty. I felt nervous being left in charge of these women in case they refused to work for me. I needn't have worried. Most of them are so used to the drudgery that they barely notice who is supervising them and just apply themselves to the task in hand. All, that is, except for Ellen.

Today she had the job of ironing a large pile of sheets. I noticed her watching me whilst she waited for the iron to heat up on the stove. I approached her and asked if everything was all right.

"I always wonders what makes ladies like you come and work in a place like this," she said tilting her head to one side and eyeing me with curiosity.

I was taken aback and did not know what to reply. "I suppose we hope to do some good," was all I could think of to say.

She looked at me then as if she was trying to decide whose good I was working for – hers or mine. To change the subject I said, "I think the iron should be hot enough now."

She picked it up using a tea-towel and spat on the soleplate to test the temperature. Her spittle sizzled on the hot surface and she reluctantly turned to the pile of sheets that needed ironing.

I left her to her work, pretending to go and check on how the other women were progressing with their stirring, scrubbing, rinsing and wringing, but Ellen's words kept coming back to me, what makes ladies like you come and work in a place like this?

After chapel the women are permitted to take some exercise in the gardens. I joined them for the fresh air, glad to be away from the heat of the laundry room. As I was strolling around thinking about today's sermon (on the Good Shepherd who goes in search of the one lost sheep) I became aware of someone close behind me. I turned and saw Ellen no more than a couple of feet away. To prevent her asking me any questions about myself I asked her about her previous life and what, specifically, had brought her here.

Hers wasn't a long story and was, no doubt, fairly typical – a father who squandered the family's meagre income on drink and then turned up one day floating in the Thames; a mother who fell ill and died of cholera; brothers and sisters taken into the workhouse; Ellen's fall into prostitution.

"Could you not have found some honest employment?" I asked

her.

She paused by an old apple tree, running her fingers over its gnarled trunk. "Honest employment?" she scoffed. "As a servant? Who'd want to do that?" I was unable to think of a satisfactory answer but at that moment the bell rang for the women to return inside and Ellen started walking back to the house. I watched her, noticing the stoop of her shoulders and the way she dragged her feet. I wondered what would become of her when she left this place.

There is one more thing to record before I retire for the night. A most unusual incident. Earlier this evening I felt in need of a glass of water and went downstairs to fetch one. The house was in darkness. Mrs Payne retires early and Betsy must have been in her room (she has a small sleeping space at the back of the kitchen.) Anyway, on my way back up the stairs I heard sounds coming from Madeleine's room. Footsteps and muffled voices. She clearly had visitors although she had not mentioned this at dinner and I had not seen anyone arrive at the house. As I approached the first floor landing I heard a sharp rapping sound and then a female voice shrieked so loudly that I jumped, spilling some of the water, and had to grab hold of the banister for fear of falling. I froze, listening. Was someone hurt and should I call for Mrs Payne or Betsy? Then I heard Madeleine talking quite calmly, although I could not make out what she was saying and I did not like to eavesdrop. But it sounded from the tone of her voice as if everything was quite in order. I continued on my way to the next flight of stairs, glancing at her door as I did so. And this was the strange thing. What struck me as most peculiar was the fact that there was no light showing under the door. Were Madeleine and her guests all sitting in the dark?

31

It was late. Tom had spent the whole afternoon and most of the evening trawling through the files on his dad's computer, emerging from the study only briefly to make himself a slice of toast and marmite. His phone call to Peter Hart had been a success. Peter had sounded friendly on the phone and had even offered to meet him tomorrow in Starbucks opposite St Paul's Cathedral. Tom didn't think he would find anything else useful in *Outlook*, so he'd moved on to the files under *My Documents*.

He'd found hundreds, if not thousands, of unprinted photos that had been downloaded from his dad's digital camera and then probably never looked at again. A quick scan through the photos brought back so many memories that he'd had to shut that folder quickly before he broke down.

There were also at least ten years' worth of essays that his students had emailed to him, organised into folders by year and academic term, and his own notes for lectures and tutorials over the same time period. His dad had always regarded teaching, not research, as the fundamental part of his job and because of this his students had been devoted to him.

Tom checked his watch. It was already eight o'clock in the evening and he was hungry, but he wanted to check the *Research* folder before he logged off. He double-clicked and the screen filled with an alphabetical list of files on everything from *Ascension of Queen Victoria* to *Zoological Gardens*. He could see from the date stamp that most of these files were years old.

Tom stifled a yawn then clicked twice on the *Date Modified* tab. The two documents that jumped to the top of the list were *Isabelle Hart – notes* and *Highgate Vampire*.

32

Wednesday, 9th February 1870 - midnight

I must try and describe what I have seen tonight before I forget; although, in truth, what I witnessed was so astonishing I think the memory of it will live with me forever.

The mystery regarding Madeleine and her guests from the previous week has been explained. It came about thus:

Madeleine and I were dining alone, Mrs Payne having retired early with a headache. Betsy was serving dinner, her customary stew, and moaning about the "feckless" scullery maid, Daisy, who had disappeared for over an hour this afternoon when she should have been scrubbing the pots and who deserved nothing better than a good box around the ears. I have learnt not to pay heed to Betsy's gossip, but Madeleine was very attentive to what Betsy was saying. She suggested that Mrs Payne may have sent Daisy on an errand to the chemist to obtain a remedy for her headache, but Betsy scoffed at the idea, saying that Daisy was a 'dark horse' and 'no good ever came of employing people like that.' Betsy strongly suspected her of 'dallying' with Sam, the baker's boy, which, inexplicably, made Madeleine smile.

Then resuming her usual composure, Madeleine informed Betsy that she was expecting some visitors this evening. Betsy received this news with a roll of her eyes and a grunt but Madeleine was unperturbed by her reaction.

When Betsy had returned to the kitchen Madeleine leaned towards me and said, "Would you like to join us, Isabelle?"

I thanked her for her invitation but said that I did not wish to intrude if she had friends paying a visit, and then she explained that her visitors were not personal friends as such, but clients.

I must have appeared confused for she smiled and said in a smooth voice, "I am a spirit medium. I have been blessed with a gift for communicating with the spirit world and people come to me when they want to receive news of relatives who have passed to the other side." As she spoke she held my gaze with her penetrating green eyes and I felt goose bumps on my arms.

So she was a spirit medium. I had heard talk of such people but had never met one. It explained the noises I had heard from her room the other night.

"Do not look so alarmed," she said with a little laugh. "Why not come as an observer to this evening's sitting?"

Although I was nervous at the idea, I did not like to refuse her invitation which seemed well meant. Also, I must admit I was curious. Madeleine assured me that I would see miraculous things. I wondered if she had guessed my story and was, in her way, trying to be of some service to me. Anyway, I had no reason to decline the invitation without appearing rude, so I went to her room on the first *floor at the appointed time of eight o'clock and I will now confide to the pages of this diary, as accurately as I can, what occurred there.*

When I arrived at Madeleine's room I found three other people already there - an eminent gentleman with an exuberant moustache and ginger whiskers who said he was from 'The Ghost Club.' He introduced himself as Mr Gatesby and explained he was conducting research into the phenomenon known as Spiritualism; a wealthy-looking American lady by the name of Mrs Waterman who, she informed me whilst twisting a black-edged handkerchief around her fingers, was in mourning for her daughter, Abigail, who had passed away three months ago suffering from consumption; and Mrs Waterman's female companion, a timid-looking woman with mousy brown hair called Miss Simpson who hovered in the background and said little.

Madeleine invited us to sit at a circular table which was covered in a dark red cloth that hung to the floor. I sat down with Mrs Waterman on my right, then came Miss Simpson and Mr Gatesby. Madeleine lit a candle on the mantelpiece and then turned the oil lamp down so low that the room was in virtual darkness. Then she took her place at the table between me and Mr Gatesby. Madeleine instructed us all to lay our hands flat on the table which we did.

I was apprehensive and held myself so still that I became aware of my beating heart. It was hammering so loudly I felt sure everyone would hear it. Outside it had started to rain and the wind had picked up. A sudden gust caused the rain to lash against the window panes. My attention turned to the cemetery and I wondered if Madeleine was, even now, making contact with the spirits of those who were buried there.

Although I could barely see her in the darkness, I was acutely aware of Madeleine sitting to my left. She was breathing deeply and seemed to be holding herself very rigid. When she spoke her voice sounded ethereal as if it was coming from a long way away.

"I am searching for the spirit of Abigail Waterman. Is she there? Abigail can you hear me?"

A loud sniff from Mrs Waterman.

Then Madeleine spoke again, "Is Abigail there? Please give us a sign that you can hear me."

Silence.

Then a faint tapping sound was heard. At first I thought it was the wind blowing a branch against the window, but it became louder and more insistent and was coming from somewhere inside the room. The hairs on the back of my neck stood on end and I pressed the palms of my hands even more firmly onto the table.

Madeleine asked the "spirit" if it wanted to "appear" to us. I had no idea what that meant, but suddenly there was a rapping so loud and violent that I nearly jumped out of my seat and then the table started to lift and tilt so that I snatched my hands away from the cloth and think I must have cried out in alarm.

"Calm, calm," said Madeleine in a voice like silk. The table stopped moving and the raps became less agitated.

"You see," Madeleine said, "the spirit wants to come but it cannot do so whilst I sit with you all at the table. It wants me to go into my cabinet." She turned to Mr Gatesby and asked if he would help her prepare. She told him to bring the light so that he could see what he was doing and satisfy himself that everything was in order.

Mr Gatesby picked up the oil lamp from a nearby table, turning it up just enough to light his path, and followed Madeleine over to the corner of the room where a black velvet curtain hung from a rail attached to the walls. There was a door in the corner but when Mr Gatesby asked about it Madeleine shrugged and said it was just a cupboard and always locked. Mr Gatesby tried the handle and it was indeed locked. The only piece of furniture behind the curtain was an upright chair with some lengths of silk cord draped over the back.

Madeleine requested Mr Gatesby to fasten her to the chair with the silk cord.

"Is that absolutely necessary?" I blurted out. It seemed such a bizarre request that I couldn't help myself. Madeleine assured me this was quite normal and was for her own safety. The spirits could sometimes be violent. I did not like the sound of that but as no one else seemed concerned I held my tongue.

Madeleine sat down on the chair and held out the cords to Mr Gatesby who was only too happy to oblige. He tied her to the chair with the silk cords, wrapping one around her upper arms and another around her waist. The third cord he used to blindfold her.

"Tighter," she said. "You must pull the cords tighter or the spirits will not come." He made an effort to tighten the cords. "Is that better?" She nodded before closing her eyes and dropping her head forwards.

Mr Gatesby pulled the curtain across the front of the cabinet and then turned out the light before resuming his place at the table.

We sat in the dark and waited.

There was no sound save for the ticking of the clock on the mantelpiece and the rain lashing against the window pane.

As my eyes acclimatised themselves to the dark I could just make out Mrs Waterman's upright figure on my right. I couldn't see Miss Simpson or Mr Gatesby who were sitting too far away.

I think I must have closed my eyes. The darkness was making me sleepy.

A groan.

I jerked my head up and opened my eyes wide. Sighs and moans were coming from the spirit cabinet. They grew louder. Then there were thumps and bumps and the rustling of material.

Madeleine cried out as if in pain.

Was she hurt?

I wanted to go to her but no one else stirred and I didn't dare try to find my way across the room in the dark.

Then silence.

I looked towards the cabinet straining my eyes to see anything in the gloom.

At first I thought I was imagining it but after a moment I was sure that a light was emerging from behind the curtain. As I watched, the light seemed to grow and take shape. Then it started to glide across the room. It wasn't a bright light, more a gentle glow and as it came closer I saw that it bore the outline of a female form.

I was utterly transfixed by this spirit, if that is what it was, and for a moment forgot about my companions around the table. I was reminded of their presence all of a sudden when Mrs Waterman cried out, "Abigail, is that you?" I can only surmise that Mrs Waterman recognised in this ethereal figure the spirit of her recently departed daughter.

Abigail, if that's who it was, came closer. She lifted a ghostly hand towards Mrs Waterman's face. The poor lady was so overcome with, I suppose, a mixture of grief and shock that she shrieked and fell into a faint, sliding off her chair and falling, with a crash, onto the floor.

After that everything seemed to happen at once. Miss Simpson and I jumped to our feet, as did Mr Gatesby, knocking over his chair. Mr Gatesby fetched the light whilst Miss Simpson and I knelt down beside the prone figure of Mrs Waterman.

Miss Simpson turned her over and felt for her pulse. "Can you fetch some smelling salts please?" she asked me.

"Of course."

I ran downstairs to the kitchen where Betsy was sitting with her feet up, reading a letter. She didn't look too pleased at being disturbed, but when I explained the situation to her she fetched the smelling salts from a drawer and followed me upstairs straight away. Betsy knelt down beside Miss Simpson who had lifted Mrs Waterman's head onto her lap, and waved the salts under Mrs Waterman's nose. I am pleased to say that she revived in a matter of seconds.

"She'll be all right now," said Betsy in her matter-of-fact way. "I'll go and fetch her a glass of water," and she got up and went back downstairs.

I was not aware of what the spirit was doing during this time, occupied as I was with fetching Betsy and ensuring Mrs Waterman was fully recovered. By the time we had lifted a shocked Mrs Waterman back onto her chair the spirit had vanished.

Betsy returned then with the glass of water and Miss Simpson held the glass to Mrs Waterman's lips, insisting that she take a sip.

Whilst this was happening Mr Gatesby pulled back the curtain on the spirit cabinet to reveal Madeleine, still tied to her chair but in some disarray with her hair strewn around her face. She sat with her head collapsed onto her chest and looked exhausted. Mr Gatesby was murmuring to himself, "Incredible, quite incredible."

For my part, I wondered at what I had seen and trembled.

33

Lauren jumped in fright.

The sudden noise had startled her, until she realised it was only her mobile phone ringing. She pulled it out of her pocket and answered the call with shaking fingers. Reading about séances late at night was clearly not a good idea.

"Hello?" she asked. In her confusion she hadn't noticed who the call was from and, given what she'd just read in the diary, wouldn't have been at all surprised if it was her long-dead grandfather calling from the other side.

"Hi Lauren, it's Tom."

Relief at the sound of his voice flooded through her. Of course it wasn't a dead person phoning her. Whatever had she been thinking? She was so happy to hear his voice and there was so much she wanted to tell him about the diary that she almost missed what he was saying and had to ask him to repeat it just to make sure she'd understood correctly.

"I said, can you meet me tomorrow outside St Paul's, at about one thirty?"

"Yes, of course," she said. Was he asking her out? Was this a date?

"Great." There was a pause as if he wanted to say more. "OK, well, see you tomorrow."

"Sure. Looking forward to it."

He hung up.

Don't go, she thought. *I like talking to you.*

She stared at her phone. She wanted to call him back so that she could hear his voice again. He'd said something about meeting a man called Peter Hart but she didn't know what about. Her thumb hovered over the screen whilst she struggled to decide what to do.

In the end she put the phone down. She'd see him tomorrow. She'd just have to be patient. It was late and if she didn't get some sleep she'd arrive at St Paul's looking like the walking dead. And she couldn't risk that happening.

34

The Trials and Tribulations of a Household Maid in the Year of Our Lord 1870, continued...

There ain't no peace for the wicked in this house. There I am thinking at last I've done all my jobs for the day and I'm just sitting down to read a letter from my sweetheart, Will, who works over in the cemetery, when the new lodger, Miss Hart, comes running down the stairs like she's seen a ghost. I stuff the letter back inside my pocket and jump to my feet.

"Lord," I say, "whatever's the matter?" It turns out that a lady has had a fainting fit at one of Miss Fox's gatherings. I tell you, they keel over at the slightest little thing do ladies.

I fetch a bottle of smelling salts from the dresser drawer and follow Miss Hart back upstairs. As Miss Hart said, the lady's lying in a swoon and her companion, a dull mouse of a woman if ever I saw one, is fussing over her, as if that's going to do any good.

"Excuse me, Miss," I say kneeling down and unscrewing the lid off the smelling salts. "This'll have her back on her feet in no time." I wave the bottle under her nose and, as I predicted, she comes to with a moan.

"Oh Mrs Waterman," cries the companion. "Thank goodness you're all right." She'd be better if she didn't mess with Miss Fox I thinks to myself but I don't say nothing.

I goes off to fetch her a glass of water and when I come back I see that the gentleman what was present has pulled back the curtain in the corner of the room. Miss Fox is sitting there on a wooden chair looking like a rag doll with her head slumped on her chest and her hair strewn all over her face and I thinks to myself, she's the one what wants the smelling salts but again I don't say nothing.

Miss Fox has been messing around with them spirits again and I don't like it. The dead are dead I always say, and it don't pay to go calling them back to the land of the living.

PART FIVE
FRIDAY 13 MARCH 1970

35

Home from school at four o'clock. Corned beef sandwiches for tea followed by strawberry flavoured Angel Delight and a slice of Battenberg cake. Then a pot of PG Tips whilst watching *Dad's Army* on the television huddled around the gas fire for warmth. Father smoking his pipe. Mother doing her knitting. Bed at nine-thirty.

That was the sum total of life for sixteen year old Alan Nesbit, only child of prematurely ageing parents Donald and Jean Nesbit. Like the black and white television they watched every evening, Alan saw his life playing out in shades of grey, and, like the programmes his parents enjoyed, completely devoid of any drama.

For some time now Alan had become aware that modern life was passing him by. Whilst his contemporaries embraced psychedelic-coloured shirts and bell-bottoms, Alan still wore the clothes his mother bought, or knitted, for him and which looked like the kind of things his father wore - brown, shapeless and old-fashioned. He never listened to pop music because they didn't own a record player and his father declared it to be a load of *screeching and caterwauling* and not *proper music*.

Then there were mealtimes, which he had come to dread. He sat at the table now as he did every night. A slice of pink and yellow Battenberg cake with its sickly yellow marzipan coating lay on his plate. It was the only thing of colour in his drab world. Yet how he hated it.

He'd liked Battenberg cake once. When he was five. He'd made the mistake of saying so and his mother had bought it continuously ever since. That had taught him the consequences of careless talk.

He broke off a quarter of the cake – pink – and forced himself to put it in his mouth. A crumb went down the wrong way, making him cough. He pushed his plate away. He wasn't going to eat any more of that revolting cake.

"Not hungry love?" His mother dabbed at the last crumbs of her cake with fingers worn rough by the laundry she still did by hand. She distrusted modern machines, preferring instead a bar of soap and a scrubbing brush.

Alan shook his head.

"What was that?" Alan's father looked up from his own plate. They didn't usually talk at mealtimes. They weren't conversationalists, his parents.

Alan looked at his father and all he could think of was, *why does Dad always wear that mustard coloured, hand knitted tank top? It's so ugly.*

"No. I'm not hungry."

His father grunted. Alan knew what was coming. He'd heard it before. Too often.

"A young man like you should eat everything on his plate and be grateful for it. Back in the War people knew what it was to go hungry. We had rations then and we didn't waste a drop. Young people today don't know how lucky they are. When I was your age I signed up to fight for King and Country. You spend too much time in that bedroom of yours…" Blah, blah, blah. Alan wished he could turn his father off the way he turned the television off – with a push of the button. "…they should never have got rid of national service. Today's young people…"

Alan stood up.

"And where do you think you're going?"

Alan ignored him and walked out of the room, letting the door slam behind him. There was no point trying to talk to his father. Nothing Alan ever did was good enough for him – he didn't work hard enough in school, he wasn't any good at sports, he had no backbone and, like all young people today, was completely lacking in moral fibre and any sense of responsibility. So his father said. But the old codger never let up. He just couldn't accept that his moment of glory in the war – working as a warden on the streets of Camden – was over. Couldn't accept that the world had moved on, that things were different now. Alan was never going to be able to please him so there was no point in trying.

But what Alan knew deep down was that he craved praise and recognition. Just one word would have been enough. But he was never going to get it from that hard-hearted bastard.

He paused at the foot of the stairs. He could hear his mother trying to smooth things over, "Let him be a while, Donald. He looks a bit pale to me. Maybe he's going down with something." That was his mother all over. Always trying to placate things and never seeing the real problem underneath. He could hear his father's raised voice and his mother's pathetic pleading, arguing over, what his father termed, his delinquency. The walls in this house were too thin. He didn't want to listen to his parents' voices, least of all his father's. He needed something to drown them out.

He turned and went into the front room – the best room in the house, reserved for watching television in the evening and entertaining visitors. Not that they did much of that. He thought of it as the brown room because the wallpaper was covered in brown and orange swirls, the carpet was a shade of mud, the curtains were mustard and the tatty old three-piece suite was covered in brown velvet with yellowing antimacassars on the arms and backs to hide the worn patches. He switched on the television and turned the volume up loud so he wouldn't have to listen to his parents' voices on the other side of the wall.

As acts of rebellion went, it might not look much, but in this house of set routines it was tantamount to declaring Armageddon. The television never went on in the evening until after his parents had washed up and put all the crockery and cutlery away in the sideboard. Then his mother would settle down with a cup of tea and watch shows like *The Generation Game*. His father always insisted on watching *The Nine O' Clock News* during which he would harrumph continuously over the moral collapse of the nation. BBC1 was the approved channel but was switched off as soon as *Doctor Who* or *Top of the Pops* came on because both of those programmes were, according to his father, symptomatic of the general decline in moral standards pervading the country. They hardly ever watched BBC2 which mainly broadcast long-haired weirdoes from the Open University talking about particle physics. ITV was, according to his father, trash. There were no other channels.

BBC1 was showing a repeat of *Laurel and Hardy*. They were a pair of bumbling idiots that Alan had no time for. He changed over to BBC2. It was displaying the test card – a young girl and a clown sitting in front of a blackboard. It always gave Alan the creeps. He pressed the third button for ITV and waited whilst the screen flickered into life. It was the local news on Thames TV. What a load of old shite. Nothing interesting ever happened locally.

He went to switch the television off when the newsreader said something that made him pause.

Unexplained events at Highgate Cemetery. Possibly of a supernatural origin.

What was this?

Intrigued, Alan sat back down on the sofa and watched the television. He'd heard of Highgate Cemetery, just a few stops up the Northern Line, but had never been there. The picture on the screen changed from the newsroom to an outdoor shot of three people standing beside tall iron gates with tombstones clearly visible in the background.

Wow. That was some creepy-looking cemetery with all the crosses and tombstones. He'd only ever seen graveyards like that on *Scooby Doo*. Imagine visiting a place like that. At night.

The young female television reporter, wearing a fashionable mini skirt and holding a huge microphone, flashed a smile at the two men she was about to interview. Alan leaned towards the television to hear what they had to say.

The interviewer turned to the man standing nearest to her, a pale, thin guy with shoulder length fair hair. "You say you came to Highgate Cemetery at midnight on the twenty-first of December last year. Can you tell me why you did that and what you saw that night?" She thrust the microphone towards the young man and waited for him to speak. When he did, he spoke softly and seemed to choose his words with care.

"There had been reports about a supernatural phenomenon in the cemetery."

The reporter's smile widened. "How fascinating. Can you give us any details?"

The fair-haired man leaned towards the microphone. "A passer-by claimed to have seen a tall, dark spectre hovering above the ground in the middle of the cemetery. He says the spectre hypnotised him. Then one night an old lady was walking her dog by the top gates when she saw a tall dark figure floating towards her from inside the cemetery. The figure had glaring eyes but vanished suddenly."

"So you decided to investigate for yourself on

December the twenty-first. Is there any significance in that date?"

"I chose December the twenty-first, the eve of the Winter Solstice, because that is when it is easiest for supernatural beings to materialise."

"You mean ghosts are more likely to be walking around at the time of the Winter Solstice?" It was obvious from the thrill in her voice that she was enjoying this assignment.

"If you want to put it like that. So, anyway, I set off for the cemetery late at night. As I walked up Swain's Lane I had the feeling that I was no longer alone. When I reached the top gate I tried to see if I could find a rational explanation for what the old lady claimed to have seen – what she took for a dark figure might have been a shadow from a tombstone or from a tree moving in the wind."

"And what did you find?"

The man took a deep breath and continued more slowly. "I could only see about twenty yards into the cemetery – beyond that everything was black. But there was a movement in the blackness – an animal or something was scurrying through the undergrowth – and then, suddenly, no more than five yards from the gate I saw a tall, dark shape." He paused as if remembering the vision.

"Fascinating," breathed the reporter, her eyes wide. "Please go on."

"There was a dark figure, staring at me with two bright eyes."

"Was it a man?"

The man shook his head. "I don't think so. I couldn't make out any features. But I sensed it was malevolent."

"What an amazing story," enthused the reporter. "Thank you so much." She then turned to the other man who had been lurking in the background, waiting his turn. He had dark, curly hair and was wearing a buttoned-up black suit which made him look like an undertaker. But he clearly wasn't an undertaker because he was holding a crucifix and a pointed wooden stake which he waved menacingly under the reporter's nose. She flinched and stepped backwards before asking her first question.

"What do you make of what we've just heard?"

This dark-haired man spoke with much more confidence than the first guy.

"There can be no doubt that what we have in Highgate Cemetery is a King Vampire."

The interviewer's smile faltered for a fraction of a second. "Do you mean…?"

The man continued without waiting for her to finish her question. "The only way to deal with such a creature is to drive a stake through its heart, chop off its head and burn the body." He brandished the stake in her face as if to demonstrate.

Nervous giggle. "Yes, well, what the viewers would like to know is…"

"My friend here," he turned to the first man who looked somewhat alarmed, "will be returning to Highgate Cemetery this evening to carry out the dangerous mission of hunting down and killing the vampire," – he then looked straight at the camera and spoke directly, it seemed, to Alan – "and I invite *you* to join him."

The fair-haired man looked as if he wanted to protest but the reporter, who was fiddling with her earpiece and probably receiving instructions from her editor to cut the interview right there, turned to the camera and said, "Well, there you have it. Confirmed sightings of a mysterious, tall, dark figure haunting Highgate Cemetery which may, or may not, be a vampire. These really are extraordinary times we're living in. Now back to the studio for the weather forecast."

Alan stood up and turned off the television. Something exploded inside his head. It was a revelation. A call to arms.

He had discovered his purpose in life.

No longer would he be the unpopular geek at school, the loser who was never picked for the football team, the moron whose school bag was constantly being stuffed down the toilet and the down-trodden son who was shouted at by his father for not eating the bloody Battenberg cake. Alan was sick of being pushed around. He wanted respect and he wanted praise.

But respect had to be earned. Alan knew that. And here was a way for him to earn the adulation of his classmates and even the respect of his father. He'd be a hero. His Dad's moment had come in 1939 with the outbreak of World War Two. Alan's time was now. 1970.

I invite you to join him. Alan had looked into those piercing eyes and felt the words were for him and him alone. He was being called. This was his vocation. It was his God-given duty to go to Highgate Cemetery this evening and kill the vampire.

It was fate. He'd never given it much thought before, but that was what it was. When he looked back over the evening, even the course of his whole life, he could see now that everything had been leading up to this moment; the stifling boredom of his life; the bullying at school; the Battenberg cake that made him gag; the lecture from his father that made him leave the table and come in here and switch the television on. It all made perfect sense. Even the fact that his parents hadn't followed him in here and told him to turn the television off. It was fate, pure and simple.

Alan versus the vampire. Like David and Goliath. He was going to take on this blood-sucking demon and he was going to win. And God help anyone who got in his way.

Alan stepped out into the hallway and listened. His parents were in the kitchen doing the washing up. He left them to their mundane existences, crept upstairs and took some money out of his piggy bank to pay for the tube fare. Then he slipped out of the house, closing the door noiselessly behind him.

36

The trees closed in around her, their roots threatening to trip her up. Any moment now they would transform themselves into stone columns and angels, obelisks and urns, ivy-clad crosses and mausoleums. The woman in black would be kneeling beside the statue of the sleeping angel. She would stand up. She would take Lauren's hand. She would start to speak.

But this time there was something else. A knocking sound.

Lauren spun around. *Who's there?*

The knocking was rhythmic and persistent. *What's happening? Are the dead trying to escape from their coffins?*

In terror Lauren started to run, tripped over a fallen log and felt herself falling, falling, falling…

She woke with a start. Her heart was thudding against her ribcage and her nightshirt felt damp from sweat. These dreams she was having were turning her into a wreck. She lay there staring at the ceiling. Maybe she should talk to someone.

Then she realised something. The knocking sound was continuing. It hadn't just been in her dream – it was here in the house.

What the…?

Then she remembered. Of course. The builders. And she was supposed to be on tea-making duty because Wendy was at the hospital this morning.

The banging was reverberating inside her skull. It would be impossible to get back to sleep. She rolled over and reached out a hand for her watch. Eight o'clock. Way too early.

Bang, bang, bang.

The hammering was making the house shake.

Lauren hauled herself out of bed and made a quick

dash for the bathroom, praying that she wouldn't meet Neil or his apprentice on the stairs whilst she was wearing her skimpy nightshirt.

Then, showered and dressed, she ventured up to the attic.

The room was already unrecognizable from how it had been two days ago. Half the floorboards were up, exposing the joists and pipes below the floor. Neil was on his knees peering into the dusty gap between the floor and the ceiling of the room below, whistling to himself. The apprentice, a spotty lad of about seventeen, was levering the skirting off the far wall using a chisel and hammer – hence the banging. Lauren hovered in the doorway, not daring to walk on the exposed joists in case she lost her balance and put her foot through the ceiling of the room below.

"Hi there, can I get you some tea?"

Neil looked up. He was a stocky man with rosy cheeks and close-cut ginger hair.

"Thanks love, that'll be grand. Milk, two sugars please. For both of us."

"Coming right up."

She might as well get used to it. Despite her previous intentions, she was obviously going to be making cups of tea all week.

She delivered two steaming mugs of sweet milky tea to the men in the attic then sat down at the computer with Isabelle's diary. She was determined to read more of the diary before she had to go and meet Tom. If only that banging would stop for a moment.

37

Thursday, 10th February 1870

I must try and put my past life behind me but memories of it still haunt my dreams.

Yesterday evening after the séance I was so agitated by everything

I had witnessed that I was unable to sleep for many hours. When I did eventually fall into a restless sleep I dreamed I was back in my old home.

It was that fateful Christmas Eve.

The wind had been rising all afternoon and by the evening there was a ferocious storm howling outside. Gusts rattled the window panes and the coals hissed when raindrops fell down the chimney. It was a cruel night and I pitied those poor souls who did not have the warmth and comfort of a home as I did.

Despite the storm raging outside, I felt safe in the drawing room of my parents' London house, little thinking what dangers could reach me here amongst my family.

The Christmas tree sparkled with decorations and beneath its boughs the presents lay in little piles, waiting to be shared on the morrow.

Nathaniel, my brother, was playing the piano and Helen, his fiancée, was singing a song about a robin in her clear, sweet voice. She sings like an angel. Mother sat in her armchair embroidering a handkerchief and father stood in front of the mantelpiece smoking his pipe. I busied myself with a tapestry I had been working on for some time – a pastoral scene of meadows and shepherds.

A knock at the drawing room door.

Jenny, the maid, entered to announce the arrival of our guest for the evening.

He was a friend of Nathaniel's. His name was – I tremble even now to write it down – Edward.

Helen and Nathaniel ceased their song. Mother laid aside her embroidery. Father adjusted his cravat.

We waited for Edward to appear.

At the first sight of his friend in the doorway, Nathaniel jumped up from the piano stool, welcoming Edward with warm words and ushering him into the room.

What a sight.

He looked as if he had passed through the storm of the apocalypse. His black hair was swept across his pale face and his coat tails and trousers were wet from walking in the rain. He shook Nathaniel's hand, thanking him for his welcome and bowing his head as he did so. He was a good six inches taller than my brother. He kissed Mother's hand, making her blush, then Helen's and then he came to me.

He took my hand in his icy fingers and lifted it to his lips, all the time looking at me from under dark lashes. I shivered at the coldness of his touch but was unable to look away from those eyes which were a startling shade of blue.

"My good fellow," said Father breaking the spell, "come and stand in front of the fire. What a dreadful night to be out."

Whilst Nathaniel poured Edward a glass of whisky and Father spoke to him about politics, I became aware of his blue eyes watching me. I tried to continue working on my tapestry but my hands were trembling and I pricked my finger with the needle. A bead of blood swelled up and dripped onto the satin of my dress.

38

Tom paid for his drink, a Caramel Frappuccino, and sat down at an empty table for two with a clear view of the door. He took a sip of his drink, enjoying the feel of the cool liquid in his mouth.

He was in Starbucks opposite the west doors to St Paul's Cathedral. When Tom had phoned Peter Hart yesterday, Peter had said how sorry he was to hear about Tom's father and had agreed to meet him the very next day in his lunch break at one o'clock. Peter had suggested this branch of Starbucks because he worked at the Stock Exchange on the other side of Paternoster Square. Tom didn't mind. It was another good excuse to get out of the house.

Tom checked his watch. Five to one. Good – he wasn't late. He looked around the café in case Peter was there already. Three women in business suits were sitting on a squishy leather sofa sipping cappuccinos. A couple of American tourists in baggy shorts and baseball caps were rifling through a London A-Z and perusing a leaflet about the London Eye. A group of teenage girls were seated around a table, laughing and tucking into chocolate muffins. No, it didn't look as if Peter Hart was there yet. Tom took another sip of his drink and watched the door.

Tom was hoping that Peter Hart would be able to tell him a bit more about Isabelle's diary. The document on his dad's computer had told him nothing. It looked as if his dad had started to transcribe the diary, as Lauren was doing, but hadn't got much further than the first couple of paragraphs. Maybe he'd struggled with the handwriting as well. Or maybe he'd just run out of time. Quite literally.

On the stroke of one the door opened and a man walked in. Tom guessed at once it was Peter Hart. He was in his mid-to-late fifties but looked like he kept himself fit. He was tall and slim, with dark hair and was carrying his suit jacket slung over one shoulder. He ordered a pot of Earl Grey tea from the counter and came over to Tom's table.

"Tom?" he asked setting his tray down on the table and holding out his right hand. "I'm Peter."

"Hi," said Tom shaking his hand and taking an instant liking to Peter Hart. "Thanks for coming to meet me."

"Not at all." Peter sat down and poured himself a cup of tea. Tom waited, not sure where to begin.

Peter broke the silence. "I just want to say how sorry I was to hear about your father's accident. I hadn't known him long but I could see he was a fine man and an excellent scholar."

Tom nodded his thanks and sipped his Frappuccino to stop himself from getting all emotional. He didn't want to screw up this first meeting. He put his drink down and ventured a reply, hoping his voice wouldn't crack. "How did you get to know him?"

"It's quite a long story."

"That's OK. I'm not in a hurry."

Peter leaned back in his seat, crossing one leg over the other. "Back in the late nineteenth century my great, great grandfather, Nathaniel Hart, was a lepidopterist."

"That means he studied moths and butterflies right?"

Peter's face lit up. "Exactly. Most people don't know what I'm talking about but I can see you do. In 1875 he published *Butterflies of the British Isles – A Nature Lover's Guide*. It was long regarded as the definitive work on the subject of native butterflies and is beautifully illustrated with his own watercolours. Anyway, when my own father passed away earlier this year I had the job of clearing out his house and in the attic I discovered a chest of the most amazing things – notebooks, drawings, watercolour sketches - that had belonged to Nathaniel. All his research notes and sketches had been passed down through the generations but my father, grandfather and great grandfather hadn't done anything with them so I thought it was about time somebody sorted it all out. But I only have a small apartment in Canary Wharf – I haven't got the space to store boxfuls of memorabilia no matter how much I'd like to."

Peter poured himself another cup of tea. Tom could see he was really warming to his subject and waited for Peter to continue. "Nathaniel specialised in the Lycaenidae family of butterflies," explained Peter, "specifically blue butterflies. In his diary, which was also in the box, he wrote at length about his travels all over the South Downs hunting for the Silver-studded Blue, the Chalkhill Blue, the Adonis Blue and the Holly Blue amongst others."

Tom stifled a yawn by downing most of his drink which was no longer cold but room temperature. All this stuff about butterflies was interesting up to a point but Tom really couldn't see what it had to do with his dad or Isabelle's diary. He shifted in his seat.

Peter pointed at Tom's drink. "Can I get you a refill?"

"No, I'm good, thanks. Did you find anything else in the chest?"

"Well, yes, as it happens. This is the interesting bit."

Tom sat up straighter.

"There were two diaries in the box."

At last.

"One diary belonged to Nathaniel and the other belonged to his sister."

"Isabelle?"

"Exactly. I was particularly interested to find Isabelle's diary because a few years ago I tried to research my family tree and Isabelle had been all but erased from the family records. It was odd - I found her birth certificate but then nothing else. No marriage certificate. No death certificate. It was as if she had just vanished into thin air." Peter held his hands up as if to demonstrate that he wasn't hiding a miniature Isabelle in his palms.

"What do you think happened to her?"

Peter took another sip of tea and looked thoughtful. "Possibly there was some sort of scandal, which the family thought best to conceal."

"By pretending she didn't exist?"

"It was a different age back then in the nineteenth century. We shouldn't judge too harshly."

Tom wasn't sure what Peter was getting at but decided to let it pass. "So you gave Isabelle's diary to Dad? What made you do that?"

Peter smiled. "I met your father at a drinks party at UCL for alumni."

"Sorry, for what?"

"Old students. You know the sort of thing – they invite old students back for a social gathering and you spend the evening feeling that you've wasted your life because your contemporaries are now running the BBC or have a prominent position in the government. And then at some point in the evening the Chancellor of the university makes a speech about the state of university funding and we're all supposed to go away and make a donation to the university's hardship fund."

"So you met Dad there?"

"Yes, and we got talking. I told him about Nathaniel's papers which I'd recently discovered and he told me he was researching the history of Highgate Cemetery for a book."

This was news to Tom. "He never said."

Peter shrugged. "I think he was keeping quiet about it. It wasn't part of his main university work. I gave him Isabelle's diary to read because it mentions Highgate Cemetery quite a lot. In fact she…" His voice trailed away.

"What?"

Peter shook his head. "It doesn't matter."

"Did you meet Professor Nesbit at this drinks do?" It had occurred to Tom that Peter might have some insight into the professor that it would be useful to know about.

Peter put his cup down on the table and Tom noticed a subtle change in his manner, a stiffening of his posture and a more serious expression on his face. "No, he wasn't at the drinks party as it happens, but I know him from a very long time ago."

"Oh?"

Peter leaned across the table and dropped his voice. "Have you heard of the Highgate Vampire?"

39

Friday, 11th February 1870

It is a cold, blustery day. The weather is too unsettled for me to risk a visit to the cemetery so I find myself turning to the pages of this diary as a form of solace.

Yesterday I wrote about the dream I had after the séance. It has brought everything back to me so vividly that I feel compelled to write about it here. Maybe then I will be able to put past events behind me.

So it was Christmas Eve.

We were warm and safe in the parlour with the fire crackling in the hearth and the warm smells of cooking wafting from the kitchen. Nathaniel joined Father and Edward in the discussion about politics and Helen sat down next to me on the sofa, admiring the tapestry and talking excitedly about their plans for the wedding. But I was distracted and, I am ashamed to say, only half-listened to what she was telling me.

My attention was constantly drawn towards the three men, now seated in armchairs around the fire and discussing the merits of Gladstone versus Disraeli.

No, I must be honest. My attention was drawn to one man and that was Edward. Now that he no longer looked as if he had just blown in on the storm, I could see that his features were very fine indeed - high cheek bones, a strong jaw, piercing blue eyes.

It was those eyes. I was sure he kept looking in my direction, even whilst he appeared to be deep in conversation with my father and brother.

By the time Jenny called us to the dining room I was trembling from head to foot and was convinced my agitation must be plain for everyone to see.

Edward offered me his arm as we made our way to the dining room. I took it, feeling the heat rise to my face. No one had ever had such an effect on me before.

I remember little of the meal. I think we had roast goose or something similar. I do remember I was seated next to our guest. How could I forget? He raised his glass to mine, our eyes locked and I knew in that moment I was lost.

In the New Year he became a regular visitor to the house, usually on the pretext of some business or other he was conducting with Nathaniel, but I am sure he came to see me. We were never alone, of course. That would not have been the proper thing at all.

But then came that day in the spring. My face burns with shame even now at the thought of it.

Edward called, so he said, to see my brother but Nathaniel was still not back from the office. Mother suggested to me that I might take our visitor on a stroll around the garden. I consented willingly.

It was warm for the time of year and the apple trees were in full blossom. We strolled past the flower beds nearest to the house, admiring the spring bulbs and the roses which were just coming into bud. Then Edward offered me his arm and we struck out across the lawn towards the shrubbery. Years ago Father had planted yew hedges which had grown into dense, green walls creating enclosed spaces in the garden where you could find welcome shade on a hot day.

As we entered one of those enclosed spaces now, shielded from the view of the house, Edward took me in his arms and drew me to him. He kissed me. I felt as if the world was spinning. But then…

I cannot go on.

No, I must.

Then he became rougher with me. He forced me onto the ground and…

My hand is trembling and I can barely write.

I was ignorant of the ways of the world. I had no idea what a man could do to a woman. But I was soon to find out. It all happened so quickly and my fall from grace was complete.

He left me there, shocked and weeping.

When dusk began to fall I returned inside, resolved that I would speak of what had happened to no one.

But a couple of months later I discovered I was with child. The shame of it was too much for Mother to bear. She hid me away, in a convent.

My daughter, Emily, was born on a bitterly cold January day with the wind howling outside the convent walls. She was a sweet but sickly creature and not made for the harshness of this world. She died not long after birth.

Born out of wedlock and unbaptised as she was, I could not give her a proper Christian burial. I took my poor darling to Highgate Cemetery and God led me to the kind grave digger who saw my distress and helped me bury my daughter by the sleeping angel.

I think I will go to the cemetery after all. I do not care about the weather. I wish the wind would come and blow me away.

40

The café seemed suddenly very quiet. The man at the next table rustled his newspaper. Someone clinked a teaspoon against a saucer. The coffee machine hissed.

The Highgate Vampire.

"I came across something about it on Dad's computer yesterday," said Tom, keeping his voice down. "Dad had started a document about it, but he hadn't got very far with it, just a few bullet points that he'd copied from Wikipedia. Something about March 1970?"

Peter nodded. "That's right. March 1970. I was sixteen at the time. About the same age you are now?"

"Yes," said Tom. "So what happened?"

Peter seemed reluctant to speak. "I was young," he said, shrugging his shoulders. "You know how it is, you go along with what your friends suggest because you don't want to be left out of the group and labelled boring. I got caught up in the events of the time as did a lot of people. As did Alan Nesbit. Yes, I know it's hard to imagine him as a teenager, but even he was young once."

Tom was intrigued. "What events?"

Peter leaned forwards and said in a lowered voice, "That there was, or is, a vampire haunting Highgate Cemetery."

Tom laughed. "Surely people didn't think…" But he stopped when he saw the expression on Peter Hart's face, a mixture of uncertainty and embarrassment. Maybe he just didn't like being reminded of his younger, more foolish self. Or maybe he really did think there was something weird going on in the cemetery. Something which, for all his intelligence and sophistication, he couldn't explain.

"You can read about it," said the older man. "It was reported at the time in the local newspaper, the *Hampstead and Highgate Express* as it was then called." He started pouring himself another cup of Earl Grey.

Tom thought for a moment then decided to put the question that was forming itself in his mind. It was a long shot, but he wanted Peter's opinion. "Could this Highgate vampire business have anything to do with my dad's death?"

Peter put the teapot down. "Why do you say that?" From the tone of Peter's voice, he was at least taking the question seriously.

"I don't think Dad's death was an accident. I had a

meeting with Professor Nesbit where he acted very strangely indeed. He took a memory stick from Dad's study at home and he's been trying to get his hands on Isabelle's diary."

"I see." Peter sipped his tea and frowned as if gathering his thoughts. When he next spoke he seemed to be choosing his words with care. "I wouldn't like to speculate, and please don't think I'm making an accusation, but Professor Nesbit is, how shall I put it, obsessed with Highgate Cemetery. If he felt your father was, I don't know, interfering somehow, or had access to some new information about the cemetery or the vampire, then I suppose it's possible that he might do something…rash. Where is the diary now by the way?"

"My friend Lauren is reading it. She's better at deciphering the handwriting than I am. She'll keep it safe."

"Good. Keep it for as long you need it."

Tom wanted to ask Peter what he meant by "something rash," but Peter had finished his tea and was looking at his watch.

"I'm afraid I'm going to have to go," he said, standing up. "Got to get the economy back on its feet and all that. But you know where to find me if there's anything else you want to talk about."

"Thanks for coming to meet me," said Tom, standing to shake Peter's hand.

"My pleasure." He picked his jacket up off the back of the chair and walked out.

Tom finished the last mouthful of his drink and prepared to leave. What Peter had said about Professor Nesbit certainly put a new light on things. A vampire hunter? The professor couldn't be right in the head. Tom wondered if there was a way he could find out the truth.

41

Lauren steered clear of a group of French school children in identical red baseball caps who were milling about outside St Paul's showing no interest whatsoever in Wren's architectural masterpiece, and sat down on the cathedral steps to wait for Tom. It was nearly half past one so he shouldn't be long now. Shielding her eyes from the sun, she squinted over at Starbucks to see if she could see him. A tall, slim man walked out of the café carrying his suit jacket slung over one shoulder. Less than a minute later Tom appeared.

Lauren jumped to her feet and waved to him as she hurried down the cathedral steps. He saw her and came over. There was a slight frown on his forehead as if he was deep in thought.

"How did it go?" she asked, "your meeting with Peter Hart?"

The frown cleared and he smiled properly for the first time since she'd met him. "Great, thanks. He's a really good bloke."

They started walking across Paternoster Square, skirting around camera-clicking tourists and a party of elderly Japanese led by a tiny woman with a huge golfing umbrella pointed at the sky like a lightening conductor.

"So is Peter Hart related to Isabelle?" asked Lauren.

"Yes. His great great grandfather was Nathaniel Hart, and Nathaniel was Isabelle's brother so that must mean…" He frowned, trying to work it out.

Lauren laughed. "I think that mean's she's his great, great, great aunt if she's the sister of his great great grandfather."

Tom looked bewildered. "If you say so."

"So anyway, what did he tell you?"

"Well he went on for ages about how he found the diary in his father's attic and about Nathaniel's interest in butterflies, but the really interesting bit was when he mentioned Alan Nesbit."

"Who's he?"

"*Professor* Alan Nesbit, I should say," and there was no hiding the contempt in Tom's voice as he spoke the name, "head of department at University College London and my dad's…colleague."

"So what about this professor?"

Tom turned to look at her. "Have you heard of the Highgate Vampire?"

"The what?" Lauren tried to keep her voice light, but she felt a shiver run up her spine.

"In 1970," explained Tom, "Professor Nesbit went on a vampire hunt in Highgate Cemetery. According to Peter Hart, Nesbit has been obsessed ever since then with the idea that a vampire haunts Highgate Cemetery. What do you make of that?"

Lauren felt the blood drain from her face. She stopped walking and stared at Tom. "You're kidding, right?"

"I'm just telling you what Peter said. What's the matter, are you OK?"

"Yes, it's just…" Lauren wanted more than anything to tell Tom about Saturday night - the cemetery, the bulbs of garlic lined up like toy soldiers in front of the catacomb, the man with the axe. The horror of it all was still so real. It had been too dark to see the man's face properly, she wouldn't recognise him now if she saw him in the street, but she would know his voice. Angry and grating. It haunted her dreams. But she couldn't admit to trespassing in the cemetery at night. Not to Tom whose father had only just been buried there. He'd think she had no respect for the dead. She shook her head. "No, I'm fine. Really. I was just surprised by what you said, that's all."

They walked on in silence. Lauren wanted to ask Tom about Alan Nesbit, but didn't want to risk upsetting him. "When you gave me Isabelle's diary, you said you thought your dad had been…" She hesitated to say the word, not sure how Tom would react.

"Murdered?" Tom completed the sentence for her.

Lauren nodded, relieved that Tom was able to discuss it more rationally this time. "So what I don't understand is where does Alan Nesbit fit into all this?"

This time it was Tom who stopped walking and looked at her with a deadly serious expression on his face. "I have this hunch that Alan Nesbit had something to do with my dad's death. But I need to get some evidence before I go to the police."

"Right," said Lauren, her head spinning as she absorbed this new chilling piece of information. There was no doubt she and her friends had had a lucky escape on Saturday night, assuming it was this Alan Nesbit person they'd encountered in the cemetery. Who else could it have been?

"And how are you going to get this evidence?" she asked.

"Well, I've had an idea," said Tom, his face brightening. "There's someone at UCL who might be able to help us. Do you mind if we go there now?"

"Sure," said Lauren. "Why not?" They had reached St Paul's station and Lauren saw no harm in going along with Tom's plan. She was just glad he wanted to include her this time and hadn't rushed off like he usually did.

They descended the steps to the underground and made their way to the platform where a train was just pulling in.

"So what have you read in the diary?" asked Tom as they jumped aboard.

As they sped along the Central Line, Lauren gave Tom a brief résumé of what she'd read so far.

"So you're saying that Isabelle was an unmarried mother who was cast out by her family and who buried her dead baby in secret in Highgate Cemetery?" he asked.

"That's about it," said Lauren.

"Well that would explain why she was erased from the Hart family tree."

They changed onto the Northern Line at Tottenham Court Road. This time the train was too packed for them to continue their conversation. They only just managed to squeeze themselves on board.

"Watch out," said Tom as the doors started to close. He put his hand against the small of her back to prevent her being trapped by the doors and Lauren felt her stomach flip over. She spent the rest of the journey acutely aware of the closeness of him; his broad shoulders; the muscles in his arms as he gripped the overhead bar and the way his body swayed with the movement of the train. Normally she hated tube trains when they were packed, but she had never minded less about being in such a confined space. She was disappointed when Tom peered out of the window and said, "This is our stop." They were at Warren Street.

Back at street level, it was only a short walk to the University College building on Gower Street.

"Who are we going to see?" asked Lauren as she followed Tom up the steps into the university. She assumed it wasn't Professor Nesbit. She couldn't help glancing over her shoulder, as if the mad professor might leap out from behind a pillar, brandishing his axe, but the reception area was empty, save for a couple of students with armfuls of books.

"Nancy Letts," said Tom. "She's the department secretary."

Tom went up to the reception desk whilst Lauren stared with wonder at the figure of Jeremy Bentham. *What a weird place this is,* she thought to herself.

They found Nancy in her office, with the door open, frowning at a computer screen, her desk overflowing with paperwork. Tom tapped on the open door. "Hi there, Nancy. I hope we're not disturbing you."

"Tom," exclaimed Nancy swivelling round on her chair, "fantastic to see you. I need a break from all these application forms. They're doing my head in. Come on in."

"This is Lauren," said Tom, walking into the office.

"Nice to meet you," said Nancy getting up to shake Lauren's hand. She looked from Lauren to Tom and back again. It was obvious from the knowing smile on her face that she had just put two and two together and come up with five. "Can I get you both a drink? Fizzy water OK? I've got some in the fridge."

"Yes please," said Lauren. They sat down in the office whilst Nancy trotted off to the kitchen, her heels clicking on the wooden floor. A minute later she reappeared with two glasses of sparkling water.

"So, what's happening in the world?" asked Nancy perching on the edge of her desk. "I don't get to hear any gossip these days with everyone on holiday."

Tom proceeded to tell Nancy about his meeting with Peter Hart. When he got to the bit about Alan Nesbit, Nancy's mouth fell open and her eyes grew round as saucers. "What, you don't say old Nesbit goes chasing after vampires in his spare time do you? Well I never." She shook her head in astonishment. "I always said there was something not right about him," she added in a conspiratorial whisper.

"The thing is," said Tom, "I need to find out what's going on with Professor Nesbit because I think he had something to do with...with...what happened to dad. So I was wondering if you might be able to help."

Nancy looked thoughtful and nodded, as if the idea of Professor Nesbit "having something to do" with Jack's death was of no surprise to her. "Of course I'll help you out," she said, patting him on the arm. "What do you want me to do? I could start by taking a look around his office."

"Well, if you don't mind..."

Nancy laughed. "Of course I don't mind. He's not in today, thank goodness, so as soon as I've finished logging these applications I'll take a peek, see what I can find out. How does that sound?"

"Brilliant," said Tom. He stood up. "Can I give you my

mobile number?"

"Write it down here," said Nancy, passing him a pad of post-it notes and a pencil. "I'll give you a call this evening to let you know what I've found." She dived under the desk and resurfaced with a bulging handbag that she started to search through. Not finding what she was looking for she started shifting piles of paper off her desk onto the floor.

"Ah, here it is," she said retrieving a battered old mobile from under a stack of application forms. "I'll give you my number too. Can never remember it though," she laughed. She found her number on the phone, scribbled it onto a yellow sticky and handed it to Tom. "If there's anything else I can do for you, call me."

"Will do," said Tom, pocketing the note.

"Thanks for the water," said Lauren.

"You're welcome," said Nancy, giving her a conspiratorial wink.

They returned to Warren Street and caught a train back up to Highgate. Lauren sensed that Tom was feeling more relaxed and for the first time they chatted about ordinary things like which schools they went to and what A-levels they were planning to take. They had English in common, but Lauren wanted to combine it with French and German, whereas Tom was thinking of doing History and Geography.

All too soon Lauren realised they had reached her house on Highgate Hill.

Should I invite him in for a coffee?

"Listen," said Tom thrusting his hands into his pockets and staring at the ground, "I was, umm, wondering, about tonight… if you've got nothing planned that is, whether or not you might like to, umm…"

"Yes?" prompted Lauren encouragingly.

"If you'd like to…"

"Hey, Lauren!" Lauren whipped her head round at the sound of her name being called from across the street.

Chloe was waving at her and running across the road, darting between a black cab and a double decker bus.

Not now, for crying out loud.

Tom fell silent and stood awkwardly, shuffling his feet.

Chloe looked from Tom to Lauren, giving Lauren a look that clearly said, *so is this the secret boyfriend?*

Lauren refused to rise to the bait and kept her tone neutral.

"Hello, Chloe. How are things?"

Tom looked at his watch.

"Yeah, great," said Chloe. "Doing anything tonight?"

Lauren glanced at Tom who had moved off to one side and was fiddling with his mobile phone.

"I don't know," said Lauren, pointedly. "I was just talking to Tom here…" She gave him what she hoped was an encouraging smile. She was sure he'd been about to ask her out before Chloe had appeared out of thin air and screwed everything up.

"I better be going," said Tom. "I'll catch up with you later." She felt her heart sink as he turned and walked down the hill.

"What's the matter?" asked Chloe. "Was I interrupting something?"

"Yes, as a matter of fact," snapped Lauren.

"Oops, sorry." Chloe smiled sheepishly. "Anyway, I was going to ask if you want to come out tomorrow. *Saints and Sinners* are doing another gig. They're doing a re-run of Saturday's concert because it was interrupted. Megan's dead keen to go."

I bet she is, thought Lauren. She remembered the crush of bodies, the deafening noise and then the panic when the lights went out. Quite frankly she wasn't in the mood. She was cross with Megan for always dictating what they did and she was cross with Chloe for barging in on her conversation with Tom.

"Actually, I'm busy tomorrow night," said Lauren. "And there's stuff I have to do now, so I'll be in touch,

OK?"

Chloe looked a bit put out. But this time Lauren was determined to have things her way. She wasn't always going to dance to Megan's tune.

"I'll see you around," she said walking up the garden path to the front door, leaving Chloe standing on the pavement.

42

Lauren's friends were a nightmare.

First there was the scary one who'd made him feel guilty for standing on the pavement and breathing, and now he'd encountered the dippy one who'd screwed up his opportunity for asking Lauren out on a date. Or maybe, he realised with a sense of defeat as he pushed open the front door of his house, the problem was with himself. He'd had plenty of opportunity all afternoon to ask her but he'd put it off, leaving it to the very last minute. And then it was too late. He was just too sensitive around girls. Lauren was the only girl he'd met with whom he could be himself. All he wanted to do now was go up to his room and lose himself in some loud music.

He stopped at the foot of the stairs. There were voices. Laughter. He recognised with distaste the high pitched cackle his mother always used when she was trying to impress someone and which always irritated him. She was talking to someone in the lounge. He listened and heard a man's voice which, with a shock, he recognised.

What the hell is he doing here?

After everything Tom had learned today this was the final straw. He pushed open the lounge door and walked in.

The conversation stopped immediately. His mother and Alan Nesbit turned to face him.

"Sorry, am I interrupting something?" He knew he didn't sound sorry. He walked up to the coffee table and helped himself to a chocolate chip cookie. He noticed with some surprise that his mother had gone to the trouble of making tea in the best china teapot and had laid out two cups and saucers. Why all the fuss? And when had she been out to buy chocolate chip cookies of all things when there was still hardly anything to eat in the house?

"Tom," said his mother in a voice that was too bright. "I wasn't expecting you home."

"I do live here."

A flicker of embarrassment in her eyes. "Yes, of course you do. Anyway, Alan, I mean Professor Nesbit called round to see how we were getting on. He brought the biscuits."

That would explain it.

"Please, call me Alan," said Professor Nesbit leaning forward to pick up his cup from the coffee table. "No need to be formal. We're all friends here."

Are we? thought Tom biting into his cookie. He wondered if Professor Nesbit had told his mother about their conversation at UCL.

An awkward silence descended on the room. His mother lifted the lid on the teapot and peered inside. "It's nearly empty, let me go and make a fresh pot." She picked up the teapot and hurried out of the room leaving Tom standing there with a mouthful of cookie. Alan put his cup back on the coffee table. For a moment neither of them spoke.

"So you came to see how we were getting on?" asked Tom. He couldn't keep the sarcasm out of his voice.

Alan shot him a look of contempt. "I think you know why I'm here."

"Do I?"

"Look, I haven't got much time so let's not pretend ignorance here. Before he died your father was working on something to do with Highgate Cemetery. But what were the precise details?"

"How should I know? You're his colleague. Didn't he

discuss his work with you?"

Alan scowled and Tom knew he'd hit a raw nerve.

"Academics don't have time to tell each other everything," he blustered. "So come on, you must have some idea. Didn't he chat to you at the weekends? I know you used to go out fishing together."

"You know nothing," said Tom, clenching his fists. He wanted to punch Professor Nesbit and had to force himself to stay calm.

"There's a book isn't there?"

Tom couldn't trust himself to speak. He turned away from Professor Nesbit and stared out of the window, crossing his arms in front of him.

"Your silence betrays the fact that I'm right," said Professor Nesbit with satisfaction in his voice. "No doubt you think you're being very clever keeping it hidden, but I will find it."

At that moment the door opened and Tom's mother reappeared with a fresh pot of tea.

Alan stood up and resumed his ingratiating voice. "I'm sorry but I have to be going. It's been a pleasure."

"Oh, what a shame." She sounded genuinely disappointed. Tom wanted to puke.

"Nice talking to you Tom."

Tom said nothing but picked up another cookie and walked out of the room.

43

Friday, 18th February 1870

I have been busy at the penitentiary all week, taking my meals there with the other Sisters so have not seen Madeleine since the night of the séance. In truth, I have avoided her because she disturbs me so. It has been a relief to spend my time at the penitentiary where the routines of the laundry and kitchen have helped to calm my nerves.

I have discovered that Sister Christina is a poet and, in fact, the sister of the artist Dante Gabriel Rossetti whose work I admire. She is very religious and has great dedication to her work. I feel she could teach me much.

At today's chapel service Reverend Renshaw spoke to the women about the importance of being baptised. It seems that many of the young women there have not been baptised. He told them that only those who are baptised can enter the Kingdom of Heaven.

As I sat at the back of the chapel listening, every word he spoke was like a knife cutting into me. What, I wanted to ask, about those who die before they can be baptised? I was clenching my fists so tightly that Ellen, who was sitting next to me, put a hand on my arm and gave me a look that mingled curiosity with sympathy. I tried to relax after that. I must not let my feelings give me away.

When I returned home this evening I was still in a state of agitation. At dinner I felt Madeleine's eyes on me but the presence of Mrs Payne prevented us from discussing anything more meaningful than the weather which has been very unsettled of late.

When dinner was over and we were climbing the stairs, Madeleine stopped when we reached the first floor landing and turned to me.

"Forgive me," she said, regarding me with her bright green eyes, "but I couldn't help noticing you are a little preoccupied this evening. Is there anything I can help you with?"

I hesitated a moment, remembering what happened when Madeleine had "helped" Mrs Waterman. I must confess I was nervous. But I also realised that I wanted her comfort. As much as I admired Sister Christina, I did not feel I could talk to her openly. And what I had witnessed in Madeleine's room the other week made me feel there was a bond between us, even if I didn't fully understand it. I was curious to know what she, who had experience of the spirit world, would say about Reverend Renshaw's sermon today. So I said, yes, there was something she could help me with.

We went into her room. She turned the oil lamp up so that the room was bathed in a warm glow. The coals in the grate were burning orange. The round table where we had all sat was still covered in the dark red cloth but looked more like a table in a parlour where one would sit to drink tea or play bridge. I glanced over at the cabinet but the curtain was pulled across and there was nothing to see.

Madeleine invited me to sit with her on the sofa in front of the fire and then she asked me about my day at the penitentiary. I told her that I had spent the morning supervising the women in the laundry and then I told her about the chapel service and Reverend Renshaw's sermon on the importance of baptism. I also told her about my concerns on this subject although I did not mention anything specific to myself.

She listened carefully to what I had to say then she shook her head.

"He means well, your Reverend Renshaw," she said with a hint of a smile on her lips, "but he does not understand the spirit world as I do."

"Tell me what you understand," I said.

She closed her eyes for a moment as if gathering her thoughts, then she opened them and spoke slowly and clearly. "Whether a soul spends eternity in Heaven or Hell is not a simple matter of faith or doing good works. Protestants lay greater emphasis on faith and Catholics still believe in the power of good works, but it is not as simple as that. When someone dies, their spirit passes through hierarchies in the spirit world."

"Hierarchies?" I asked. "You mean, they move from one level to another?" I did not fully understand her meaning.

"Let me explain," she said. "What I am trying to say is that spirits can still grow and move towards a state of perfection, even after they have left the physical body behind. So it doesn't matter if the person was baptised when they were alive or if they did lots of good works."

"But Reverend Renshaw says that in the Bible…"

She laid a hand on mine and put a finger to my lips. "Hush. Do not concern yourself with Reverend Renshaw. Does Reverend Renshaw have personal contact with spirits? Does he have the gift of communicating with those who have passed to the other side? I doubt it. What better way is there to arrive at an understanding of God than through direct contact with the spirit world?"

I thought of Sister Christina with her devotion to the Bible and the cross which she wears around her neck. I thought also of the painting of the crucifixion hanging in Sister Burn's office. I tried a different argument.

"The Sisters at the penitentiary believe they are doing the work of God in bringing the women back into the Christian fold, teaching habits of industry and piety."

"Oh, I'm not saying that industry and piety are not desirable qualities in a person," said Madeleine, shrugging her shoulders. "But you saw for yourself a manifestation from the spirit world at the séance last week. Do you not trust the evidence of your own eyes?"

It was true. I could not deny what I had witnessed even if I did not fully comprehend it.

"I could conduct a private séance for you," said Madeleine. "That is, if there is anyone in the spirit world with whom you would like to make contact."

I looked into her eyes and, despite the warmth of the room, felt a shiver up my spine.

"I…I…." My voice faltered. I was afraid. I pulled my hand away from hers and stood up, my legs shaking. "I'm sorry, I'm tired," I said. "I must go to bed." Then I hurried from the room before the tears started to fall.

44

Nancy typed the final details of the last applicant into her spreadsheet and pressed save. Tomorrow's post would bring a whole new batch of applications, but for now she was done. It was tedious work and after a while all university applicants started to sound the same – *expected to get 3 As at A-level, plays the flute/violin/trumpet/piano (grade 8), enjoys reading serious novels and works as a volunteer in the local old people's home.* Who were they kidding? They couldn't all be top-class students and model citizens to boot who spent their evenings delving into literary classics and their weekends happily listening to doddering old folks harping on about life during the war. Nancy wasn't a fool. She hadn't worked in the university for the last ten years without forming an opinion or two about your typical student and she'd never yet met one who lived up to their application form.

It had been a welcome relief from work when Tom had turned up with his nice young friend. Nancy hadn't been entirely sure if they were an *item*, but she hoped so. The poor boy needed someone supportive in his life right now. And who'd have thought it, eh? Old Nesbit chasing vampires? Well, well, well. What would his students say to that? Come to think of it, maybe they wouldn't be surprised. She doubted they discussed the finer points of his lectures or the warmth of his tutoring style down the bar. There was something of the *undead* about Nesbit that must be quite scary for new undergraduates. And he'd always treated her, not as a valued member of the department as Jack had done, but as if she was something he'd picked up on the sole of his shoe.

Nancy checked her watch. It was four o'clock. She wasn't supposed to leave work until five, although no one would notice if she left ten minutes early. She planned to drive down to Rotherhithe and visit her mum for the evening. She usually came to work on public transport but today she'd brought the car so she wouldn't have to travel home on the tube late at night. She looked at the next job in her in-tray – the Archaeology Department had ordered some new machine or other for spying underground without actually digging and Professor David Jones wanted her to check on its progress and find out when it was going to arrive. Well the archaeological thingummy could wait another twenty minutes. She'd promised Tom she would help him and she intended to do just that. It was a shame she didn't have a machine that would enable her to examine Professor Nesbit's office without venturing in there. She was going to have resort to old-fashioned digging.

She poked her head out into the corridor and listened. It was a quiet afternoon. Most of the lecturers and tutors were off on their summer holidays. It was only loners and weirdoes like Professor Nesbit who hung around all year without ever taking a break, but even he hadn't been in today so hopefully that meant he wasn't going to show up.

Nancy took the master key to the department from a drawer in her desk, picked up some paperwork to do with student loans and made her way down the empty corridor.

Professor Nesbit's door was closed. She leaned forwards and listened but no sound emerged from inside. Straightening up, she gave three short, sharp knocks just to be sure.

No answer.

Right then, best get this over with quickly.

With a final glance up and down the corridor to make sure no one was coming, Nancy slipped the master key into the lock, turned it, and, with a beating heart, let herself into the office, shutting the door quietly behind her.

The air smelt stale and musty. She was tempted to open a window but she knew she mustn't waste time. But where to start? She dumped the paperwork on the edge of the desk and went over to the bookcase.

The wooden bookcase that occupied a corner of the room was over six feet high and four feet wide. It was jammed full of books, some of them upright and others piled on their sides. Nancy started at the top, scanning the spines and working her way down from left to right.

She didn't really know what she hoped to find. Other than a dictionary and a thesaurus, they were all history books with titles such as, *The Battle for Power - Church and State in Tudor Times*, and *The Black Death – A Social History of the Plague*. There was nothing as incriminating as *How to Catch a Vampire* or *Vampire Hunting for Dummies* – now there was a good title. Someone should write that one. There wasn't even a copy of *Dracula*.

She abandoned the bookcase and took a moment to look around the room. Old copies of the local paper, the *Ham & High*, were lying on the floor by the armchair. There were a couple of mouldy mugs and an open carton of milk on a small, round table. Nancy turned her nose up in disgust and went over to the desk. There was nothing on the desk except an old desktop computer and a memory stick. She opened the top drawer of the desk and peered inside. It was full of rubbish – old pencils and pens, a stapler, a box of drawing pins, a pair of scissors and a small silver key.

She tried the bottom drawer of the desk. It was locked. Interesting. She took the silver key out of the top drawer and tried it in the bottom drawer. It fitted perfectly and turned with a satisfying click. She crouched down and pulled open the deep bottom drawer. It was the type of drawer she herself used for filing paper folders and documents. She wasn't expecting to find anything different in this drawer. She was wrong.

Inside was a large cardboard box of the sort used by removal firms. It only just fitted inside the drawer.

Feeling like a child on Christmas morning, Nancy lifted the flaps on the box and peered inside.

On the top of the box was a tatty old A4 cardboard wallet. She opened the wallet and pulled out a pile of newspaper cuttings, most of them yellowed with age. She flicked through them. They were all about Highgate Cemetery. One of the headlines read, *Why do the Foxes Die?* Another read, *Does a Vampyr walk in Highgate?* Tom had been right. Nesbit *was* interested in vampires.

She slipped the cuttings back into the folder and laid it to one side, keen to see what else the box contained. The next object was a newspaper parcel. She unfolded the sheets of newspaper and discovered thirty or more bulbs of garlic and a wooden crucifix. *Of course,* she told herself. Garlic and crucifixes were supposed to keep vampires away. The crucifix was old and worn. It looked like the sort of tat you could buy at any junk shop. She picked up one of the garlic bulbs, feeling its papery skin against her fingers. It was just starting to sprout a green shoot from its tip. Otherwise, it looked fresh and plump, as if it had been bought recently. She laid it back with the others and lifted the newspaper parcel out of the box onto her lap so she could see what was underneath.

Oh my Lord!

Lying neatly side by side were half a dozen wooden stakes, their ends sharpened to a deadly point. And...

The door handle rattled.

The hinges creaked.

The door opened.

Nancy jumped to her feet, garlic bulbs bouncing like misshapen balls over the floor. She watched them roll away, not daring to look up. One of the garlic bulbs came to rest by a shoe. A black shoe. She lifted her gaze. The shoe belonged to Professor Nesbit who was standing in the doorway looking as if he would like to turn her to stone.

Her stomach lurched. He'd caught her red-handed, snooping in his room. She'd seen what was in the box. He was obviously a nutter, a lunatic, worse. Tom had implied he was a murderer for Christ's sake! And here he was, looking at her as if he would like to consign her to the fires of Hell. When he spoke his voice was emotionless.

"What are you doing in my room?"

"I...I...." There was nothing she could say to explain what she was doing there. She wished she could click her heels together and vanish like Dorothy in *The Wizard of Oz*.

She grabbed the paperwork that she'd brought with her off the desk. "I was just dropping off some papers for you to look at." It was an obvious lie and no way explained why the desk drawer was open and the contents of the box scattered over the floor. She felt her cheeks burn with shame and embarrassment.

"*Get out*," he hissed. "*And don't ever come in here again.*"

She didn't need telling twice. She ran for the door and didn't stop running until she reached her office. She slammed the door shut and sank down on the chair at her desk, her heart thudding so hard she thought it would burst out of her ribcage.

She grabbed her mobile phone and started typing a text with fingers that wouldn't stop shaking.

45

Friday 13 March 1970

Alan darted a glance up and down the platform at Kentish Town to make sure his father wasn't tracking him down like a sniffer dog. It would be just like him to come storming down the escalator and make a scene in front of the other passengers. But there was no sign of the old buffoon, thank God. He wished the train would hurry up.

A distant rumble in the tunnel, getting louder and louder. *At last.* A rush of cold air swept along the platform and the northbound Northern Line train hurtled into view, travelling so fast that Alan was afraid it wouldn't stop. With a screech of metal wheels on metal tracks the train came to a halt. It seemed to Alan that the doors took forever to open. But at last they slid apart and, clutching his ticket between fingers clammy with sweat, Alan jumped on board and threw himself into the first seat he came to.

He kept his head down, staring at discarded newspapers and sweet wrappers on the floor. He wasn't used to taking the tube in the evening and prayed he wouldn't meet anyone he knew in case they asked him where he was going.

At Tufnell Park a man and a woman, laid-back and both with equally long hair – hippies, obviously - sat down opposite him. He could hear his father's voice in his head - *scruffy layabouts, pair of wasters.* Alan envied them their carefree attitude to life. And what legs! The woman was wearing an unbelievably short skirt which would make Alan's mother go, *tut-tut.* Alan couldn't take his eyes off those long legs which she stretched out in the space between the seats, one leg casually draped over the over. The woman caught him looking at her legs and blew him a kiss whilst her companion stared out of the window. Alan blushed and looked away.

They arrived at Highgate station and Alan nearly tripped over those long legs in his hurry to get off.

"Hey, take it steady man," the woman's companion called after him in a long drawl. "Chill out." The woman laughed.

The doors opened and Alan jumped onto the platform. The last thing he felt like doing was *chilling out*. That guy had probably been smoking pot, he was so laid-back. Didn't he know there was a vampire on the loose? He should look after that woman of his before she was attacked.

Alan spotted the *Way Out* sign and headed towards the escalator. Once outside he stopped and looked about him. He was on a busy main road. Opposite was a row of small shops with their lights off and shutters down. It was already dark and the cars and buses going up and down the hill had their headlights on. There was no cemetery anywhere in sight.

The people who had got off the train at the same time as him had all disappeared. He wasn't familiar with this area of London – they didn't come this way, his family. *Highgate's a bit posh, not for the likes of us,* his mother would say. He shook his head to get rid of his mother's voice and started to walk away from the tube station in what he hoped was the right direction – he couldn't very well ask a passer-by the way to the cemetery without drawing attention to himself.

He crossed the main road and found himself in a street of large, old houses, set back from the road. Nothing like the pokey house he lived in. These houses were all three or four storeys high with flights of stone steps up to the front door and spacious front gardens.

Three young people, two guys and a girl, all dressed in black, pushed past him. He was about to protest when one of the men lifted his hands into the air, bared his teeth and made a play of lunging at the girl, pretending to bite her neck. The girl tossed her long dark hair over her shoulder and shrieked with laughter.

"Stop arsing about you two," said their companion. "If you do that in the cemetery people will think *you're* the vampire and someone will try to drive a stake through your heart."

The girl hooted with laughter.

Alan's heart skipped a beat. These people were obviously not serious vampire hunters like he was. To them it was all a joke. But they were going to the cemetery too. All he had to do was follow them.

Alan kept his distance so they wouldn't realise he was tailing them. The would-be vampire and the girl were now walking with their arms around each other. They addressed their companion as Peter and made jokes about blood-sucking demons and ghouls that stalked the cemetery at night. Peter, who was more serious, just nodded at them and sauntered along with his hands in his pockets as if he wasn't all that interested in what they were about to do. Alan wished they would hurry up. They turned into a road called South Grove. *How much further?* Alan wondered.

As he walked Alan became aware of growing numbers of people heading in the same direction. There was a buzz in the air. He could sense it. These people were all going to the cemetery to hunt down and kill the vampire.

Alan felt a surge of excitement, but also a sense of threat. He wanted to be the one to find and kill the vampire. He hadn't come here to work as part of a team. This was going to be his moment of glory; the turning point in his life that would transform him from a *loser* into a *hero*; that would win him the respect of his classmates and his father. He only needed other people to help him find the cemetery. Once he was there he would work alone.

A moment of panic. He'd lost sight of the people he was following. Then he caught a glimpse of them turning left into a road called Swain's Lane. Alan followed. It couldn't be much further, surely.

Swain's Lane was dark and narrow, hemmed in on both sides with high walls. It led steeply downhill and, in his eagerness to reach the cemetery, it was hard not to break into a run. But in the gloom it was difficult to see far ahead. Some people were carrying flashlights. A few even held flaming torches high above their heads, casting long, flickering shadows along the ground. Alan regretted he hadn't thought to bring a torch, even a box of matches. But that would have been impossible. The only torch at home was kept under the kitchen sink and he couldn't have taken it without his parents noticing and asking awkward questions. He felt like an amateur amongst a bunch of pros but it made him even more determined to prove himself.

Suddenly he found himself at the main cemetery gate. This wasn't the entrance he'd seen on the television, but hopefully that didn't matter. He looked up and saw a grand gothic building with towers and battlements which, in the moonlight, loomed over him like Dracula's castle.

He'd lost sight of the people he had been following but that didn't matter. They had served their purpose in leading him here. He had no need of them now. He was itching to get inside the cemetery walls and fight the vampire. He'd never felt so alive. His nostrils twitched in the cold night air. He thought he smelled blood.

He noticed some people were carrying wooden stakes filed sharp at one end and small, white bulbous vegetables that Alan had never seen before.

"What's that?" he asked a girl with long hair who had a string of these bulbs around her neck and who was handing them out to anyone who wanted one.

"Garlic," she said. She broke one off from the string and handed it to him. "Take it," she said when he hesitated.

"What's it for?"

"Protection."

Alan grasped the bulb in his hand. Its outer skin was

dry and papery.

The girl disappeared into the crowd before he could ask her how a piece of vegetable matter was supposed to protect him. He thrust the garlic into his pocket and turned his attention to how he was going to get into the cemetery.

The boundary wall must have been at least ten feet high but hordes of young people were scrambling over the top using ropes and giving each other a leg up. Some of the men were clearly drunk and were clutching beer cans. Many carried makeshift weapons made from fence posts and other bits of wood. Alan saw the group he'd followed from the tube station who were helping each other over the wall. He approached them, was offered a leg up and, before he knew it, felt himself being hoisted over the top.

He jumped down and landed with a thud on the ground. He was in the cemetery.

46

Tuesday, 22nd February 1870

I left the house early this morning so that I could visit the cemetery before going to the penitentiary. A funeral cortège was progressing along Swain's Lane but I managed to cross the courtyard and climb the steps up from the colonnade before the horses turned in at the gate. I walked slowly, lingering by the gravestones of strangers and wondering what these people had been like in life. My own family has a catacomb in the Circle of Lebanon, a very grand part of Highgate Cemetery, where my grandparents and an elderly aunt were laid to rest. My mother and father and dear brother, Nathaniel, will no doubt one day be laid there too. I, however, shall not.

I made my way to the sleeping angel where my own little angel lies buried in an unmarked grave. Primroses were starting to spring up out of the earth.

When I laid Emily into the hole that the gravedigger had dug for me, I entrusted her to the care of the sleeping angel. Since then I've had the feeling that the angel is not really sleeping but is keeping

*guard over my darling baby girl. I feel she protects this part of the
cemetery from anything bad.*

*I cleared some fallen leaves from the angel and tidied back a
tendril of ivy that had started to creep over her feet. Then I said a
quiet prayer before hurrying away, lest anyone who has relatives
buried nearby should make an appearance and enquire as to whom I
was paying my respects.*

*I returned home and continued to work on the sampler which I
am stitching in memory of Emily. I am including in the design a verse
by Sister Christina, and also a butterfly. Maybe I was thinking of
my brother who studies these delicate creatures.*

*Sewing the sampler is the least I can do since I am unable to
wear proper mourning dress. People would ask questions about who
had died and I would have to lie, telling them it was some distant
relative, a cousin, or whoever. There is enough deception in my life
without piling on even more. When I am not working on the sampler
I keep it stored away in my box which I hide under a loose
floorboard. I cannot afford to be too careful. Betsy likes nothing better
than a bit of gossip.*

*Whilst I sewed I thought of what Madeleine had said, about the
spirit world, and what I saw with my own eyes at the séance with
Mrs Waterman. I'm not yet ready to do a sitting with Madeleine.
But she is waiting for me to come to her. I sense it.*

47

At the sound of her mum's key in the lock, Lauren
checked her watch and saw, with surprise, that it was
already half past five. The afternoon had flown by. Since
the unfortunate encounter with Chloe and her
disappointment over Tom, she'd returned to the diary and
had managed to lose herself in the task of deciphering
Isabelle's handwriting and transcribing the diary extracts
onto the computer. She'd also looked after the builders,
conveying a steady supply of tea – milk, two sugars - up to
the attic and returning the mugs to the kitchen where they
sat in a dirty pile by the sink.

She slipped a bookmark into the diary and turned off the computer. Wendy had stopped in the hallway to talk to Neil who was stomping down the stairs in his hobnailed boots. That gave Lauren just enough time to load the dishwasher. By the time Wendy appeared in the doorway the kitchen looked almost respectable.

Wendy lifted her Go Green canvas shopping bag onto the kitchen worktop and pulled out a large square object wrapped in brown paper.

"I picked this up from the framer's on my way home."

The sampler. Lauren laid it down on the kitchen worktop and pulled back the brown paper.

The embroidered cloth had been pressed flat and mounted in a glass-fronted frame with a simple black border. Lauren held it up to catch the light from the kitchen window.

"Thanks, Mum, it's beautiful. I'll hang it on my bedroom wall."

"I'll get a hook for you," said Wendy, fetching the DIY toolkit from the under stairs cupboard.

Wendy hammered the hook into the wall and Lauren hung the sampler above her bed. As she gazed at the tiny stitches she thought about everything that Isabelle had suffered. She still didn't know what had happened to Isabelle or why she wanted justice but the truth would surely be revealed in the diary soon.

48

Journal of Mr. Nathaniel Hart, Esq. March 1870

I have cancelled my intended visit to Shoreham-by-Sea where I was planning to hunt for the Chalkhill Blue butterfly on Mill Hill where it is said to live in abundance. I would have journeyed there after visiting Ashdown Forest where I was fortunate enough to acquire a fine Silver-studded Blue specimen, however, I received extremely troubling news from Helen this morning whilst I was breakfasting in my lodgings. Helen has informed me by letter that she paid a visit to the convent only to discover that Isabelle left the convent weeks ago and has disappeared without a trace. When Helen enquired as to her whereabouts, the nuns informed her that they assumed she had returned to her family. Helen fears for Isabelle's safety, and so do I.

Helen is such a good soul that I rejoice she is soon to become my wife. But that happy event must be put on hold whilst my sister is in jeopardy. I know Helen will understand as she cares for Isabelle as if she was her own flesh and blood.

Moreover, I feel keenly my own culpability in Isabelle's plight. It was I who introduced her to the scoundrel who is responsible for her situation, little knowing what a cad he was. I berate myself that I ever called him "friend." If he was to be found I would challenge him to a duel but I fear the rascal has fled these shores and is even now on a vessel bound for some distant land, never to return.

Mother thinks only of the shame that has fallen on the family. She thinks more of the family's reputation in society than she does of her own daughter. I care little about what others think. I will not abandon Isabelle to her plight.

I have secured a seat for myself on the stagecoach that departs this afternoon and so will return to London with all haste. I will search every street, every house of charity, every Godforsaken hovel until I find Isabelle and can bring her back to the family where she belongs. May God grant me mercy.

PART SIX
TUESDAY 17 JULY

49

Tom couldn't sleep. The night had been hot and sticky, but the main reason he had been awake since before six was because he was desperate to call Nancy. He knew she'd been in Nesbit's office yesterday because she'd sent him a text shortly after five o'clock. It hadn't contained a lot of information. He reached for his mobile on the bedside table and read the message for the hundredth time.

OMG u r right. Garlic, stakes & axe in Nesbit's office. Newspapers cuttings from 1970. Can't talk now. Call me 2moro. He found me in there.

So Nesbit *was* a vampire hunter. The garlic and other grisly equipment confirmed that. But what worried Tom most of all were the words *He found me in there*. He'd tried calling Nancy yesterday evening but her phone had been switched off and just went straight to voicemail. Tom dreaded to think what Nesbit might do if he'd found Nancy going through his stuff.

He looked at the time on his phone. Still only seven fifteen. Too early for him to call her.

To pass the time he took an extra-long shower, allowing the water to wake him up. Then he dressed and went downstairs to make himself a slice of toast and a mug of coffee. The digital clock on the microwave said 08:03. Still too early to call.

The ceiling creaked. Footsteps upstairs. His mother was getting up. He heard her go into the bathroom. Tom picked up his plate of toast and his mug of coffee and hurried upstairs to the sanctity of his dad's study, kicking the door shut with his heel. He knew he was being a wimp, avoiding his mother like this, but at the moment he could only think about so much at once.

He sat down in the comfy chair where his dad had liked to read and ate his breakfast. Then he passed as much time as he could continuing to sort through his dad's emails. By five to nine he couldn't wait any longer. He picked up his mobile and dialled Nancy's number.

It went straight to voicemail. *Hi, this is Nancy Letts. I can't take your call right now so please leave a message after the beep.*

He hung up. This was getting frustrating. Where was she? Why wasn't she answering?

He tried to think of the most logical explanation and, remembering the trouble she'd had finding her phone yesterday, decided she'd probably left it lying around somewhere. Yes, that must be it. Well there was a solution to that problem. He rummaged in the in-tray on his dad's desk and pulled out a department letter that had the number of the university in the header. If he couldn't reach her on her mobile, he'd try her office. After a couple of rings the receptionist answered.

"Hello, it's Tom Kelsey. Can you put me through to Nancy Letts please?"

There was a sound on the other end of the phone like ragged breathing. When the receptionist spoke her voice wobbled and then cracked. "I'm sorry," she began. "But…"

Tom's blood ran cold as he listened to what the receptionist was telling him. This could not be happening.

50

Thursday, 3rd March 1870

Betsy was not in the best of spirits today at lunch time. She served cabbage soup but there was no bread to accompany the meal because it had been eaten by rats. She informed us that she had sent Daisy, the scullery maid, to fetch arsenic from the chemist but Daisy had come back with completely the wrong thing – some strange powder that glowed in the dark – so the girl was, according to Betsy, obviously an imbecile and not to be trusted and she, Betsy, didn't have time to go to the chemist because she had to bake more bread and see to the laundry and she was expecting a coal delivery and so it went on.

Since I was not required at the penitentiary today, I offered to go to the chemist and fetch the arsenic. It was a simple thing to do and would not take me long, but Betsy looked at me in surprise.

"That ain't your job," she said as she splashed a ladle of cabbage soup into my bowl.

"Really, I don't mind," I said. "The exercise will do me good."

Betsy shrugged as if to say, well suit yourself. For my own part I was happy to have a reason to go out. When I'm not occupied at the penitentiary I am liable to spend the hours pining away in my room. Also, I could feel Madeleine's eyes on me, watching and waiting. But I'm not yet ready to tell her more.

When we had finished lunch I put on my bonnet, wrapped a shawl around my shoulders and walked to the top of Highgate Hill where the chemist's shop occupies a prominent position on the street corner. The sign outside the window reads, G. K. Birtwhistle & Son, Apothecary. In the window was a pyramid of bars of Pears Soap and a display of Epsom Salts. I pushed open the door and a bell above the doorway jangled to announce my arrival.

The chemist, an elderly gentleman with tufts of white hair on his temples and a pair of pince-nez balanced on his nose (Mr Birtwhistle senior, I presumed), was busy dealing with a gentleman customer who was seeking a remedy for his gout and was complaining that nothing he'd tried thus far had worked. I was happy to wait as I was in no hurry to return to the house.

The walls of the shop were lined with wooden shelves stocked high with bottles of medicines, pills, ointments, lozenges and tinctures for every conceivable ailment. Judging by the quantities in stock, laudanum, belladonna and opium were much sought after, as were those remedies named after their inventors – Clarke's Blood Mixture, Dr James' Fever Powders and the cure-all Fowler's Solution.

Eventually the gentleman afflicted with the gout hobbled away, the chemist having assured him of the efficacy of a new remedy, and Mr Birtwhistle turned his attention to me, eyeing me curiously over the top of his pince-nez as if trying to diagnose my particular complaint.

I requested some arsenic to use as rat poison and, with a nod of his head, he fetched a sack of white powder from the storeroom and proceeded to fill up a glass bottle which he stoppered with a cork. He handed over the poison as if it was nothing more innocuous than a bottle of cough syrup. I requested him to put the bill on Mrs Payne's account and he wished me good day.

By the time I left the chemist's a thin, grey rain was starting to fall so I returned to the house with all speed and delivered the poison to Betsy in the kitchen. A sullen, whey-faced girl, who I assumed to be Daisy the scullery maid, was scrubbing pots at the sink. She gave me an insolent stare when I entered but Betsy told her not to be so idle and she returned to her cleaning task.

Betsy was kneading dough at the large wooden table, her sleeves rolled up and her forearms coated in flour. She'd taken her bad mood out on the dough and was in better spirits than she had been at lunch time.

"You got it then?" she asked, looking at my basket.

"Yes." I reached into the basket and gave her the bottle.

She examined the bottle carefully, nodding with approval. "That's the stuff you should've bought," she said to Daisy holding the bottle out to her. "I'll put it up 'ere with the soap powders and mind you don't go messing it up with the sugar otherwise there'd be a very nasty accident." She laughed and wiped the back of her hand across her cheek leaving a streak of white flour.

I watched her put the arsenic on the shelf and said I hoped it would do the job of eliminating the rats.

"Oh, it'll do that all right," she laughed. "That stuff'd kill a horse."

51

Belladonna, laudanum, arsenic – it was a miracle anyone survived the nineteenth century. Lauren remembered something she'd seen once on television about poison being a woman's weapon of choice. Killing someone with poison didn't require superior physical strength or skill with a weapon. Just a sprinkle in an unsuspecting husband's dinner each night, the poor fellow would quickly contract a debilitating stomach upset, and within a few weeks the widow would be claiming the life insurance. Easy-peasy.

She turned over the page and was just about to start reading the next diary entry when she was startled by a loud knocking at the front door. Her first thought was Megan. She always hammered the door with gusto. Lauren hoped Megan hadn't come round to give her stick for not going out last night. As she made her way down the hallway and unlocked the door, Lauren tried to think how she should defend herself.

But it wasn't Megan.

It was Tom. Her heart jumped for joy.

"Hey Tom! Great to see you." Maybe now they could finish the conversation that Chloe had interrupted yesterday. She opened the door wide. "Come in."

He was standing on the doorstep, hands thrust inside

his jeans' pockets, shoulders hunched. His eyes were red. Something was wrong.

Lauren's feeling of elation vanished in an instant.

"What's the matter?" she asked.

"It's, it's…" his voice cracked. He looked as if he was on the verge of tears.

"Please tell me," said Lauren, putting out a hand and touching him on the arm.

He took a deep breath, swallowed hard and said in a voice that was barely more than a croak, "It's Nancy. She's dead."

Lauren felt as if she'd been struck a blow to her chest and for a moment she couldn't breathe. A strangled cry escaped from her mouth. She'd only met Nancy once but she was the sort of person you couldn't help taking an instant liking to. Nancy was so full of life and excitement, so bubbly and generous. How could she be dead? Lauren didn't want to believe it. But one look at Tom standing so miserable and forlorn on her doorstep told her it was true.

"Come in and tell me what happened." She pulled Tom inside the house and took him through to the lounge where he sat down on the sofa. He seemed to be in a state of shock, pale and wide-eyed. She wished Wendy was here. Her mum knew how to handle a crisis whereas Lauren didn't have a clue. She sat down next to him and waited for him to speak.

Between sobs Tom told her about the text Nancy had sent yesterday; about the garlic, the stakes and the axe. Lauren listened in stunned silence. A shiver ran up her spine at the word *axe*. It must have been Professor Nesbit in the cemetery on Saturday night. How close had she and her friends come to being attacked? She pushed the thought from her mind and tried to concentrate on what Tom was telling her.

"I phoned Nancy's mobile this morning but there was no answer, so then I phoned the university and the receptionist told me…" he stopped to catch his breath, "she told me that the transport police had just been in to report that Nancy had been killed in a car accident yesterday evening. She couldn't give me any details."

God, how awful. Lauren didn't know what to say. There was nothing she could say that would make things any better so in the end she just put her arm around Tom and they sat, without moving, for ages.

Tom mumbled something which she didn't catch.

"Sorry?" asked Lauren.

"I said, it's all my fault."

She pulled back from him. "What do you mean?"

Tom stood up, punching his right fist into his left palm. "This has got something to do with Professor Nesbit. I'm sure of it." He started to pace the room, running his hands through his hair. "Nesbit found Nancy in his office," he said, turning to face Lauren. "He must have been furious. Maybe he messed with her car, or something. I don't know."

Lauren was taken aback. What had happened to Nancy was a terrible tragedy, of course, but wasn't Tom jumping to conclusions? "You don't know that," she said. "Maybe she was so shaken by the fact that he caught her, she just wasn't concentrating properly when she was driving home." Even as she said it, Lauren knew it sounded feeble.

Tom shook his head. "No. I don't think so."

"So what are you going to do now?" she asked.

"I'm going to the police," said Tom. "They need to know about Nesbit and his weird obsessions. He's a serial killer! I'm sure of it."

"Do you want me to come with you?" asked Lauren.

Tom thought for a moment then shook his head. "Thanks, but I can handle this."

Lauren was disappointed but tried not to let it show. "Good luck," she said as she opened the front door. "Let me know what happens."

He turned to wave as he walked down the garden path. "Will do," he called back over his shoulder.

Lauren couldn't help wondering when she'd see him again.

52

Journal of Mr. Nathaniel Hart, Esq. March 1870

Oh, what a frustrating journey I endured today. The stagecoach was held up near Reigate due to the misfortune of one of the horses losing a shoe. We were obliged to stop at the local blacksmith's where we found the fellow in a stupor from having partaken of too much liquid refreshment with his midday meal. I helped the coach driver to rouse the miscreant and when I was satisfied that he was engaged in his proper occupation of restoring the horse's shoe, I joined my fellow travellers at the local inn.

As a result of this delay I did not arrive in London until well past eight o'clock in the evening by which time it was too late to begin searching and Helen bade me wait until the morning when I should be more refreshed.

Mother simply refuses to discuss the problem of Isabelle. She has forsaken her daughter which I cannot understand.

Helen, the good soul, has made some discreet enquiries about where to begin searching. She says we must look in the penitentiaries – I shudder at the word – and other such houses that take in fallen women. Tomorrow the search begins.

53

"Can I help you?" The librarian moved the pile of recently returned books to one side and smiled at Lauren.

"I was wondering," said Lauren, "if you have anything about the Highgate Vampire?" After Tom's visit Lauren had been too unsettled to go back to reading the diary. She needed to get out of the house, but at the same time she wanted to find out more about this supposed vampire that roamed around Highgate. The library had seemed as good a place as any to start. She just hoped the librarian wouldn't think she was some kind of nutty vampire hunter intent on breaking into the cemetery.

The librarian, however, didn't bat an eyelid as if questions about vampires were as common as *Do you have information about local yoga classes?* or *Do you have the latest crime/romance/thriller novel?*

"Certainly," beamed the librarian. "In fact, I can show you copies of the *Hampstead and Highgate Express* from February and March 1970. We have quite a little archive here. Follow me."

The librarian led Lauren over to a table in the local history section of the library and asked her to wait a moment. Then she disappeared into a side room and came back with a box marked *Hampstead and Highgate Express 1970-1972*. She put the box down on the table, removed the lid and lifted out a pile of old newspapers.

"The ones you want," said the librarian, "are all from February and March 1970. They're ordered by date." She flicked through the pile and pulled out a handful of papers from the bottom. "There you go. You should find what you're looking for in these."

Lauren pulled the pile of newspapers towards her. She hadn't expected anything like this. Wasn't this what her history teacher called *Primary source material?* It was miles better than just reading stuff on Wikipedia.

"The first mention of anything strange is in the letters' page in the Sixth of February edition," said the librarian, helpfully. "I'd start there if I were you."

"Thanks," said Lauren. She found the Sixth of February edition and, with a growing sense of excitement, started to turn the pages.

The paper was dry and yellowed with age and Lauren wondered if she shouldn't be wearing a pair of those white cotton gloves you saw people wearing on history programmes. She found the letters' page and scanned it. Amongst the usual stuff about missing cats and complaints to the council about rubbish collection she found a letter from a man who reported seeing a *grey figure* near Highgate

Cemetery in Swain's Lane. The writer believed the figure to be supernatural and he wanted to know if anyone else had seen anything similar. Lauren put the paper to one side and turned to the next edition.

Nothing unusual was reported for a couple of weeks, but the edition dated the Twenty-seventh of February had a startling headline - *Does a Vampyr walk in Highgate?* Things had clearly moved one from just a *grey figure.*

Fascinated by this bizarre headline, Lauren turned to the article in which the writer explained how a Romanian nobleman who practised black magic, a so-called *King Vampire of the Undead,* had been transported to England in a coffin in the early eighteenth century and buried in the place later to become Highgate Cemetery. Roused from the dead by modern Satanists, this medieval nobleman was apparently the vampire that was now haunting the cemetery. The solution, according to the writer, was to stake the vampire's body, chop his head off and burn the whole lot.

Lauren shivered. This was scary stuff. She looked towards the desk where the librarian was checking out some books for an old lady and chatting about the hot weather. *It's just a pile of old newspapers,* she told herself. *There isn't really a vampire in Highgate Cemetery, is there?*

She put the *King Vampire* article away and turned to the edition from the Sixth of March. The front page headline asked *Why Do the Foxes Die?* The writer of the letter printed on the Sixth of February reported seeing dead foxes in the cemetery whilst the proponent of the Romanian nobleman theory argued that the dead foxes proved the existence of the vampire.

There was nothing in the edition dated Friday the Thirteenth of March. Lauren picked up the following week's paper and found an article discussing the events of the previous Friday. She read how, following a televised news report on the Highgate Vampire, hundreds of young people had swarmed into the cemetery that night, scaling the ten foot high wall. The police had been outnumbered and unable to control the crowds. They had only succeeded in making a handful of arrests. Lauren scanned the names of those picked up by the police. One name jumped out at her. Alan Nesbit had been arrested after the police found him collapsed, unconscious, on the ground.

54

Friday 13 March 1970

Alan stood up and looked around, trying to get his bearings. He was in an open, paved area. Behind him the towers of the Victorian gateway were silhouetted against the moonlight. Ahead of him the cemetery lay shrouded in darkness.

It was clear there was no proper leadership, no organisation. There was no sign of the men he'd seen interviewed on television. People were running around in all directions, whooping and shrieking, beams of torchlight flickering like fireflies. He didn't recognise anyone – not the people he had followed from the tube station or the girl who had given him the garlic - they were just shapes in the dark.

As his eyes acclimatised he could just make out a curve of arches straight ahead. People were disappearing through the central arch. He decided that must be the way into the heart of the cemetery, and followed them.

A steep flight of stone steps led upwards from the central arch. High brick walls on either side cut out any light so Alan was unable to see where he was putting his feet. In his haste, he tripped on the steps' damp and uneven surface, cutting his palm on the rough stone. He brought his wounded hand to his mouth and tasted the blood, sweet and metallic. Would the vampire be able to smell his blood? He wiped his hand on his jeans and walked more carefully up the rest of the steps, keeping his eyes and ears alert for any signs of danger.

At the top of the steps he emerged onto a rough earth path. Either side of the path the blackness was impenetrable but the occasional flash of torchlight showed him a chaotic jumble of lop-sided gravestones, angels, crosses, broken columns and classical urns, all of it entangled with twisted trees, creepers and brambles.

Alan had never been anywhere so mysterious. He had never been so close to death. He had never felt so alive.

He walked straight ahead until he came to a crossroads where the path branched off in different directions. Most people were following the path to the right, up the hill.

Alan hesitated. He didn't want to just follow the crowd. He wanted to find the vampire himself. Maybe if he went in a different direction he would strike lucky. But he would need a weapon. He reached up to the low-hanging branch of a nearby tree and tugged hard. The branch came away in his hands with a sharp crack. The end where he had severed it from the trunk of the tree was splintered enough to make a sharp point. Now he was ready.

Holding his makeshift weapon in one hand he turned left. He hadn't gone far before he lost sight of the path under a tangle of undergrowth and found himself treading over graves. It was hard going. Tendrils of ivy entwined themselves around his arms; brambles clawed at his legs; tree roots and broken headstones threatened to trip him up; nocturnal animals startled him by scurrying across his path; branches scratched at his face like dead men's fingers.

Something swooped low overhead, brushing against his hair. He froze. What was that? A bat? Was it a sign that the vampire was close? Clutching his weapon tighter, he looked up but couldn't see anything in the inky blackness.

He stumbled on until he came to an area of ground that wasn't so overgrown with trees and brambles.

In a sudden gust of wind the moon appeared from behind a cloud and, just for a second, Alan glimpsed the figure of a woman lying on the ground, her head on her arm.

Alan inhaled sharply. He couldn't quite believe what he had just seen, but there was no denying the truth of his own eyes. There, on the ground, in front of him was…*a victim of the vampire.*

A feeling of triumph surged through him. He was vindicated in his decision not to follow the crowd but to trust to his own instincts. He should proceed with care. The vampire must be close at hand, was probably even now hiding behind one of the headstones, watching and waiting to make Alan his next victim. Well just let it try.

Dark clouds rolled in front of the moon, blotting out the light, so that the woman was no longer visible. But he knew what he had seen. He only had to walk forwards and he would find her lying there, drained of her lifeblood, teeth marks on her neck.

He gripped the makeshift stake tight in his fist and walked towards the woman.

His mouth was dry and his heart was pounding against his ribcage. He needed to draw the vampire out so that he could attack it. He remembered the wound on his hand from when he had tripped on the cemetery steps. He squeezed it now to encourage more blood to come to the surface and held his injured palm out in front of him like bait.

Where was the woman? She couldn't be more than a few feet away. He didn't want to trip over her so he knelt down and crawled the last few metres, reaching out with his injured hand until he felt something under his fingertips. Something cold. Like stone.

Stone?

It can't be.

Desperately, he ran his hands over the body in front of him, feeling the features of her face, her slender arms, the dip of her waist and the curve of her hip, and, behind her back…her angel's wings.

Angel's wings?

What he had taken for a poor, defenceless woman, a victim of the vampire, was nothing but a stone angel, lying asleep on her side. No, she wasn't *asleep*. Statues didn't *sleep*. It wasn't even a *she*. It was nothing but a lump of carved rock, a stupid, inert, piece of stone and it had made a fool of him. Humiliation at his mistake flooded through him. Even though there was no one to witness his embarrassment, he felt shamed, mortified.

How dare it!

He sprang to his feet and struck the angel with the tree branch, hitting her again and again until his arms ached and the wood splintered in half.

It was on him before he knew what had happened.

A blackness descended on him which was so intense he couldn't have seen his own hand in front of his face if he'd tried. Something much stronger than himself forced the broken tree branch out of his hands and flung it, with a crash, onto the ground. What was happening? His mind raced. It was as if he was caught up in a whirlwind. He gasped for breath. His legs shook. His heart thudded.

He tried to move backwards, away from the angel and away from whatever was engulfing him, but his sense of balance had deserted him and even though he couldn't see anything he felt as if the world was spinning around him.

He had to get away from this accursed place. It was evil. This was the vampire's doing, he was sure of it, and he vowed that one day he would get his revenge.

He tried to run, but a tree root tripped him up and then he was falling, falling, falling…

He put his hands out to save himself but it was too late. He hit his head against the stone plinth on which the angel lay sleeping.

For a brief moment stars danced in front of his eyes. Then everything went black.

55

Wednesday, 9th March 1870

Something happened at the penitentiary today. I felt there was something amiss when I arrived there, a tension in the air, like a storm about to break. The weather has been foul recently: cold, grey fog that hangs over Highgate like a shroud and a thin, spiky drizzle that chills you to the bone. The women have not been able to take their daily exercise in the orchard but have been confined indoors, washing, cooking, sewing, reading the Bible. These women are not used to remaining indoors for extended periods. In their former lives, they spent much of their time on the streets, in all weathers.

Whilst I was hanging up my cloak and arranging my muslin cap on my head, Sister Burns came to me and asked if I would take over from Sister Christina supervising the work in the laundry. Of course, I agreed. I do whatever I am asked to do and do it willingly.

The air in the laundry was more humid than ever. Hot and damp, it clung to my clothes as soon as I entered the room. I spotted Ellen straight away. She was stirring one of the steaming wooden tubs with a pole which she grasped tightly with both hands so that the whites of her knuckles showed. Her face was bright red from the hot steam and wily strands of her red hair had escaped from her bonnet. From the intense look in her eyes I sensed an energy about her, a fury that I hesitated to disturb.

I went first to the women doing the ironing to check that everything was all right with them. The poor things were wilting in the heat and the irons looked heavy and cumbersome in their hands. I told them they were doing a good job and then proceeded to the women operating the mangles. They too were finding it difficult to work in the oppressive atmosphere so I praised them for their efforts, eliciting a small smile of gratitude. They are not accustomed to receive words of acknowledgement. Finally, I made my way over to the wooden wash tubs.

Ellen did not look at me even though she must have seen, out of the corner of her eye, that I was standing no more than a couple of feet away. She kept stirring, stirring with a manic energy as if she had been told she must not stop until she had washed all the blood and mud out of the uniforms of the entire British army. Her manner alarmed me and I was worried she might make herself ill if she continued in that frenetic way.

"Calm yourself, Ellen," I said to her in a gentle tone. "Those sheets must be clean enough now for the angels of Heaven to sleep on."

She stopped abruptly and glared at me. "The devil can sleep on them for all I care." Then she resumed her stirring, working faster and more furiously than ever before.

I put out my hand and held the top of the pole, forcing her to stay still. We stood like that for a moment, staring at each other over the tub of steaming water. "Ellen," I said, my voice shaking, "whatever is the matter? Please tell me if something has upset you."

For a moment I thought she was going to wrench the pole from my grasp and resume her manic stirring, but then she let her hands fall to her sides and hung her head, her energy spent. I laid the pole gently against the side of the tub. The other women had slowed in their work to watch us. "It's nothing," I said to them. "Ellen is just a little tired. Please continue with your work." Then I led her to a seat by the window and sat her down. Outside the fog was as thick as ever.

"Dear Ellen," I said, "please tell me what is the matter."

Her shoulders heaved and she let out an audible sob. "Reverend Renshaw says I must stay here for at least another six months. He says I'm not ready to leave. He says I'll just go back to my old life."

"And will you?" I asked.

She shrugged. "I'm not going to be nobody's servant, if that's what he thinks." Her old defiance was reasserting itself and I was glad.

If she did not wish to work as a servant, who was I to tell her what to do?

She looked at me more closely then and said, "What about you? Why don't you go back to your old life?"

Her question startled me. How much of the truth has she guessed, I wondered? "What do you mean?" I asked her, trying to keep my voice neutral.

"You always look sad," she said then. "Like you lost something

you used to have."

Like you lost something you used to have.

Ellen's words struck deep into my heart. Maybe sensing that she had hit a raw nerve, she squeezed my hand in a gesture of friendship and then returned to work calmly and without complaint.

For my part, I went through the motions of supervising the women in the laundry and, later, in the kitchens, but all the while I thought about the life I had left behind – the comfortable house in London where my parents and brother lived; the dashing young officer who had stolen my heart and then treated me with such brutality; and Emily, the child born to me in disgrace and shame and who now lies buried in secret in the cemetery beside the sleeping angel.

Yes, I had lost something. Everything, in fact. Material comforts meant nothing to me anymore, but what wouldn't I give for a moment in the presence of my baby girl who had passed to the other side. And there was someone who could help me. Madeleine.

56

Tom pushed open the heavy doors to the police station and stepped inside. The sharp smell of disinfectant on the linoleum floor brought back the painful memory of coming here with his mother to identify his father's body in the morgue. That had been the worst day of his life. He'd hoped to never have to come here again.

But he had come back because he was determined to speak to DCI McNally about Alan Nesbit. It was obvious to Tom that the Professor was a madman. He couldn't yet prove a connection between his dad's death and Nancy's that would stand up in a court of law, but after what Nancy had discovered in Nesbit's desk at work, Tom was in no doubt that the professor should be investigated. It was for the police to discover the true facts.

An elderly man, clearly in some distress, was standing at the front desk reporting a missing cat that he believed to have been kidnapped. He kept repeating what he had already said and the desk sergeant looked bored and weary.

There was a row of plastic chairs lined up against the wall. Tom sat down on the chair nearest to the desk and waited his turn. His eyes flickered over the notices pinned to a board on the opposite wall – *Don't Drink and Drive, Report Drug Abuse, Report Domestic Violence.*

How about *Don't Kill your Colleagues?* They should have that one, thought Tom.

He checked his watch, wishing the man at the desk would hurry up. A faulty fluorescent light flashed on and off.

Eventually the man with the missing cat was led away by a young police woman who looked like she'd be better at offering sympathy and support than the sergeant.

Tom stood up and went over to the desk. The sergeant looked at him with a blank expression.

Tom cleared his throat. "I'd like to see Detective Chief Inspector McNally please."

"And you are?"

"Tom Kelsey. My father was found drowned in his car two weeks ago. DCI McNally dealt with the case."

"Right." The desk sergeant had obviously used up his meagre supply of sympathy on the previous gentleman. He picked up a phone and pressed a button. "Is DCI McNally free? There's a boy here called Tom Kelsey who wants to see him…Right…OK."

The sergeant put the phone down. "This way." He led Tom to an interview room that was furnished with nothing more than a Formica-topped table and four plastic chairs, two on each side of the table. There was a pane of darkened glass on the wall that Tom guessed was a one-way mirror for senior officers to secretly observe interviews with suspects. *I'm not the criminal here,* he felt like saying.

"Wait here," said the officer. Then he closed the door behind him, leaving Tom on his own.

Tom sat down on one of the plastic chairs and, for the hundredth time, went through in his head what he planned to say to DCI McNally. The purpose of this meeting was to convince McNally that Alan Nesbit had a hand in his dad's death and in Nancy's fatal accident, and should be arrested and questioned.

For starters, there was the theft, as Tom saw it, of the memory stick and the way Alan Nesbit seemed to be worming his way into their lives. Then there was Tom's meeting with Alan Nesbit at UCL and the way in which the professor had evaded his questions, but made it clear he was after Isabelle's diary. Thirdly there was Nancy's discovery of the box containing the vampire-hunting equipment and her fatal car accident which Tom was convinced was no accident at all. And finally, Lauren had phoned him an hour ago to tell him what she had read about Alan's part in the Highgate Vampire incident. They were obviously dealing with a lunatic and Tom wanted the police to act before Alan Nesbit harmed anyone else.

Five minutes later the door opened and DCI McNally walked in carrying a lever arch file. A balding man in his late fifties with bags under his eyes and carrying too much extra weight around his middle, McNally gave the impression of a man who'd seen it all and wasn't keen to see any more. Tom couldn't imagine him as a young, enthusiastic officer. He didn't look happy to see Tom. Tom guessed he must be nearing retirement and probably wanted an easy life – no cock-ups or difficult cases in his last year, nothing to get in the way of the comfortable retirement package and congratulatory send-off. Tom couldn't have cared less about the Inspector's retirement plans and got straight to the point.

"Inspector, I think Dad was murdered. I don't think it was an accident that his car ended up in Highgate Ponds. I want you to re-open the case."

The Inspector sat down heavily on one of the chairs opposite Tom, pulled a handkerchief out of his trouser pocket and wiped his forehead which glistened with sweat. He showed no sign of being remotely interested in what

Tom had just said. Instead he opened the file and glanced at the first few sheets of typed paper. "When your dad's car was recovered from the lake there was nothing to suggest foul play." He closed the file as if to say, matter closed. Move on.

Tom leaned forward on the desk. "Yes, but I think Dad's colleague at University College had something to do with it. His name is Professor Alan Nesbit. He's a vampire hunter and…"

"A what?" The Inspector looked as if he thought Tom was taking the mickey.

"He's obsessed with vampires," said Tom, "and he keeps a box of garlic with a stake and an axe in his desk at work."

McNally frowned and Tom thought he saw something, a memory maybe, flicker in the Inspector's eyes, but then it was gone. "And how do you know about this box?"

"Nancy Letts, the department secretary, found it, but then Nesbit caught her going through his stuff and that evening she was killed in a car accident which I'm sure wasn't an accident. Maybe Alan Nesbit tampered with her brakes or something."

The Inspector leaned back and crossed his arms. "You're making a lot of assumptions here and not a lot of sense."

Tom knew it all sounded far-fetched and maybe he'd rushed in too quickly. He decided to take a step back and start at the beginning.

"The day after Dad's funeral, Alan Nesbit came round to our house and took -" he refrained from saying *stole* "- a memory stick from Dad's desk. I went to see him at UCL and he made it clear that he was trying to get his hands on a Victorian lady's diary that…"

The Inspector held up a hand. He looked like he'd heard enough. "What is this? Vampires and Victorian diaries? I haven't got time for all this gibberish. What's your point?"

"My point," said Tom trying hard to keep his voice steady, "is that Alan Nesbit has been acting suspiciously and I think there might be a connection between his obsession with vampires, the diary I mentioned and the fact that Dad ended up drowned in Highgate Ponds."

"Look," said the Inspector rubbing his forehead with his hand, "I'm paid to investigate the facts of cases, not to fantasise over improbable links between nutcases with hoards of garlic and unfortunate cases of careless driving."

"But Inspector, you don't understand."

A vein started to throb in the Inspector's right temple. "I understand perfectly well that there isn't a shred of evidence against this Alan Nesbit, even if he is a lunatic which I can quite well believe. Now, if you'll excuse me I have work to do keeping real criminals off the streets." He stood up.

"Please, Inspector, can't you just send someone round to interview him?"

The Inspector picked up the file and started walking towards the door. "Forget it. And don't make me arrest you for wasting police time. You have absolutely no concrete proof whatsoever. The case is closed. I'll show you out."

He held the door open and Tom had no option but to get up and leave. It had been a waste of time coming here, he could see that now. He needed more proof, but the question was, what?

57

Saturday, 14 March 1970

Alan woke with a start. *Where the hell?* Then he remembered. The cemetery. The vampire. The angel.

The morning had dawned, damp and foggy. He was shivering with cold and his temple felt like someone had taken a sledgehammer to it. But that wasn't the most immediate problem.

A great beast of a dog was standing over him, fangs barred, saliva dripping. The animal's front legs straddled Alan's shoulders, its rear legs straddled his thighs. It was watching him with jet black eyes.

Alan hated dogs.

In the cold morning air the dog's breath misted over his face and stank of raw meat. Alan noticed with fear the tense, rippling muscles in the animal's chest and shoulders. He sensed the animal was poised, ready to attack if he so much as moved a muscle.

An involuntary cry, more like a whimper, escaped Alan's lips and the dog growled at him. Alan screwed his eyes tight shut wishing it was a nightmare but knowing it was all too real. Where had this hound of Hell come from and how was he going to escape from it?

The dog barked, loud and sharp, and the pain in Alan's head felt like it would split his skull in two. Then he heard voices and footsteps crashing through the undergrowth.

"Over here, Sir. Cuthbert's found something."

Alan opened his eyes a fraction and, without turning his head, glanced to one side. In the grey light of early morning he saw a young uniformed police officer, bright eyed and keen, striding towards him. In his right hand he carried a truncheon.

"Good boy, Cuthbert. Sit." To Alan's relief the dog wagged its tail, then stepped to one side and sat, its pink tongue lolling.

The young police officer was followed seconds later by an older policeman who seemed to have trouble keeping up with his younger colleague. The older man took one look at Alan and turned to the young officer.

"Good work, McNally. Arrest the bugger and get him sent down to the police station. I don't think he'll give you any trouble judging by the state he's in. We'll get these bloody vandals and lock 'em up if it's the last thing we do."

58

Monday, 14th March 1870

This evening Madeleine invited me to her room. I had not set foot inside her room since the séance with Mrs Waterman and, remembering the events of that evening, I was a little hesitant. Even though I had resolved to put my trust in Madeleine, believing that she was the only person who could help me, still I felt a reluctance and a shyness to talk openly to her.

In truth, I did not know what to expect. What would she do? If I was on my own would I have to sit at the table, in darkness? Would she want to go into her cabinet and would she ask me to tie her to her chair with the silk cords? Really, I did not think I could bear to do such a thing.

Maybe sensing my unease, she led me to the sofa which is positioned in front of the fireplace.

"Please make yourself comfortable," she said, sitting down next to me. I folded my hands in my lap and tried to appear calm but I could not look her in the eye. She reached out and took one of my hands in hers, holding it gently. This gesture forced me to look at her and it was as if her green eyes could see into my soul.

"Dear Isabelle, I feel that there is a great sadness in you." It was not a question, more a statement of fact. As I have said, it was as if she could see into the very depths of my being. I gave the briefest of nods, wondering what else she could see.

She closed her eyes a moment, then said, "I sense you have something in your past which is causing you distress and which you feel you must conceal."

My heart started to beat harder and I could feel the colour rising to my face. How much could she possibly know? Madeleine gave my hand a little squeeze and leaned closer.

"Maybe you feel that society will shun you for the secret that you hold?"

This time I found my voice. "Yes, yes that is correct. But how did you…"

"Ah," she said, a smile creeping over her lips, "it is part of the gift I possess. The same gift which enables me to communicate with

those who have passed to the other side also helps me to read the hearts of the living."

I must have looked somewhat taken aback at those words because she said in a lighter tone of voice, "Please, do not alarm yourself. I am not a mind reader," she gave a little laugh, "but everyone has an aura that surrounds them. And yours I see is pale blue. A sad, cold colour."

"I see," I said.

"But you should know that I never judge clients and their situations. It is not for me to say who is righteous and who is not, who is to be saved and who damned. I am merely a medium through whom the spirits speak and if, in the process, I can bring some small measure of comfort to people in need..." She looked at me enquiringly.

I did not know where to start and stared into the dying embers of the fire. She rose, then, and went over to a small table where there was a decanter of sherry and two small glasses. She filled the glasses and carried them back to the sofa, handing one of the glasses to me. I took a sip. The liquid was smooth and sweet.

"Tell me," she said, "you must have family." Again, it was a statement of fact, not a question.

I must have reacted badly to the mention of my family because she put a hand onto my arm and said, "We don't have to talk about them if they are not relevant."

"No, it's not that."

"So they are part of your..." she hesitated as if choosing her words with care, "...story."

I took another mouthful of the sherry which warmed me and gave me the courage to speak. "They have disowned me," I said in as steady a tone as I could manage, "so I must pretend they do not exist."

"Yes," she said, nodding her head. "I thought it was something like that. You have the air of someone who has been cast out."

At the words cast out my breath caught in my throat.

"Is there no one in your family to whom you can turn?" she asked.

I glanced away, thinking of my dear brother Nathaniel and sweet

Helen, his fiancée. But I cannot allow them to become tainted through association with me, so I must forget them too. I turned back to Madeleine and shook my head. "No. There is no one."

"But there is someone you wish me to make contact with? Someone who has gone over to spirit?"

I nodded, my eyes starting to burn with tears.

"And this person, is young, old?"

"Young."

"Ah, how young?"

"Six days."

"I thought so. A baby. Your baby."

I couldn't hold back the tears any longer and wept openly. Now Madeleine knew the worst of me. There was nothing left for me to hide from her.

59

August 1970

"Look at this, Jean. It's a bloody disgrace."

At the sound of his father's irate voice Alan looked up from his homework which he was doing at the dining table, the tea things having been cleared away half an hour ago. He wished his parents would go into the other room and leave him in peace, but his mother was busy knitting and his father was reading the local paper with much harrumphing and occasional snorts of disgust. Donald Nesbit now folded back the page of the *Hampstead and Highgate Express* and held it out so his wife could see.

"People who do this sort of thing are obviously delinquents with no sense of right or wrong, and want locking up for good in my opinion. We should never have got rid of the death penalty."

Same old, same old...

With a sigh, Jean Nesbit laid her knitting to one side and took the paper from her husband's hands. She glanced at the story, her face creasing into furrows of revulsion. She handed the paper back. "I'd much rather not read about things like that, thank you very much," she said picking up her knitting and starting to count the stitches.

Later, when his parents were watching the Nine O'clock News and Alan knew he wouldn't be disturbed, he went outside to the bin and retrieved the paper that his father had thrown away. He took it up to his bedroom and started to read the article that had caused such outrage.

The story that had angered his father and revolted his mother was exactly the sort of story Alan was keen to read about. It was one more piece in the jigsaw that he was trying to solve - two schoolgirls had found a decapitated female corpse in Highgate Cemetery.

Alan drank in every word. He read, with growing excitement, how the corpse had been taken from one of the vaults used for aboveground burial and how the girls had found it, lying in the middle of the path, with a stake through its heart.

A stake through its heart.

The previous week the same newspaper had reported dead foxes in the cemetery. Their throats had been cut and they had been drained of blood.

Evil forces were at work in the cemetery.

Alan knelt down by the side of his bed and pulled out a cardboard box. The box already contained newspaper cuttings about the events of March the thirteenth and anything else he'd been able to find out about vampires. He kept it hidden under his bed because he didn't want his parents to discover it. They still had no idea where he'd been that night back in March when he'd walked out. Even though he'd been arrested, because of his age and the fact that he was carrying nothing more harmful than a bulb of garlic, the police had let him off with a warning and hadn't bothered informing his parents.

Taking a pair of scissors from his bedside table, Alan cut out the new article and placed it carefully in the box. It was another clue in what he had decided would be his lifetime's work – finding and killing the Highgate Vampire.

60

The Trials and Tribulations of a Household Maid in the Year of Our Lord 1870, continued…

I were that fed up today that I had to get out of that house and calm myself down a bit. I don't know what that Madeleine gets up to in that room she rents, but I don't like it. There I am, doing a spot of cleaning and tidying whilst the young madam's out and I pick up a length of thin, chiffon cloth what was lying on the floor of the *cabinet* as she calls it, although it looks like an alcove with a curtain to me. Anyway, I'm folding up this piece of cloth nice and neat when suddenly I gets this burning in my fingers. *Dear God,* I shriek, *what is this? The Devil's bed sheet?*

I drop it faster than a hot potato and run to the kitchen where I plunge my hands into a bucket of water. When I look at my fingers, they're all red at the tips like the skin's inflamed. I'll have to have a word with Mrs Payne. She should be more careful about who she lets lodge here.

I were supposed to be baking bread this afternoon but my fingers are so sore I thinks to myself, sod this, I'm off to see if Will's done with digging graves for the day. Then maybe we can spend a moment or two somewhere quiet, you know, like in the Dissenters. *They* don't mind a bit of larking about. So I sets off for the cemetery, and who do I see going through the cemetery gates but Miss Hart. *Well,* I thinks to myself, *here's a turn up for the books.* I never knew she had someone buried in there. She never said. But then she don't say much.

So I follow her in, keeping my distance mind, and she goes straight over to that place where the sleeping angel is lying on the ground. Now, I've always thought, it would be nice to have an angel looking after your grave, but if I were buried here I'd rather have one standing up and looking about, not dozing on the job. I wants an angel what's going to look after me proper.

Anyway, I hide behind a big stone urn whilst she kneels

down and places a bunch of primroses on the ground near the angel. Then she gets up and leaves.

Well, I don't know what to make of that.

I walk back to the cemetery gates where I see Will. He's busy talking to Mr Hills, the cemetery supervisor, so I hang back till they're finished. Then I goes up to Will and says, "You'll never guess who I saw just now over by the sleeping angel?"

He nearly jumps out of his skin. "Who?"

"The lady what lodges in Mrs Payne's house. Miss Hart. I wonder who she's got buried over there?"

Will loves talking about this place, he's always going on about who lies where, so I thinks it's a bit strange when he turns away from me and says, "I don't know nuffink."

PART SEVEN
WEDNESDAY 18 JULY

61

It was no good. She just couldn't concentrate on Isabelle's diary today. The florid handwriting swam in front of her eyes and every time she turned to the computer screen to type up what she'd just deciphered she found she'd forgotten half the words.

Lauren tried to tell herself it was because Neil was making a racket lugging the new bathroom suite up the stairs and also because the weather had turned unbearably humid as if a storm was on the way, but really it was because she couldn't stop thinking about poor Nancy.

It was unbearably shocking to think that someone could be so full of life one minute and dead the next. And had they inadvertently caused her death, as Tom seemed to think, by asking her to spy on Professor Nesbit? Did that make them guilty of…what? Being an accessory to murder?

She wondered how Tom had got on at the police

station yesterday and wished he'd call. She tried his mobile but it was switched off. Her own phone was nearly flat so she switched it off, went into the kitchen and plugged it into the charger. Then she sat back down at the dining table and re-opened the diary.

A sharp knock at the front door made her jump. It had to be Tom. Lauren pushed the diary to one side and ran down the hall. She yanked open the front door.

It was Chloe.

"Oh, hi," said Lauren, trying not to let her disappointment show. "How are things?" She felt awkward. The last time she'd seen Chloe she'd been cross with her for barging in on her conversation with Tom at a crucial moment. And she'd turned down the invitation to go out with her friends on Monday night so she guessed she wasn't flavour of the month right now.

"Can I come in?" asked Chloe in a small voice. "I need to tell you something."

It was then that Lauren noticed how pale Chloe looked. And she had dark rings under her eyes as if she hadn't slept properly. "Yes, of course. Come in. Whatever's the matter?"

Lauren took her through to the living room and sat down with her on the sofa where only yesterday she'd sat with Tom and heard the terrible news about Nancy. From the way Chloe was picking at the skin around her fingernails and looking as if she might burst into tears any minute, it looked as if Lauren was about to hear yet more bad news.

"I called round yesterday," said Chloe. "But you were out."

"I had something to do at the library," said Lauren, recalling the old newspaper articles she'd read.

"Oh." Chloe tried, unsuccessfully, to stifle a sob.

"Look, please tell me what's going on," said Lauren, putting her arm around her friend.

Chloe pulled a tissue out of her sleeve and dabbed at

her eyes. "I wish you'd come with us on Monday night," she sobbed. "Then maybe none of this would have happened. Megan listens to you more than she does to me."

Hardly, thought Lauren, but she didn't say anything.

Chloe dried her eyes and blew her nose. "We went to the same place as Saturday night. It wasn't as crowded and there was no trouble this time."

"Go on."

"So afterwards, Megan persuaded Rick to walk back with us."

That creep?

"Honestly Lauren, it was awful. She was all over him and I felt like a right gooseberry. Anyway, Megan insisted that we walk down Swain's Lane and when we reached the broken railing she wanted to go back inside the cemetery."

"You're kidding! After what happened last time?"

"I didn't want to go back in there," said Chloe shaking her head. "I thought it was too dangerous with that lunatic on the loose. And besides, I was cross with her for making me feel like a spare part, so I told her I wasn't going in and I walked off."

"Wow."

"But now…" Chloe started to weep so that the tears streamed down her cheeks, "now M-M-Megan's… b-b-been h-h-hurt… and it's my fault for leaving her in that dangerous place with that monster Rick."

"But what happened to her?"

Chloe took a deep breath. "I don't know exactly. She didn't go home on Monday night. The police came to our house at six o'clock yesterday morning. Megan's mum had raised the alarm at half past five when she got up to go to the loo and saw that Megan wasn't in her room. I had to tell the police everything about Monday night, about when I'd last seen her and what she was doing. I told them about Saturday night too, to explain why I hadn't gone back into the cemetery. I had to tell them the truth Lauren. I didn't know what else to do."

Lauren took hold of her friend's hand and gave it a squeeze. "No, you did the right thing." They should have told the police about the madman in the cemetery on Saturday night, even if it meant getting into trouble themselves. "Did the police find Megan?"

Chloe nodded. "Yes. They went straight round to the cemetery. Megan was lying on the ground unconscious."

"Shit. And what about Rick? Where the hell was he?"

"Looks like Rick did a runner. Obviously the police want to speak to him."

"And how is Megan now?"

"I phoned her mum this morning. She says we can go round. She thinks it would do Megan good. That's why I'm here – to see if you want to come."

"Yes, of course. We'll go straight away."

62

The police were a bunch of incompetent arseholes. No, they were worse than that. What angered Tom most was that they weren't just incompetent, but they didn't care. It had been a waste of time going to see Inspector McNally yesterday. He should have known the Inspector wouldn't be interested. McNally was only interested in his police pension and retirement plans and just wanted to wind his career down without any bothersome cases to solve.

Tom was rapidly coming to believe in the truth of the saying, if you want something done properly then you have to do it yourself. Well he wasn't going to waste any more time. He grabbed his backpack and headed off in the direction of Hampstead Heath. He wanted to take one more look at the place where his dad's car had gone into the water. Maybe there was something he'd missed the first time.

He cut across Waterlow Park and down Swain's Lane. The weather had turned close and sticky and the tourists waiting outside the entrance to Highgate Cemetery were mopping their foreheads with handkerchiefs and taking large gulps from litre bottles of water. Lauren had said her mum gave guided tours at the cemetery. He wondered what Lauren was doing now. He should have called her after he'd been to the police but he'd been too angry at McNally's response and had gone home and spent the evening playing computer games. He'd tried her phone this morning but it was switched off. So then he'd found her home number in the phone directory but her mum had answered and said she'd just gone out with a friend and did he want to leave a message? He couldn't think of what to say so he'd said he'd call back later and then he'd hung up. Pathetic.

The Heath was strewn with half-naked bodies, sprawled on the grass. Even many of the hardy dog walkers who strode around in all weathers were collapsed on the ground, their pets panting at their sides. As Tom approached Highgate Ponds he could hear the shouts of children's voices and the splash of refreshing water. But Tom wasn't here to enjoy himself. He made his way to the largest of the ponds and watched as a gaggle of geese landed on the water, their screeches splitting the air.

Then he started to walk around the edge of the pond keeping his eyes glued to the ground in front of him. He was determined not to miss anything. Crisp packets, sweet wrappers, a child's bouncy ball. Nothing escaped his attention. Something glinted in the sun. He bent down to pick it up. It was a name tag from a dog's collar. He dropped it and carried on walking.

He reached the spot where his dad's car had gone into the water. To his right, the gate from Merton Lane was closed. He hoped the contractors who'd left it open had received hell from their managers. He began to examine the ground in this area in minute detail, not caring if passers-by thought his behaviour a bit odd.

He walked up to the gate leading to Merton Lane and

retraced his steps back towards the water. Any tyre tracks which had once been here were now obliterated by the constant to-ing and fro-ing of people, dogs and pushchairs.

He was beginning to think he wasn't going to find anything when he spotted a piece of white card trampled into the ground by muddy feet. He bent down to pick it up. It was creased and dirty but when he turned it over he recognised it immediately. He had one just like it in the back pocket of his jeans. He pulled his dad's invitation to Professor Barlow's retirement dinner out of his pocket and compared it with what he had just found on the ground.

Professor Barlow
Invites
Professor Alan Nesbit
To his retirement dinner
Friday 22nd June 2012, 8pm
University College, London.
Dress is Black Tie
RSVP by Friday 8th June 2012

Yes!

Tom had to stop himself from jumping up and down and punching the air. Finally, he had what he needed. Proof that Alan Nesbit had been at Highgate Ponds the night of the dinner. The night his dad's car had gone into the water.

Tom dropped both invitations into his backpack and started to run home. The police had to believe him now.

63

Alan sat down at his desk with the copy of the *Ham & High* he'd picked up from the newsagent's on his way into work that morning. He'd already read the lead story more than a dozen times but still it thrilled him, like a drug, and now that he wasn't being jostled by commuters on the tube he re-read it, savouring the details.

Under the headline *Missing Girl Found in Cemetery* Alan read how a local girl, sixteen years of age, had been found, unconscious, in the early hours of Tuesday morning in Highgate Cemetery. She had entered the cemetery through a gap in the railings on Swain's Lane, late on Monday night. The police mounted a search for her when her mother raised the alarm. A friend confirmed that she had last seen the missing girl entering the cemetery with the drummer of a local band. The same band, the paper noted with relish, that had been playing at an underground venue the night police raided it for drugs. It was not clear what had happened to her but the newspaper blamed the drug culture which was blighting the respectable, middle-class community of Highgate.

Alan tossed the paper aside. *Hah! Idiots.* What did they know? Nothing.

Of course it wasn't drugs or drug addicts that were to blame for what had happened to this girl. There was something much more sinister prowling around the cemetery than a bunch of crack cocaine users. It was no surprise to Alan that she'd been found next to the sleeping angel. Wasn't that the place where evil lurked?

Alan hadn't gone to the cemetery on Monday night and, in his absence, the vampire had taken the opportunity to attack. If Alan had been there with his garlic and his crucifix he might have been able to save the girl. But Alan had had other things on his mind on Monday night.

The discovery of Nancy in his room, rifling through his box of equipment had roused in him a fury so violent it was a miracle he hadn't strangled her there and then. What if she'd gone to the police accusing him of storing murderous weapons in his desk drawer? He couldn't let that happen. It had been the work of moments to tamper with the brake fluid in her car and the results had been even more successful than he'd anticipated. Her car had ploughed into the back of a Polish lorry in Rotherhithe Tunnel, killing her instantly. After that, he'd decided to lie low for a couple of days.

Alan took a pair of scissors from the top drawer of his desk and carefully cut out the article. Then he unlocked the bottom drawer and placed the article in the wallet of newspaper cuttings he kept in the box. Next he opened the newspaper package, removed the crucifix and slipped it into his pocket. He re-wrapped the package of garlic and then placed it, together with the axe and a handful of the stakes, in the black holdall he kept under his desk.

He checked his watch. It was eleven thirty. He was due to meet Jack's widow at twelve for lunch. He'd invited her out in an attempt to win her over by flattery; in an attempt to get his hands on Isabelle Hart's diary. But he realised now the widow was an irrelevance. He'd been wasting his time with her. He would fob her off with some excuse and then go to the cemetery and lie in wait. He had a feeling that today would see the fulfilment of his lifetime's ambition - to capture and destroy the Highgate Vampire.

64

Lauren tapped on Megan's bedroom door. "It's us, Lauren and Chloe. Can we come in?"

No reply.

She tried again and this time thought she heard a muffled response so she opened the door and peered in. Megan's mum had told them to go straight up; had said how glad she was they'd come; that Megan needed some company.

Lauren stepped inside, followed by Chloe who closed the door behind her.

It was dark and stuffy in Megan's bedroom. Lauren suppressed an urge to pull back the curtains and open the window to let in some fresh air. A poster of *Saints and Sinners* had been ripped from the wall and was lying in shreds on the floor. Dirty clothes were strewn higgledy-piggledy around the room. There was a pungent smell of incense from a stick that had almost burnt itself out.

Megan sat slumped on her bedroom floor, leaning against the side of the bed, her arms on her knees and her head hanging forward. Her hair fell limply in front of her eyes. She was plugged into her iPod, the volume up so high that Lauren and Chloe could hear the throb of the bass. She pulled the earplugs out and looked up at her friends.

Lauren had never seen Megan look so awful. Her hair was flat and unwashed and she had dark rings under her eyes. She was beginning to think they shouldn't have come round so soon, maybe left it a day or two to give Megan a chance to get herself together.

Chloe rushed over and threw her arms around Megan. "I'm so sorry," she sobbed. "I should never have let you go into the cemetery with Rick."

"Don't say that bastard's name," Megan hissed. Her voice sounded hoarse.

"OK, I won't. I promise. But I'm still sorry."

"Yeah, well thanks, but it wasn't your fault." She rubbed her eyes with her knuckles. "Look, I'm sorry I got angry just now."

"Forget it," said Chloe sitting down beside Megan.

Lauren knelt on the floor in front of them. She didn't know what to say. She hadn't been there on Monday night but even if she had, could she have stopped Megan from going into the cemetery with Rick? She doubted it.

"Will you tell us what happened?" asked Chloe gently. "We just want to help, that's all."

Megan looked down at the floor, pursing her lips together. "OK, I know it was stupid of me," she began, "but I thought if I took Rick" - she almost spat the name - "into the cemetery and showed him around then he might stop thinking of me as Matt's little sister and start thinking of me as...as..." Her voice started to crack and she didn't finish the sentence.

"So what happened after you went into the cemetery?" prompted Chloe.

Megan grabbed a tissue, blew her nose hard, and sat up straighter. She seemed to be getting some of her old pluck back. "I wanted to show him the garlic bulbs although I had no idea if they'd still be there. I thought he'd find them amusing."

"And were they there?" asked Lauren, unable to keep the alarm out of her voice.

Megan shook her head. "No, they'd gone unfortunately. It was a bit of a let-down."

"What about that weirdo with the axe? Did you see him?" asked Chloe.

Megan shook her head again. "No, he wasn't there either."

Well, that's a relief, thought Lauren.

"So what happened in there?" asked Chloe. "You two seemed to be getting on really well when I left you."

"Well, we walked around for a bit. I told Rick about the garlic bulbs and our encounter with the mad axe-man but I'm not sure he believed me." She paused and took a deep breath. "Then we walked further into the cemetery. Much further than the three of us did the other night. We could hear foxes calling to one another. And I'm sure there were bats flying around. It's a really creepy place in the dark. There was just enough moonlight to see where we were going and I was looking at all the stone angels who looked almost alive, then we found this statue of an angel lying on her side, like she was asleep or something and..." her voice trailed off. She bit her lip.

Chloe prompted her. "And did you and Rick..."

"Actually," said Megan clenching her fist, "he got a bit aggressive. He'd been drinking and I think he might even have taken some drugs. We'd been walking with our arms around each other, nothing more. But then he suddenly turned into this sex-crazed maniac. He seemed to think I'd

taken him in there for one thing only. He was all over me."
She closed her eyes and took a deep breath before
continuing. "He pushed me onto the ground next to this
angel and then…"

"What?" said Lauren and Chloe together.

"I was shit scared," said Megan, looking at her friends
with wide staring eyes. "I shouted for someone to help me,
even though I knew there was nobody around. I couldn't
help it. Then this really weird thing happened. It's hard to
explain." She stopped and frowned, as if trying to find the
right words. "It was like, one minute he had me pinned
down on the ground and he was too strong for me and I
was panicking and then…I don't know how to describe
it… it was like some black shadow or something came
swirling out of the trees and…and engulfed him."

"What do you mean 'engulfed' him?" asked Lauren.

Megan threw her hands into the air. "I don't know, it
was like this supernatural force or something. I know that
sounds crazy, but that was how it was. This dark *thing*
swallowed him up and then it was like he was being
dragged off me – I can't really explain it any better – but I
swear there was no one there."

"So what happened to him?"

"He totally freaked out." She laughed. "He didn't
understand what was happening and it scared the shit out
of him. I could see the whites of his eyes. He was pissing
himself. He jumped to his feet and ran like he was being
chased by the devil."

"So what did you do then?"

"This is where it all gets a bit hazy. I remember getting
to my feet," said Megan slowly. "I wanted to find my way
out of the cemetery but when I tried to walk everything
started to spin and I felt dizzy. After that I don't
remember anything. I guess I must have fainted or
something. Maybe from the shock of what had happened
– I don't know. I was still lying there when the police
found me the next morning."

"That is well weird," said Chloe shaking her head in disbelief.

"I'm just glad you're OK," said Lauren. "Sounds like it could have been a lot worse."

After that they chatted about inconsequential stuff and Megan was much more like her old self. But something was bothering Lauren. What was it Megan had said? *An angel lying on her side, like she was asleep.*

There was only one such angel in the cemetery as far as Lauren knew - the sleeping angel.

It was where Isabelle had buried her baby in secret. And from what Megan had told them, it sounded as if some power was at work there that had saved Megan from Rick's unwelcome clutches. What was going on? Lauren was sure it had something to do with Isabelle's story. She had to read the rest of the diary and find out what had happened to Isabelle.

65

Tom arrived home dripping sweat and out of breath. As he barged in through the front door his mother was coming down the stairs. She was dressed up. Figure-hugging purple dress, black Chanel handbag, red lipstick.

Whatever, he thought. It was no concern of his. But he was glad he'd caught her before she went out. He had to show her what he'd found. She'd have to listen to him now.

"I've just been back to Highgate Ponds," he said.

"Oh?" she sounded surprised as if she couldn't think why he'd want to go there.

"I found something." He started to undo his backpack.

"Can this wait until later?" she asked. "I'm in a bit of a hurry. I'm meeting someone for lunch."

"But…"

"There's fresh bread in the kitchen. Can you make yourself a sandwich?"

"Sure, but can I just show you…"

She looked at her watch. "I'm sorry, but I really must go. Alan will be waiting."

"What?" The backpack fell from his hands and crashed onto the floor. He couldn't believe what he'd just heard. "You're meeting Professor Nesbit for lunch?"

She turned to look at him. "Tom, I know it's been difficult for you since your father died, but Professor Nesbit has been very understanding and kind."

"But…"

"I'm sorry Tom, I'm not going to discuss it now. He's turned out to be a good friend. There's nothing more to it than that." She rummaged in her bag and pulled out her car keys. "I'll see you later." She turned and walked out of the house.

Tom stared at the front door, willing her to change her mind and come back. But, of course, she wouldn't. What was wrong with her? Why wouldn't she listen to him? *Dammit.* He gave the backpack a resounding kick and sent it skidding across the parquet floor. It crashed into a radiator. With a sigh Tom walked over and bent down to pick it up. On a shelf above the radiator was a photo of himself and his dad. He studied it now. It was of the two of them on the Ridgeway in Oxfordshire after they'd been caught in a freak storm that had ruined what should have been a gloriously sunny summer's day. They were soaked to the skin and covered in mud but they were laughing. It had been a good day. They'd come through it together.

And then it hit him. There was only one person Tom wanted to be with right now, even if he was buried six feet underground. He left the house and headed off in the direction of Highgate Cemetery.

66

Thursday, 17th March 1870
I visited Madeleine for my first proper sitting with her last night.

She said we should meet alone, after dinner, when the house would be quiet and there was no risk of being disturbed by Betsy carrying hot chocolate to her mistress' room.

I tried to fill the hour after dinner by working on my sampler but I was all fingers and thumbs and couldn't sew a straight line for love nor money. In the end I unpicked the crooked stitches and folded the sampler away in my box, hiding it in its safe place under the loose floorboard.

When I heard the clock in the hall strike nine, I crept down the stairs to Madeleine's room and knocked on the door. All around me the house lay quiet and still. I thought I heard a whisper of voices in the room, but when she opened the door and invited me in I saw that she was alone and guessed that she must have been communicating with the spirit world.

The oil lamp was turned down low as it had been for the séance with Mrs Waterman so the room was in virtual darkness. The coals in the grate emitted a soft glow, but there was no other light in the room. I glanced, with some trepidation, at the corner where Madeleine's spirit cabinet stood but the curtain was pulled across and the whole corner was shrouded in darkness.

"Welcome, Isabelle," she said in a velvety voice. "You have come at just the right time." I did not know what she meant by that, but let her guide me to the sofa in front of the fire where we had sat the last time I was with her.

She sat down next to me, folding her hands in her lap.

"This evening," she said, "I will try to contact the spirit world to see if there is news of your daughter. That is," she added, "if you still wish me to proceed."

Did I wish her to proceed? I am not sure. Part of me wished, more than anything, to make contact with my darling daughter, but another part of me was afraid. But I had come this far and I felt compelled to continue. So I told her, yes, I would like her to proceed.

"Very well," she said. "Now we must be patient. I will go into a trance and listen to what the spirits are telling me." At that she sat up very straight, tilted her head upwards and closed her eyes. I gazed at the dying embers in the fire.

We must have sat like that for ten minutes or more. Madeleine's breathing became heavier and deeper, whilst mine only became shallow and rapid. I was aware of my fingers trembling.

Suddenly she spoke as if to someone or something that only she could see. "Yes!"

"What is it?" I ventured.

She relaxed her posture and turned her face towards mine. Her cheek looked flushed in the light from the fire and her eyes glittered.

"Oh Isabelle," she said. "This is a very special night."

"Why is that?" I asked. Had she made contact with Emily already? It seemed too much to hope for.

"My spirit guide wants to come," she said.

"What is a spirit guide?" I asked.

"All mediums have a spirit guide," she explained. "These are people who have passed into spirit. They help us understand and communicate with the spirit world and they bring us messages from those who have died, particularly from those who are unable to communicate on their own."

"I see," I said, although I did not fully understand what she was telling me or how this spirit guide might appear.

"But first I must go into my cabinet." She stood up.

I did not want her to leave me alone. This was what I had feared the most. "Will I have to bind you?" I asked in a frightened voice, remembering the séance with Mrs Waterman when Mr Gatesby had bound her to the chair with three lengths of silk cord.

"No," she said. "That will not be necessary tonight. But I must insist, for your safety and for mine, that you remain seated here on the sofa."

I agreed to do as she asked. I had no intention of stumbling around in the dark and walking into spirits.

She left me then and walked over to the cabinet. On the way she turned the oil lamp down even further so that the light from it barely spread further than the small round table on which it stood. The cabinet was now in total darkness. I heard the clink of curtain rings on brass as she pulled back the curtain and again as she drew it closed. I supposed her now to be seated in the cabinet and I wished I was not alone. I began to be very afraid. The glow from the coals had faded and the heat was starting to go out of them. I sat very still, hardly daring to breathe. Outside, the sound of a carriage trundling past made me jump. I gripped the arm of the sofa.

A faint sound, like the wind in the trees, came from the spirit cabinet. I listened harder and discerned the sound of heavy breathing. I knew then that Madeleine had gone into a trance. There was a rustling like silk and then all was still. I strained my eyes in the direction of the cabinet but could make out nothing in the dark. I waited, aware of the thumping of my own heart. Then, as I had witnessed in the séance with Mrs Waterman, a delicate glow started to appear in the corner of the room. It grew, appearing to take on form and substance, until it transformed itself into the shape of a figure which shone with a pale luminous light.

I hardly dared breathe.

The figure glided across the floor towards me. Its features were obscured, whether because the room was so dimly lit or because the spirit or ghost (if that is what it was) was insubstantial, I could not tell. In outline it resembled a female form. It (she?) stopped about six feet from where I was sitting and spoke in barely more than a whisper.

"I am Eliza King, Madeleine's spirit guide. I have made the journey from the spirit world tonight because you are suffering and you want to know that your child is safe in the spirit world."

"Oh!" I cried and covered my face with my hands. It was all too much for me to bear. I wished I was not sitting there all alone. I wished Madeleine was with me. I did not know what to say to Eliza and feared she would think me a hopeless case and return to the spirit world never to visit me again. I felt hot but at the same time started to shiver. The blood pulsed in my ears. Eliza took a step closer and held out her ghostly white hand. It must have been then that I fell onto the floor in a dead faint.

I do not know how long I lay like that.

When I came round Madeleine was leaning over me, waving a bottle of smelling salts under my nose. I started to cry.

"I'm sorry," I blurted out. "It was all too much for me. Eliza must think me terribly weak. She will not want to come again."

"Eliza is not so easily put off as that," said Madeleine gaily. "In fact, she would like nothing better than to assist in a materialisation

of your daughter. She could do that for you, you know."

I looked at her in astonishment. It would mean everything in the world to me to be able to see my baby girl just one more time.

Madeleine put her arm around me and helped me back onto the sofa. "I think you should go and rest now. Eliza wants to help you, but you need to be stronger. Next time you will be better prepared."

I nodded my head weakly and returned to my room where I crawled into bed and fell into a troubled sleep, dreaming that the spirits were laughing at me.

67

Journal of Mr. Nathaniel Hart, Esq. – March 1870

Today I have searched for Isabelle in all the places I could think of - penitentiaries, houses of charity, most of them hovels that do little to help the women who lodge there.

By ten o'clock in the evening I had ventured as far as Urania Cottage in Lime Grove, Shepherd's Bush. Urania Cottage is a better-run establishment than most as it benefits from the direct involvement of one of the greatest minds of our age, the author Charles Dickens. I sincerely hoped I would find Isabelle sheltering under its roof but, alas, I was again disappointed. I did, however, speak to the warden who suggested I might need to look further afield. She gave me directions to the St. Mary Magdalene House of Charity in Highgate. Tomorrow I shall turn my feet towards Highgate. May God grant me no rest until I have found my dear sister.

68

Saturday, 19th March 1870, 11 o'clock in the evening.

It is late but I am wound up like a spring and know it would be hopeless to attempt sleep for the time being. This evening we did not achieve the hoped-for results but it will happen tomorrow – I am sure of it. When Madeleine came out of her trance this evening she was greatly exhausted from her exertions. I revived her with a little brandy and hot water and she explained that, although we had prepared well, the conditions were not absolutely perfect – the weather has been unsettled of late – and for such a delicate phenomenon as that which she intends to bring forth, all external factors must be favourable. Earlier today I overheard the baker's boy, Sam, telling Betsy that he expects the weather to improve tomorrow and he is rarely wrong on such matters. In the meantime I must try to calm my nerves and be patient. It will not be long now. All my hope and trust is in Madeleine. She will not let me down.

69

The diary stopped.

Lauren turned the pages, flicking through to the end, but there was nothing. The remaining pages were blank.

What?

She couldn't believe it. She sat back in her chair and frowned. How frustrating. Like reading a book and finding the last chapter missing. Isabelle's story couldn't have come to such a sudden end. Something must have happened after the last entry. Lauren re-read it now. It had been written late at night. The handwriting had degenerated into a scrawl indicating that Isabelle must have been tired or over-excited or both. But even so, she had been looking forward to the next day. She had been sure that Madeleine would not let her down.

Lauren examined the diary more closely, and that was when she noticed something. The last page Isabelle had written on and the following page didn't sit quite comfortably next to each other. She closed the diary and looked at the edge of the paper. There a small gap between the pages. She re-opened the diary and ran her finger in between the pages and felt the rough edge of a page that had been torn out, close to the spine.

No, surely not.

Someone – Isabelle? – Madeleine? – had ripped out the last entry. Why? What were they trying to hide? She wondered about asking Tom to contact Peter Hart, but it was highly unlikely he would have the missing page after all this time. She dropped the diary down onto the desk. Now she would never know what had happened to Isabelle. She was gutted. It was such a let-down.

Unless.

Unless there was another way.

A movement at the window caught Lauren's eye. The box sash window was pushed up about four inches to let in some air. A blue butterfly had landed on the windowsill and was sitting, preening itself. As Lauren watched it she thought back over the events of the morning; about what Megan had told her and Chloe. What Megan had described – Rick pushing her to the ground and then being engulfed in a swirling black shape – could have sounded like the fanciful ravings of someone who was out of their mind, but it hadn't. Megan had sounded calm and rational. It was as if the sleeping angel, or some other power, had come to her rescue. The sleeping angel meant something to Isabelle too. Lauren picked up the diary and flicked back through the pages until she found the bit she was looking for.

I feel she protects this part of the cemetery from anything bad, Isabelle had written.

Lauren knew the statue of the sleeping angel well. She had seen it many times when she'd accompanied Wendy on tours. As a little girl it had been one of her favourite statues, the others being Lion the dog who lay with his head on his paws over the grave of the prize fighter Tom Sayers, and the lion who lay atop the tomb of George Wombwell, the menagerie exhibitor. She'd always wanted to hug the dog, pat the lion and lie down next to the sleeping angel, but Wendy had insisted she stand up and behave herself in front of the tourists. Lauren hadn't visited any of these statues for years.

She thought about them now. Was it possible she might learn something if she visited the sleeping angel? An idea had taken hold in her mind that the end of Isabelle's story would be found in the cemetery or, more precisely, by the sleeping angel.

She stood up and went to close the window. The blue butterfly hovered for a moment outside the glass and then flew away in the direction of the cemetery. Lauren made her decision.

She checked her watch. It was three o'clock. Wendy was working in the cemetery office that afternoon archiving burial details onto the computer. That was perfect because there was only one way Lauren could think of to get into the cemetery. Sneaking in through the gap in the railings was out of the question. Besides, it had probably been mended by now, particularly after what had happened to Megan. And since the vandalism of the seventies and eighties the Friends of Highgate Cemetery had put strict access rules in place – the only people allowed in were grave owners and those on guided tours. But there was another way that would work. They were always asking for volunteers.

Lauren picked up her phone from beside the computer and speed-dialled Wendy. It rang three times before her mum answered.

"Hello?"

"Hi Mum, it's me."

"Lauren – is everything OK?"

"Yes, fine. Listen, you know you were complaining the other day about the amount of litter that gets chucked over the railings into the cemetery? Well I thought I could come and pick some up. If you still need someone, that is."

Silence.

"Mum? Did you hear me?"

"Sure I heard you. Are you feeling all right Lauren?"

"I'll be there in ten minutes. Can you meet me at the gate?"

"Of course."

She ended the call.

Lauren couldn't help feeling a bit miffed that Wendy had received her offer of help with such astonishment. But then, she reminded herself, she hadn't offered to pick up litter from an altruistic desire to improve the environment but because she wanted to visit the sleeping angel and…do what? She realised she had no idea, but she had a feeling she would find out once she was there.

She went up to her room and changed into a denim skirt that was long enough to be decent (Alice, the old lady who was Chairman of the Friends of Highgate, was a stickler for decorum) but short enough to be cool in this furious heat. She opted for a pink sleeveless top and a pair of comfortable pumps – the ground in Highgate Cemetery was notoriously rough and riddled with tree roots. She didn't want a twisted ankle.

She cut across Waterlow Park to Swain's Lane, passing the bench where she'd first met Tom. Well, after nearly knocking him over on the library steps that is. She wondered what he was doing now. She promised herself she'd call him as soon as she'd finished "collecting litter" but right now she wanted to spend as much time as she could in the cemetery.

Wendy was waiting for her on Swain's Lane outside the Victorian gothic gateway.

"Hi Mum."

"Hello dear. It's very good of you to offer to help like this." Wendy unlocked the cemetery gate.

"No problem," said Lauren, following her mum inside.

Wendy turned to look at her. "You know, I should have planned a proper holiday for us this summer instead of staying here. It was selfish of me and all because I wanted to get the attic sorted out. You must be really fed up if you've got nothing better to do than come here and pick up litter."

"No really, I don't mind," said Lauren.

"Well, if you're sure. Oh, I nearly forgot," said Wendy as they walked towards the office. "There was a phone call for you this morning. When you were out."

"Oh?"

"It was a boy. Someone called Tom?"

She'd missed him! He must have phoned when she'd been round at Megan's house. Why hadn't he called her mobile? Then she remembered she'd switched it off and left it charging in the kitchen.

"Did he leave a message?"

"No. He said he'd try again later." Wendy was watching her out of the corner of her eye, obviously angling for more information. Lauren tried to reach the office before the interrogation began but it was no good.

"So who is he?" asked Wendy.

"Just a friend," said Lauren trying to sound casual and matter-of-fact. Anyway, it was true. He wasn't anything else right at this moment.

"He sounded nice."

Lauren made a dive for the office door before Wendy could ask any more questions. No doubt she was already jumping to all sorts of conclusions.

Alice was sitting behind a wooden desk piled high with pamphlets about the history of the cemetery illustrated on the cover with the tomb of Karl Marx. She was busy pouring two cups of tea from a teapot decorated with yellow flowers. Dressed in a tweed skirt and floral blouse with her white hair brushed into a bouffant she reminded Lauren of everyone's idea of an old, slightly batty aunt but Lauren knew she had a razor sharp mind and possessed an encyclopaedic knowledge of the cemetery and its inhabitants.

"Hello dear," said Alice. "It's very good of you to come and help us out. Particularly on such a hot and sticky day. I wouldn't be at all surprised if we had a storm later. I can feel it in my bones." She gave a little laugh. "Would you like a cup of tea before you start your hard work?"

"No thank you," said Lauren. "I'll have one when I've finished though, if I may." She was keen to get going.

"Of course," said Alice. "Now, you'll need to take one of these." She handed Lauren a walkie-talkie. "Health and safety you know. In case you need to contact us in an emergency."

"Thanks," said Lauren. Tree roots had disturbed the foundations of some of the monuments and the taller ones, the angels and columns, could potentially topple over, although Lauren didn't think that a walkie-talkie would be much use if a six foot stone angel decided to come crashing down on top of her.

"And here's a plastic bag for the litter."

"Great."

"You know your way around don't you?" said Alice.

"Sure," said Lauren. She'd accompanied her mother on enough tours as a younger child that she could have given the tour herself. "I'll be back in about an hour."

"Right you are then. I'll have the kettle on."

Lauren caught Wendy's eye on the way out. She could tell her mum was bursting with questions. *So who is he? What's he like? When can I meet him?* Lauren just smiled at her and left.

She crossed the courtyard in front of the Colonnade, the sun scorching the top of her head. She wished she'd thought to bring a hat. She climbed the stone steps, grateful for the shade cast by the old brick walls, and emerged into the forest-like setting of the cemetery.

She paused for a moment, taking in the scene before her eyes, feeling as if she had been here very recently. Of course, she told herself, this was the forest of her dreams: tall, thin trees competing with each other for space and light growing up amidst a ramshackle assortment of headstones, statues, columns, crosses and obelisks; ivy clinging to monuments, shrouding them in a web of green leaves; wild flowers poking their heads up amongst the undergrowth. As a child she thought of the cemetery as a magic forest where fairies, pixies and elves lived. But what lived here now?

She started to walk along the path.

Lauren wasn't a great fan of the stone urns and Greek columns which adorned many of the graves in this part of the cemetery. She thought they were too impersonal and a bit vulgar. She preferred the angels with their wavy hair and downcast eyes who reminded her of Pre-Raphaelite artists' models, like Lizzie Siddal who was buried not far from the spot known as Comfort's Corner. Wasn't there some story about her being exhumed? Just imagine having to do that job!

The path split into different directions. The classical style catacombs of The Egyptian Avenue and The Circle of Lebanon were up the hill to her right. They had been the most coveted cemetery 'addresses' in Victorian times – like Park Lane and Mayfair on the Monopoly board. But the place Isabelle wrote about in her diary was in the opposite direction.

Lauren headed off downhill towards the sleeping angel.

70

He could see that she'd made an effort with her appearance. Figure-hugging dress, fashionable black handbag, lipstick in a shade of deep crimson. But it meant nothing to him. It wasn't that he was blind to such things, just indifferent. No woman had ever shown any interest in him so he had long ago closed his heart to the possibility of receiving and giving love. The thought that Deborah Kelsey might see him as a friend who was helping her get over the death of her husband had never entered Alan Nesbit's mind. The only thing that had attracted him to her was the fact that her husband had been in possession of a diary that might have explained a mystery about the cemetery that he'd never understood. He'd believed at one point that the diary was the missing piece of the jigsaw puzzle. But he'd begun to doubt even that.

As she browsed the menu, running her finger down the list of pasta dishes, his doubt about the usefulness of the diary crystallised into certainty. Dull, ordinary people could spend their lives weighing up all the possible choices life had to offer, like the way his mother used to waste time dithering between brands of washing powder or the way Deborah was failing to decide between seafood tagliatelle and spaghetti carbonara. But he wasn't like that. He was blessed, in his opinion, with the sort of decisiveness that got things done, that achieved results.

He'd thought she would be useful to him but he'd been wrong. He could see that now. He'd used her as a way to get to her husband's work, as a way to lay his hands on the diary. But it looked like he didn't need the diary after all. He had what he needed and that was knowledge. Knowledge of how to catch the vampire and kill it once and for all. What he didn't have was time to sit around whilst his lunch partner struggled to make up her mind.

He glanced down at the black holdall that was on the floor by the side of his chair. If she knew what was inside she wouldn't be sitting there so calmly under the whirring fans that were just about managing to keep the restaurant at a bearable temperature.

She looked up at him. "Have you chosen?" His menu was lying on the table unopened.

"I don't care for Italian food," he said. "Too much garlic."

"Well we could go somewhere else. There's a nice Chinese place round the corner."

He didn't have time for this. He pushed back his chair and stood up. "I've been mistaken about you."

She flinched at his words and it made him glad. "I don't understand…"

"I thought you could give me something I wanted, but you can't."

She blushed a deep red. She'd misunderstood what he meant, but he wasn't going to disabuse her. He bent down and picked up the black holdall. "I have important business to see to."

"But what about our lunch?" She sounded close to tears.

"I'm not hungry," he said. "But you should have the spaghetti alla puttanesca. It means slut's spaghetti."

Her hand flew to her mouth and she gave a strangled cry of distress.

He turned and walked out of the restaurant.

By the time he was descending the steps to the underground at Leicester Square he had already put Deborah Kelsey out of his mind. Only one thing absorbed his attention. He was going to go to the cemetery and he was going to finish the task he'd started over forty years ago. He was going to hunt down the vampire and he was going to kill it.

71

Reflections of Will Bucket, Gravedigger, In the Year of Our Lord 1870, continued…

Now I ain't got time for all this Spiritualist nonsense. I've heard from Betsy what that Madeleine Fox gets up to and I don't want nuffink to do with it. As far as I'm concerned, you live, you die, you get buried (at Highgate if you're lucky) and what happens after that is not for the likes of me to say. We've got thousands buried here already and if spirits really did come back from the dead you might've thought I'd have seen a few by now.

We do get a lot of butterflies though and I'd sure rather be looking at them than at the ghost of some long dead fella who probably weren't all that great in life and is unlikely to have improved twenty years after he were buried.

Big Bert and me was busy digging a new grave down in the Meadow the other day when I sees this bright blue butterfly land on a holly bush.

"Look at that," I says to Bert. "Now ain't that a fine sight?" and we both puts down our spades to get a closer look. It had pale silver-blue wings with little ivory dots and was one of the prettiest little butterflies I ever seen. I leaned closer to get a better look. It sat so still I had me face no more than six inches away from it. I could see its tiny feelers twitching in the sun. Then it flew off in the direction of *The Secret Spot* and me and Big Bert went back to digging the grave.

Like I say, I ain't got time for talk of spirits and stuff, but I likes to imagine the souls of pretty young women, like Lizzie Siddal, turning into butterflies. Not that I'd tell anyone mind you – they'd think I was barmy.

PART EIGHT
WEDNESDAY 18 JULY

72

She looked so peaceful.

The sleeping angel lay on her left side, her head resting on a stone pillow, her bare arms crossed loosely in front of her. Her robe draped itself gently over her body and legs. Her long, graceful wings were tucked behind her. Tendrils of ivy crept around the base of her stone bed and a scattering of fallen leaves lay like confetti over her slumbering form.

Lauren laid the black plastic bag and walkie-talkie aside and crouched down, tilting her head to get a better view of the angel's gentle face. Closed eyes, aquiline nose and rose-bud lips. She had lain there for over a hundred years - a real sleeping beauty.

Lauren reached out a hand and stroked the angel's right arm with her fingertips, almost expecting her to wake up. The stone was cold, despite the stifling heat of the day.

A butterfly, blue with tiny ivory dots on its wings,

fluttered into view and perched on the angel's shoulder. It sat perfectly still and Lauren couldn't shake off the feeling that it was watching her.

She stood up and started to walk slowly around the angel. Dry leaves scrunched under her feet. Behind the statue lay a tangle of vines and creepers but the ground in front of the angel was clearer. Was this where Isabelle had buried her baby? Lauren knelt down and ran her fingers over the dry, dusty ground. It was impossible to tell what lay beneath the surface. If only she had some kind of X-ray machine.

She bent down to pick up the bag and walkie-talkie. She couldn't go back to the office with an empty bin liner. She'd have to pick up *some* litter at least.

That was when she heard it.

The hairs on the back of her neck stood on end. What was that? A bird? A fox? No, more like… She stayed absolutely still, crouching near the ground, and listened. More like…the rustle of silk…then running footsteps. The crunch of twigs snapping underfoot.

"Who's there?"

Lauren jumped up. Spun round. Too quick. She felt dizzy. Black dots danced in front of her eyes. She was losing her balance.

She tried to steady herself. Stop herself from falling over. The blood was now pounding in her ears and her heart was hammering against her ribcage.

The cemetery was a blur. The sun shining through the trees was too bright and the trees were spinning before her eyes. She had a memory of being five. She'd gone to Waterlow Park with her father. She was standing in the middle of a roundabout in the children's play area. Some older children were yelling and shrieking, spinning the roundabout too fast. She screamed. *Stop!* She wanted to get off. She called to her father to rescue her. He didn't come.

Rustle. Swish. Snap.

She spun round. A woman, dressed in a long black

gown, was running through the trees. Running towards her. Her long, dark hair streamed behind her in the wind.

Suddenly it was cold.

A black cloud rolled over the sun and Lauren saw with alarm that the branches of the trees were bare, stripped of their leaves as in the bleakest of mid-winters.

The woman was close now. She slowed her pace and walked towards Lauren.

Lauren froze. She wanted to run but couldn't move a muscle. Had she fainted in the heat? Was this a dream like the one she'd been having for days now?

The woman faced her, her hazel eyes gazing into Lauren's. Her skin was pale, like ivory. Her hair tumbled over her shoulders in ringlets. Her black, silk dress was splashed with mud. She reached out a hand.

Lauren gasped. The woman's hand was ice-cold. Lauren felt herself falling into a faint. The last thing she heard before she hit the ground was the woman's voice.

"Let me tell you my story."

73

Like all grave owners at Highgate, Alan Nesbit was entitled to visit his family's grave whenever he liked. Donald and Jean Nesbit had been buried at Highgate in 1980 and 1985 respectively. His father had died of a rage-induced heart attack at the age of fifty-six and his mother had died five years later from a lifetime of over-work and under-appreciation. Alan did not mourn the loss of his parents but rejoiced at the opportunity to bury them in Highgate, thus putting himself in possession of a grave owners' pass, giving him access to the cemetery whenever he wanted it.

Alice checked his pass and admitted him to the cemetery. She wondered what he was carrying in that black leather holdall of his. It was a strange thing to bring with you. Most people brought flowers or maybe a book of poems to read. She hoped he'd brought a trowel and some secateurs. The grave where his parents lay was overrun with weeds and in dire need of some attention. She watched as he walked across the courtyard and disappeared up the steps of the Colonnade. Then she turned and went back into the office. There was work to do and she didn't have time to stand around all day.

74

Tom stood gazing down at his dad's grave. The white lilies that had lain on top of the coffin and which someone – the undertakers? – had placed on top of the grave after the earth had been filled in were dry and shrivelled. Tom bent down and picked them up, feeling their brittle stems crack under his fingers. He tossed them into a mass of leafy green ferns where they would compost down soon enough. Dust to dust.

But he hadn't come here to garden. He wanted to think. He pulled Alan Nesbit's invitation out of his pocket and re-read it. Did it really prove Alan Nesbit had been at Highgate Ponds the night his dad's car went into the water? He'd been so sure it did, but now he had his doubts. Could it have fallen out of the professor's pocket on another occasion? He imagined DCI McNally pouring cold water on his theory.

Tom wished he could speak to Lauren about it. He liked the way she kept a clear head about things. But he'd tried her mobile again before entering the cemetery and it was still switched off. Maybe she was trying to avoid him. After that business with Nancy, who could blame her? He'd probably taken advantage of her – getting her to read the diary when, with a bit of effort, he could have done it himself. After all, she must have her own life to lead. He couldn't expect her to be there just for him.

And then there was the problem of his mother. He was convinced that Alan Nesbit wasn't to be trusted but she obviously had a different idea. He couldn't understand why she'd become so dependent on that creep. But then who else did she have to turn to? Had he, himself, let her down by not trying to understand what she was going through? Maybe this was just her way of coping with a difficult situation.

"Tell me what to do Dad."

The sound of his own voice startled him. He hadn't meant to speak out loud. He looked around, embarrassed, but there was no one there. And he didn't really expect his dad to tell him what to do. He didn't believe in voices from beyond the grave. At least, not literally. But a sign?

He noticed something flickering out of the corner of his eye. A blue butterfly landed on his dad's headstone. Tom knelt down and watched it. He'd never seen one such an extraordinary colour. The pale blue wings were decorated with tiny ivory dots. The butterfly rose into the air. Then it started to fly away.

Mesmerised, Tom followed it.

75

Journal of Mr. Nathaniel Hart, Esq. March 1870

I had the misfortune to call at the St Mary Magdalene Penitentiary when the Lady Principal, the Sisters and all the penitents were on their way to daily prayers in the chapel, so there was no one available to speak to me.

I decided to take a turn in the grounds whilst I waited for the service to finish. They have a number of fine apple trees growing in the garden, many of them just starting to blossom. I was admiring one particularly old and gnarled tree when suddenly a woman appeared at my side.

I judged from her blue gingham dress that she was one of the penitents. However, her manner was anything but penitential. A stray curl had escaped from her cap and there was a sly grin playing on her lips.

"Af'noon Sir," she said, as if she was quite used to addressing gentlemen in a coquettish fashion.

I inclined my head to her not sure how best to respond. I am not accustomed to dealing with women of her ilk. I wished she would leave me alone but she seemed inclined to talk so I was obliged to converse with her.

"You are not in the chapel with the others," *I remarked.*

"Pah," *she said with a dismissive wave of her hand.* "I've heard it all before. That Reverend Renshaw says the same old stuff all the time."

"I see," *I replied.*

She took a step towards me. "You come here looking for someone?"

"Well, yes, as a matter of fact I have. I was hoping to find my sister Isabelle."

"Sister Isabelle?"

Was the girl dim-witted that she had to parrot me? "Do you know her?" *I asked.*

"Course I do. She's new here. She hasn't learnt all the ways of this place yet, but she's nice."

I could detect sincerity in her voice and decided to trust her. "Do you know where I can find her?"

She shrugged and started to turn away from me.

"Wait. Don't go, please."

"What's it worth?"

I reached into my pocket and pulled out a gold sovereign. Her eyes widened at the sight of so much money. But then she shook her head. "Put it away. I haven't got need of money here. You say you want to find Isabelle, but the question is, does she want to be found?"

"If you know where she is, please, in the name of everything that is good, tell me."

She beckoned me closer to her. I inclined my head to her mouth and she whispered something just loud enough for me to hear.

"Thank you," *I said, then,* "I'm sorry, but I don't know your name."

"Ellen, Sir. They call me Ellen."

76

Alan trod the familiar path through the cemetery, looking neither to left nor right. He had no intention of visiting his parents' grave. He hadn't been back to it since the day of his mother's funeral. Why should he? It was in a part of the cemetery that held no interest for him and he had no desire to show his respects.

He came to the point where the path diverged and took the same direction he had over forty years ago.

The girl mentioned in this morning's edition of the *Ham & High* had been found by the sleeping angel. That was no surprise. The sleeping angel was where he'd had his own terrifying, supernatural and ultimately life-changing experience the night of the vampire hunt in 1970. Instinct told him the vampire would be found by the sleeping angel. There was something dark and mysterious about that part of the cemetery, as if it possessed an energy not found elsewhere.

He turned off the path and started picking his way over the graves and between the trees. He didn't want to be seen and if anyone came by he would be able to duck down out of sight.

The fact that he was walking over the resting places of the dead was of no concern to him. He trod on the grave of Lizzie Siddal which she shared with her parents-in-law and sister-in-law, the poet Christina Rossetti. He couldn't have cared less. The sentimental drivel of Victorian poets, particularly the women, revolted him.

When he was within sight of the sleeping angel he selected a solid-looking gravestone that stood over three feet high – *Here Resteth The Mortal Part Of George Henry Carpenter 1832–1894* - and knelt down behind it. He put his black holdall to one side and unzipped it, taking the contents out one by one and laying them on the ground ready. The crucifix he slipped into his pocket.

Peering out from the behind the stone, he had a clear

view of the sleeping angel, that detested lump of rock. But there was something else that made him gasp.

A girl was lying on the ground. She was wearing a pink top and a denim skirt and her arms and legs were flung out at an awkward angle.

Another victim of the vampire.

Would the evil creature return? Alan decided to wait and see.

77

Tom was lost. And he was dying of thirst. He wished he'd brought a bottle of water with him. His T-shirt was sticking to him and when he licked his lips he tasted salt.

How big was the Western Cemetery? He had some idea it was about seventeen acres which was plenty big enough to get lost in, although right now it felt more like one hundred and seventy acres. He didn't remember there being quite so many trees. It was as if he had wandered into a magical forest and they were springing up all around him, leading him astray.

His attempt to follow the blue butterfly had failed as it was bound to do. The creature was too quick for him. He couldn't keep up, at least not in this sweltering heat. In his attempt to follow it he hadn't paid attention to where he was going and now he found himself in a part of the cemetery that was even more overgrown than normal, which was saying something. The trees seemed to be leaning in, blocking out the sunlight. Brambles and holly bushes snagged at his clothing. The path underfoot was obscured by a tangle of creepers and vines.

They really ought to cut back all this ivy before someone trips over and twists an ankle.

Maybe he would offer his services to the Friends of Highgate Cemetery – wasn't volunteering supposed to take your mind off your own troubles?

He pushed his way through the undergrowth, bending

down to shift tendrils of ivy with his hands. He felt like the prince in the fairy tale hacking his way through a briar rose to rescue the princess. He laughed, a short dry laugh. *Hah, if only it was that easy – getting the pretty girl – just draw your sword, chop down the shrubbery and sweep her up in your arms.* But in Tom's experience it wasn't as simple as that. It wasn't as if pretty girls were just lying around waiting to be rescued with a spot of pruning and a kiss. No, he was going to have to be braver than that if…

What's that?

He stopped, pushing his hair back off his damp forehead. A flash of bright pink material had caught his eye. Then he saw arms and legs.

What the…

It couldn't be. But it was. Someone was lying sprawled on the ground beside a statue of a sleeping angel.

He ran over.

My God, it's Lauren. Is she unconscious or what?

She was lying awkwardly, her arms and legs flung out at an angle and her head turned away from him. Her hair had fallen across her face. His heart thudded against his ribcage. He was no expert on first aid, but he fell to his knees and placed his index and middle fingers against her neck, checking for a pulse. It was faint, but it was there.

"Lauren, can you hear me? Wake up Lauren."

78

The Trials and Tribulations of a Household Maid in the Year of Our Lord 1870, concluded.

There I am busy baking bread and getting the stew on for the evening meal and blow me if don't find rat droppings on the pantry floor. The little buggers, I thinks to myself. I'd already used half the arsenic and caught four of them. I thought I'd done with rats for the time being but obviously not.

So I goes back into the kitchen and looks on the top

shelf for the arsenic. There's the sugar and the flour, but where's the bloomin' arsenic? Maybe it had got pushed to the back. I fetches the kitchen chair and climbs up to have a look. I'm just getting me balance when blow me if the front door bell don't start ringing like someone's trying to wake the dead.

I waits to see if Mrs Payne will answer it but she must've still been at chapel 'cause the ringing goes on and on.

"No peace for the wicked," I says to myself.

I climbs back down off the chair and starts making me way to the front door.

"All right, all right. No need to deafen us all. As if I didn't 'ave enough to do what with the baking and the rats!"

I guess it'll be some crook come to flog his wares and I'm all ready to tell him we don't need no more copper pans and to go sling his hook when I sees a gentleman standing on the doorstep.

He's out of breath and all red in the face like he's just run here, but he's still a gentleman. I can tell from his fine coat and his top hat.

I puts on me best voice. "How can I help you Sir?"

He takes off his top hat. "I'm sorry to disturb you but does Miss Isabelle Hart live here?"

Now, gentleman or no gentleman, Miss Hart has never mentioned any fancy man and I don't think I should tell this stranger whether she do or don't live here in case she don't want him to know. But he must have taken me silence for a 'yes' 'cause he starts pleading with me.

"Oh please, tell me if she does. I'm her brother and I've been looking all over London for her. I'm so worried about her."

Ah, I thinks, a brother. Now he mentions it I can see the resemblance around the eyes and the mouth. So I nods and says, "Yes she does live here as it happens."

Well, he nearly collapses with relief.

"May I come in and see her please?"

I shrugs. "If you like. But I don't think she's in."

"Please be so kind as to take me to her room."

I looks him over one more time and thinks, why not? What harm could it do? If he's a true gentleman there might be a shilling in it for me.

I shows him into the hallway and says, "Follow me, sir. Her room's at the top of the house."

He follows me up the stairs. When we gets to the top I knocks on the door but there's no answer.

"May I?" He puts his hand on the handle. I don't see what choice I've got. If he wants to look in her room I ain't in a position to stop him so I stands to one side and he goes in.

I don't go in myself but I can see the room's as empty as Our Lord's tomb. It's like I said. She's not in.

He goes over to the desk by the window and picks up a book. *Get a move on,* I thinks to myself. *I've got work to do.* I watches as he flicks through the pages of the book and then stands still as a statue, reading. I don't know what he's found but he turns pale as a ghost. He cries out, "My God, please no!" Then he rips out a page, drops the book on the desk and runs from the room, pushing past me, which ain't very gentleman-like.

He runs down the stairs without another word and he's out the front door before I've had time to get down the stairs. And no shilling for all my trouble.

Well, I thinks, what a strange fellow. But I don't have time to think any more of it. There's the bread to bake and the stew to cook. And those darn rats to get rid of.

79

He was ready. He had everything he needed. A sharpened wooden stake with a point like a hunter's spear; an axe; bulbs of garlic; a crucifix. He knew what he must do – drive the stake through the vampire's heart and then chop

237

off its head with the axe. Anything less would not result in the destruction of the vampire.

It had taken forty-two years for this moment to arrive, but now he, Alan Nesbit, was going to kill the vampire that he had been hunting ever since he had come to Highgate Cemetery that night in 1970 as a naïve sixteen year old.

He had suffered for his beliefs over the years. It hurt him, even now, to remember the humiliation he had endured – arrested by the police, ostracised by his family, ridiculed by his colleagues. But the opinions of other people had only made him more determined. People could mock him, but he would have the last laugh.

All things come to him who waits.

Alan crouched low behind the gravestone and watched the scene unfolding before his eyes.

The girl was lying beside the sleeping angel, her bare arms and legs flung out, her head turned to one side and her hair strewn across her face. The vampire (he might be disguised as a teenage boy in jeans and T-shirt but Alan was not fooled) had burst out moments earlier from the dense undergrowth that surrounded the graves in this part of the cemetery. Alan could not see his face, but that was good because it meant the vampire could not see him.

The evil creature was now kneeling beside the girl, leaning over her, bending his face to hers. Any second now he would bare his fangs and plunge them into the pure, white skin of her neck.

Alan reached out a hand for the wooden stake, his fingers closing tightly around it. It was time.

He stood up without making a sound and crept forward, like a tiger, ready to pounce.

80

Reflections of Will Bucket, Gravedigger, In the Year of Our Lord 1870, continued…

Big Bert and me, we finished our digging for the day

and was packing up to go home when the blue butterfly (I could've sworn it was the same one) flew right in front of me. Bert, well he was in a hurry 'cause he's got his eye on Nettie, the baker's daughter, and he wanted to be off so I tells him to leave his spade and I'll take it back to the storeroom. I waits for him to disappear and then I turns back to the butterfly that's still hovering nearby.

Hello, I thinks, *what do you want?* It's like it's doing some kind of a dance, flitting about right in front of me, its wings going ninety to the dozen. I picks up the spades and starts to follow it. I'm so fascinated by this blue butterfly that I ain't watching where I'm going and I nearly trips over her!

"Gawd blimey!" I shouts loud enough to wake the dead. "What the flippin' heck…?"

I drops the spades and kneels down on the ground.

She's lying face down but I knows her straight away – it's the lady what I helped months ago. She's clutching a bottle of white powder in her hand.

Lord, I thinks, please don't let me be too late. I bends down and turns her over. She's stone cold and her eyes stare back at me, unblinking.

81

Lauren is dreaming.

She's had this dream before. Many times. But she's always woken up before the final scene.

This time it feels different. This time it's for real. This time she won't wake up but will see how it ends.

She's running through an enchanted forest. The trees are in full leaf and the forest floor is carpeted in wild flowers in every shade of pink, purple, cream and yellow. The forest is alive with creatures: red-coated foxes nestle amongst fallen leaves; squirrels dart up tree trunks; rabbits hop across the path; the air is filled with the chirruping of birds; butterflies and bees hover over the flowers, drinking in their sweet nectar. She knows it can't last.

A sharp wind whistles through the trees.

A dark cloud blots out the sun.

The air turns icy. Leaves shrivel and fall to the ground, revealing skeletal branches that claw at her with dead fingers.

Still Lauren keeps running whilst all around her the forest metamorphoses. Bushes turn into gravestones and tree trunks sprout wings and become stone angels. The living forest is transforming itself into a necropolis – a city of the dead.

A fox lies in the middle of the path, its throat slit.

Lauren looks neither to the left nor the right, but keeps running until she comes to the sleeping angel.

As always in the dream the woman in black is kneeling by the angel. She stands up and turns around. She takes Lauren's hand in her own stone-cold hand and says, "Let me tell you my story…"

Lauren listens to her story and her heart goes out to this woman whose diary she has spent so much time reading. When Isabelle has finished speaking she puts a hand into a pocket of her long black dress and pulls out a bottle of white powder.

Lauren tries to shout *Stop!* but no sound comes out of her mouth. It's as if she's not really there. She tries to reach forward and grab the bottle but her arms are heavy as lead and won't move fast enough. She is impotent to change the course of history. She watches in horror as Isabelle uncorks the bottle, lifts it to her lips and pours the white powder into her mouth. Isabelle sways on her feet for a moment and her face contorts in pain. She clutches her stomach, doubles over and collapses onto the ground.

Lauren screams but the sound dies in her throat.

She hears footsteps. She turns. It's a young gravedigger. He's sauntering along, a couple of spades resting on his shoulder. He's following a butterfly and not looking where he's going. Lauren tries to call to him but she can't make herself heard.

He almost trips over the woman on the ground. "Gawd blimey," he shouts. "What the flippin' heck…?" He bends down and turns her over. Isabelle stares back at him, unblinking. He can't see Lauren and she realises that she's not really there.

"Lauren, can you hear me? Wake up Lauren."

A voice breaks into the dream. It's faint at first, but gradually it becomes louder and clearer. The voice is calling her name. It sounds insistent. Scared even.

"Lauren, Lauren. Please…"

She resists at first, not wanting to leave the dream-world. She knows now it isn't just a dream, but a lost memory that has escaped from time and has sought her out so that it can be remembered and finally laid to rest.

"Lauren, for God's sake, wake up."

Fingers on her neck checking for a pulse.

Someone thinks I'm dead but I'm not. If I don't wake up I could be buried alive.

Lauren looks once more at her dream companions. She wishes she could do something to help the poor gravedigger who is sobbing over Isabelle's lifeless body, but he can't see or hear her, separated as they are in time and space.

"I will come back," says Lauren silently. "I promise."

The dream starts to dissolve, breaking into tiny fragments that blow away like leaves in the wind. She feels as if she is rising from a deep, dark pool. The light is getting brighter. The air is warmer.

Her eyes flicker, then open.

Lauren looks directly into the bright sun and is instantly blinded by it. She screws her eyes tight shut again before opening them more cautiously. This time there are dark clouds rolling into the view and the glare of the sun is dimmed.

"Lauren. Thank God."

It's that voice again, the voice that has recalled her to

her own time. It's familiar and reassuring. There's someone leaning over her. She squints at the person silhouetted against the bright sky. *Tom?*

"Tom? Is that you?" Her mouth feels dry and her voice comes out as a croak. "What...?"

"I just found you here on the ground," he says. "Did you faint or something? Can you sit up? I didn't know what to do."

What must I look like? I must be in a right state. "I do feel a bit bruised."

"Here, let me help you." He puts an arm around her shoulders and starts to lift her into a sitting position.

"Thanks. I think I'll be..."

That's when she sees the man.

She opens her mouth to say something but her voice dies in her throat. From her semi-horizontal position she has a clear view over Tom's left shoulder and what she sees makes her blood run cold.

A man with greasy black hair, his mouth contorted into a devilish grin, has sprung up out of nowhere and is looming behind Tom, hands raised high above his head. And in his hands he is holding a wooden stake sharpened to a deadly point. Any second now he will strike. At last she finds her voice.

"Watch out!" she screams.

The lightning flashes and there is an ear-splitting crack of thunder. Tom jumps to his feet and Lauren rolls onto her side at the same instant as the man thrusts the stake downwards with a strangled cry. The wooden stake pierces the ground where moments before Lauren had been lying asleep.

What the hell is happening?

She has woken from a dream only to find herself in a nightmare.

Shaking with fear, Lauren gets to her knees. Raindrops the size of marbles start to fall from the sky, pelting her on the back of the head.

This can't be real. Where has this lunatic suddenly sprung from? Is he trying to kill me? Or Tom? Or both of us?

She scrambles to her feet. Her legs are jelly and black dots dance in front of her eyes before the blood has had a chance to reach her brain.

By the time her vision has cleared Tom has pulled the stake out of the ground and is using the blunt end to try and defend himself from his attacker. The man grabs hold of the stake and for a few seconds the two of them are locked in a fierce tug-of-war, their faces turning purple with the effort of trying to wrestle the weapon off each other.

The lightning flashes and the thunder roars. The rain is turning the dusty ground into a mud-slide so that Tom and the man start to lose their footing, slipping and skidding.

Crack.

A sound like gunshot as the wooden stake splinters and breaks in half. In a cry of fury the attacker throws away his half of the stake and tries to grab hold of the sharpened end that Tom is still holding but Tom raises it high above his head and hurls it into the distance where it lands in a blackberry bush.

The man falls on Tom with his bare hands, grabbing hold of his T-shirt and punching him hard in the jaw. The older man seems to be charged with some kind of demonic fury that gives him strength. He keeps repeating something, like a mantra, that Lauren can't understand at first but then realises is, "Kill the vampire, kill the vampire, kill the vampire…"

Tom staggers back against a gravestone. The man takes advantage of Tom's momentary loss of balance to punch him hard on the nose. Tom falls backwards, hitting the back of his head on the corner of the gravestone. The grass under his head turns crimson.

Lauren screams. She has to do something and quick. Despite the advantage of youth Tom is being made mincemeat of.

"STOP IT," screams Lauren but the man is hell-bent on his task and pays her no attention. There is no one else around to hear. She looks for the walkie-talkie but can't see it anywhere.

Tom struggles to get up but he's too badly hurt. At that moment the man pulls a short-handled axe from his coat pocket.

It's him.

It's the mad axe-man they saw in the cemetery on Saturday night. He holds the weapon with two hands and lifts it high above his head.

My God, he's really going to kill him! You've got to do something now!

In desperation Lauren looks around for something, anything, to use as a weapon, but there is nothing here other than gravestones and dead leaves.

She turns to the sleeping angel.

Help me.

It is as if time stands still for a moment. The storm quietens and in the lull Lauren sees something which she can't quite believe.

The angel opens her eyes, lifts her right arm and points at something on the ground.

Lauren looks to where the angel is pointing and sees a smooth, blank stone, about twelve inches high. It might have once been a headstone but now it is lying broken on the ground. How could she have missed it?

She grabs the stone with both hands, lifts it high above her head and slams it with all her strength onto the back of the man's head. Blood spurts out, the axe falls from his hands and he topples over, landing in a crumpled heap. He lies motionless on the ground.

Silence.

Lauren drops the stone and stares at the inert figure of the man. The madman. She can't believe what she's just done.

Have I killed him? But he was going to kill Tom. What else could I have done? My God, Tom!

She rushes over to him. She has no idea if he's dead or alive. He's lying on the muddy ground in a pool of red. He looks ghastly. His right eye is swollen shut, his lip is cut and a stream of blood runs from his nose down the side of his face. Lauren kneels down beside Tom and checks for a pulse. It's there, but faint.

"Tom, can you hear me?"

His left eye flickers and opens. The right eye remains shut.

Thank God, he's alive.

"Tom, are you OK?" *Daft question, of course he's not OK.*

Tom tries to speak but only manages a gurgling noise in the back of his throat.

"Here, let me help you." She slides an arm under his shoulders and eases him into a sitting position.

"Been better," he croaks, "but I'll live."

"Is that who I think it is?" asks Lauren pointing at the prostrate figure on the ground.

"Yes," says Tom. "That's Alan Nesbit. He killed my father."

82

Reflections of Will Bucket, Gravedigger, In the Year of Our Lord 1870, continued...

When I wants to think I likes to come and sit with Lion. Now, just to be clear, Lion ain't a lion – he's a dog. We do have a lion here at Highgate – he's lying on the tomb of George Wombwell who ran a famous menagerie, but he's too high up to sit next to. Lion, the dog, on the other hand, he's lying low down and I likes to sit with him and rest me hand on his head. It's like he's waiting for sumfink to happen and he'll wait as long as it takes. I goes there often in the days following the discovery of the lady by the sleeping angel.

Lion belonged to one of me heroes – Tom Sayers. He

were only thirty-nine when he died but he were the best bare-knuckle prize-fighter in the country. He also had the biggest funeral ever – and when I say big, I mean absolutely bloomin' enormous. Well, all right, maybe it wasn't as big as the Duke o' Wellington's funeral, but still it were dead impressive. The funeral cortège stretched all the way from Tottenham Court Road to Highgate – that's over three miles. There were ten thousand mourners and – this is the best bit – his dog, Lion, were the chief mourner. Ain't that nice?

So a stone carving of Lion lies on top of his master's grave and I know that in a hundred years, two hundred years, pillars might topple and angels might fall, but Lion'll still be lying here, head on his front paws, faithful to the last.

PART NINE
THURSDAY 19 JULY

83

The air conditioning in the hospital felt chilly after the heat of the midday sun. Lauren rubbed her bare arms, wishing she'd thought to bring a cardigan. She had, however, had the forethought to pop into Oxfam on her way to the hospital and buy a box of white, milk and dark fair-trade chocolates.

She stopped a moment to read the directions' board.

Ward six. First floor.

She hoped Tom was up for a visit. She hadn't seen him since he'd been carted off from the cemetery on a stretcher yesterday afternoon. He'd looked awful.

Lauren started to climb the stairs to the first floor. The events of yesterday were all so unreal they kept going round and round in her head, like a child's spinning top. She wanted to see Tom now to make sure she hadn't dreamt the whole thing.

After she'd knocked Alan Nesbit over the head with

the gravestone and made sure that Tom was still in the land of the living, she had spotted the walkie-talkie lying under a shrub. She called the office for help and a frantic Wendy had come running over, followed ten minutes later by Alice accompanied by four paramedics, and two policemen.

Lauren had spent an agonising few minutes whilst two of the paramedics assessed Professor Nesbit. He might have been a monster, but the thought that she could have killed him, even in self-defence, filled her with horror. But she needn't have worried. She hadn't actually killed him, just knocked him unconscious.

The paramedics lifted Tom and Alan onto the stretchers and carried them away to the waiting ambulance. One of the policemen went with them, the other took Lauren back to the cemetery office to get a statement. Alice provided tea and biscuits.

At the top of the stairs Lauren turned left, following the sign for Ward six. Wendy had told her that Alan Nesbit was also still in the hospital, but under police guard. Apparently he'd confessed to killing Tom's dad. It was shocking. Lauren couldn't get her head around it. Not only had he spent his life chasing a non-existent vampire, but he'd been so delusional that he'd murdered his colleague and attempted to murder his colleague's son.

She thought of Nancy, and the terrible waste of her life. The tragedy of all this was that they hadn't been able to catch Nesbit in time. If they had, then Nancy would still be here now. The funeral was going to be held next week.

Ward six was at the end of the corridor. Tom was halfway down the ward, sitting up in bed with a bandage round his head. His right eye was still swollen, his face was covered in cuts and bruises and his nose was obviously broken. He looked a mess.

A woman was sitting by the side of his bed, holding his hand. They were talking. Lauren couldn't see her face.

Lauren hung back by the double doors to the ward,

unsure whether to go in or not. But then Tom looked up and saw her. He waved at her to come over.

"Hi," she said, approaching his bed. "How are you feeling?"

"Terrific. Feel like I've just been in the ring with Mike Tyson. But apart from that, terrific."

The woman stood up. She'd obviously been crying because her eyes were red and puffy. She held out her hand to Lauren. "Hello. I'm Tom's Mum. Deborah. I'd just like to say thank you for what you did yesterday. If it hadn't been for you Tom might not be here now and I...I just dread to think…" Her voice cracked and she fished a handkerchief out of her black Chanel handbag as the tears started to fall. "I'm sorry," she said dabbing her eyes. "This has been a very difficult time for me. I've been trying to hold everything together since Tom's dad died and now…" She gave a sob and covered her mouth with her handkerchief, unable to go on.

Tom put out his hand and touched his mum's arm. "It's OK. Everything's going to be all right now."

His mum nodded and smiled at him. "I'll leave you two alone now," she said. "I'm sure you don't want me hanging around."

She put her handkerchief back into her bag and kissed Tom on the forehead. Then she walked out, her heels clicking on the linoleum floor.

"What was all that about?" asked Lauren.

"Long story. Tell you later."

Lauren sat down on the chair next to the bed. "I brought you some chocolates. Hope you like them."

84

Journal of Mr. Nathaniel Hart, Esq. March 1870

Helen and I returned to the house on Highgate Hill this morning to collect Isabelle's belongings. It was a task that I had been dreading and it was a great comfort to me to have Helen's gentle, unwavering support.

We were met at the door by the same maid who admitted me to the house on that fateful day when I arrived too late to save my sister. (I do not think I will ever be able to forgive myself.) The maid was more subdued than last time and looked at us with genuine sympathy in her eyes. After she had shown us upstairs, I gave her a sovereign, which she was reluctant to take, but I insisted she take it, for Isabelle's sake. She wiped a tear from her eye and ran back downstairs to the kitchens.

There were not many items in Isabelle's room for us to collect. I took her diary and papers whilst Helen folded her handful of dresses and placed them in a bag. Helen looked for Isabelle's box, but we couldn't find it anywhere and, in the end, we assumed it was lost.

As we were walking back down the stairs I noticed a door standing ajar on the first floor and I had a sense that we were being watched. I immediately thought of the spirit medium that I had read about in Isabelle's diary. I had it in mind to go to her and demand an explanation. Helen must have read my thoughts because she put a hand on my arm and gently shook her head. Helen always says we must not be too quick to judge others and no doubt she feared I would say something in the heat of the moment which I should later regret. She was probably right. Then the door closed and I heard the sound of a key locking it from the inside and I knew that the moment for confronting Madeleine had passed.

Back outside, I would have hailed a hansom cab to take us home without further delay but Helen was insistent that we should visit the penitentiary where Isabelle had worked. She wanted to meet the girl who had led me to Isabelle.

85

A week later they were sitting in the garden at Tom's house sipping chilled peppermint tea that Deborah had brought out for them in a jug. Tom was on the phone. He'd been out of hospital a few days now and the bruising on his face had gone down a lot. He looked almost back to normal.

Tom finished the call and laid his phone on the table.

"What did he say?" asked Lauren.

"He said 'yes'."

"That's fantastic."

Tom had been speaking to Richard Newgate, the principal at University College London.

"He's really keen to help us. I think he wants to make amends for the fact that one of his academic staff was a deranged murderer, although that wasn't his fault. He's already spoken to the Archaeology Department. They've got some new ground-penetrating radar equipment which they were hoping to use in Egypt but the political situation there is too dangerous. So they're willing to use it in Highgate Cemetery instead."

"When?"

"In two days' time."

86

The Sorrows of a True Penitent, in the Year of Our Lord 1870

It's quiet in the penitentiary today. Everyone's sad about what happened to Sister Isabelle. It didn't take long for news of what had happened to reach us. Sam, the baker's boy who delivers the bread, goes to the house where she lived and he heard it from Betsy the maid.

Sister Christina is supervising the laundry but she spends most of the time staring out of the window. We just get on with our work. I'm stirring the laundry and my arms are killing me. But that's nothing compared to the pain in my heart. I'm so sad about what happened to Sister Isabelle I feel like my heart's breaking. She was so nice and kind to me but I always suspected she were carrying her own burdens.

But knowing Sister Isabelle has made me want to be a better person. Like she said, I need to find some honest employment. So I keep stirring the laundry and I hope and pray that one day I will.

I'm just about to start rinsing out the linens, when the door to the laundry room opens and in comes Sister Burns. I think she's just doing the rounds, checking up on us all, and I keep my head down to show that I'm working hard. But then she comes over to me and tells me to lay the pole aside. There's people wanting to see me. That has never happened to me before and I can't think what she means.

I straighten my cap and tuck my hair back underneath. Then I follow Sister Burns down the corridor. I think she's taking me to her office, but then she turns and we go outside into the garden.

"They're over there by the apple trees," she says to me. "A lady and a gentleman," she adds like I can't see that for myself. Then she leaves me on my own and I don't know what to do.

I know the gentleman at once. It's Sister Isabelle's brother who came here the other day. He's dressed in full mourning and looks unbelievably sad. I pity him but I can't imagine what he wants to say to me.

And then there's the lady. She's also dressed in full mourning but I can see she's young and pretty with auburn hair and gentle, brown eyes. When she sees me standing there she comes over to me.

"Are you Ellen?" she asks.

I nod and hang my head, too frightened to speak.

"I'm Helen," she says. "I'm engaged to be married to Isabelle's brother, Nathaniel."

At the mention of Isabelle's name my eyes fill with tears and my breath catches in my throat.

"Come," says Helen, taking my arm through hers. "Let's take a walk around the garden and you can tell me all about Isabelle and yourself."

So we walk arm-in-arm around the garden and I tell her about how kind Isabelle was to me and about myself, though that's a sorry story which I don't like to dwell on.

When we've nearly done a whole lap of the garden she

stops and turns to me.

"Ellen," she says, "when I get married and set up home with Nathaniel, I'm going to need someone to help me. Would you come and be my lady's maid?"

For a moment I don't know what to say. I always said I didn't want to go into domestic service because I imagined it was all cooking and cleaning and doing the laundry and that all employers were mean and cruel. But looking into the face of this beautiful woman, I know that she wouldn't be like that. She's too good.

"Will you?" she asks. "For Isabelle's sake?"

I'm crying again but this time it's tears of happiness. "Oh, yes," I says. "Thank you, Miss. Thank you."

87

Two days later Lauren and Tom joined Alice, Professor David Jones from UCL's archaeology faculty and a post graduate student called Andrew in Highgate Cemetery by the sleeping angel.

Whilst the professor and the student set up their equipment, Lauren studied the angel carefully. Had the angel really woken up and pointed or had Lauren just imagined it in the heat of the moment? She knelt down and examined the statue. The angel's eyes were closed and the fingers of her right hand curled gently on the ground in the way they always had. Surely it couldn't have happened, could it? And yet... Lauren stretched out a hand and touched the cold stone. "Sleep tight," she said under her breath. Then she stood up and rejoined Tom.

"All right?" she asked him. He was standing with his hands thrust in his pockets, shoulders hunched. Lauren guessed it couldn't be easy for him returning to the place where a madman had tried to kill him.

He nodded.

"I'm glad you came," she said. He managed a smile.

It was the first time for both of them to return to the

cemetery since the attack. After leaving the hospital, Tom had been confined to the house, suffering from the after-effects of concussion, and Wendy had expressly forbidden Lauren to go anywhere near Highgate Cemetery, even though it was unlikely there would be a second serial killer lurking behind the gravestones.

After the attack Lauren had told Alice how she'd fallen asleep by the sleeping angel and how she'd had the strangest dream concerning a young woman lying down to die by the place where her dead baby had been buried in secret. Lauren had fully expected the older woman to dismiss the whole idea as fanciful nonsense and offer her another cup of tea and a biscuit. But Alice had listened thoughtfully and at the end of the conversation had said she'd always believed there was something mysterious about that part of the cemetery. "I think we should investigate, don't you?" she said to Lauren. Which was how the archaeology department of UCL came to be involved.

"OK, I think we're ready," called Professor Jones.

Lauren, Tom and Alice stood in a row watching as the professor and his student wheeled a machine that looked like a small lawn-mower with a computer screen attached, towards them. On the way over to the sleeping angel Professor Jones had explained that this equipment was a ground penetrating radar machine which would draw a picture of what, if anything, was under the surface.

"Now you will take great care not to disturb the nearby graves, won't you?" said Alice, drawing herself up to her full height. She barely reached the Professor's shoulder.

"I promise we'll be extremely careful," said Professor Jones.

The three onlookers watched for a while as the Professor and his student proceeded to cover the ground, inch by inch, and then Alice suggested that maybe they could leave them to it and go and have a cup of tea and a biscuit. The Professor promised to be in touch as soon as they'd taken the data back to the university and analysed the results.

The next day Lauren and Tom were back in the office at Highgate Cemetery, having offered to help the gardeners cut back the ivy that was threatening to swallow up many of the gravestones. Alice was giving them their instructions when the phone rang.

"Good Morning, Highgate Cemetery. How may I help you? Oh hello Professor."

Lauren and Tom exchanged glances.

"I see," continued Alice, nodding her head. "Yes, of course...Quite...I'm sure that can be arranged...I'll need to make sure we follow all the legal requirements...Thank you so much for your help...Good-bye."

She hung up and turned to Lauren and Tom. "That was Professor David Jones from the archaeology department at UCL. They've got the results of the radar. There's an unidentified coffin under the ground. It appears to contain two bodies. An adult and a baby."

"It's Isabelle," said Lauren. "I know it is."

88

Summer was coming to an end.

The first leaves of autumn were starting to fall from the trees. It was six o'clock in the morning and there was a slight chill in the air.

The little group met in the courtyard at Highgate Cemetery then made its solemn way under the Colonnade, up the steps and through the cemetery to the sleeping angel. A fox stood in the path and looked at them in surprise before scurrying away into the undergrowth.

In the weeks since receiving the phone call from Professor David Jones, Alice had worked hard to assemble all the necessary paperwork required for an exhumation and reburial. She had managed to obtain permission from the Bishop of London and the Home Office, which was not an inconsiderable achievement. The Vicar of St Michael's, the Reverend Martin Andrews, had agreed to officiate in conjunction with the undertakers, Heap & Son. Alice had asked her two most faithful grave diggers, William and Robert, to do the digging. Lauren, Tom and Peter Hart were invited to attend.

Using the data supplied by the archaeology department of UCL, William and Robert marked out the area to be dug and carefully set to work.

Lauren shivered and Tom put his arm around her, pulling her close. She looked up at him and smiled. They'd been going out for a few weeks now and things were going really well. Lauren had even introduced Tom to Megan and Chloe properly and afterwards her friends had agreed what a great guy he was.

After about thirty minutes of digging, William, the more senior of the two grave diggers, stood up straight and said, "I think we've found something."

William and Robert cleared the earth with their bare hands to reveal a plain wooden coffin. With the help of the undertakers they positioned ropes under either end, hauled it out and laid it on the ground. The wood was black from having spent so long under the ground but the coffin still held together. There was no inscription on the lid.

Alice nodded her consent for William and Robert to go ahead and remove the lid. The screws had long since rusted so William took a hammer and chisel and, ever so carefully, as if he was a renaissance sculptor working on a marble Madonna and Child, tapped away at the coffin lid until it was loose. Then he and Robert lifted it to one side and the small crowd of onlookers gathered round to peer inside.

The body had rotted away - dust to dust - but the skeleton was still visible and beside it a tiny skeleton, no bigger than a newborn baby. Lauren choked back a tear.

"What's that?" asked Alice pointing at a metal tube that lay partially hidden amongst the folds of decaying black material that still covered the skeleton. "May we see?"

Mr Heap, the undertaker, bent down and carefully lifted out the metal tube. It was about nine inches long and two inches in diameter and had not rusted. It was sealed at one end and had a screw cap at the other. The undertaker passed it to Alice who slowly unscrewed the cap and peered inside. She retrieved a scroll of paper and, ever so gently, opened it out.

Lauren recognised it at once.

It was the missing final page from Isabelle's diary. It was all the proof they needed that this was Isabelle's body in the coffin. As Alice held the precious document up to the early morning light Lauren read the now familiar handwriting.

Sunday, 20th March 1870

I am a fool.

I have been most miserably abused. Madeleine Fox is a fraudster of the basest kind, plying her trade on the most vulnerable in society, namely those burdened with grief and susceptible to being told that their loved ones are safe and happy on the other side.

I visited her this evening hoping that the longed-for materialisation of my dear Emily would happen. I desired more than anything to hold her once more in my arms. Madeleine had given me to believe that her spirit guide, Eliza King, would bring her to me. This is what Madeleine had promised me. And like the fool that I am, I trusted her.

I went to her room at the usual time. She seemed a little agitated but assured me that everything would be fine. We sat for some time on the sofa in semi-darkness, the only light coming from an oil lamp turned down low and placed on the small, circular table. After a while Madeleine retired to her spirit cabinet. I waited alone, determined that this time I would not faint. I told myself I must be strong for the sake of my child.

Eliza appeared almost at once. She did not seem to glow as brightly as she had done the first time I encountered her but I did not think anything of it. As she moved towards me I kept very still and did not feel so afraid. She came closer and, in the dim light, it seemed to me she was carrying something in her arms. I hardly dared hope.

When she had nearly reached me there was a thud and a crash and the oil lamp which was the only light in the room fell to the floor and was extinguished.

Now we were in total darkness. I jumped to my feet feeling for the table which I knew was not far away. I could hear movement in front of me. I was desperate for Eliza not to disappear.

"Are you there?" I asked.

No reply.

I reached out my hands and felt something warm.

Flesh.

I screamed.

At that moment the door opened and light flooded in from the hallway. Mrs Payne and Betsy were standing there holding lights that were turned up full.

I looked at what my hands had touched and recognised the scrawny features of Daisy the scullery maid. She was wearing nothing but her petticoats and on the floor at her feet lay a pile of chiffon cloth which glowed with a pale luminous light. In her hands Daisy held the lifeless features of a porcelain doll.

I stood as if turned to stone.

Daisy dropped the doll on the floor and ran from the room, hiding her face in her hands.

Mrs Payne marched into the room and tore back the curtain of the cabinet. Madeleine was cowering inside looking shocked and frightened. Mrs Payne started shouting at Madeleine saying she would throw her out onto the street and that there would be no more fraudsters in this house.

Betsy came over to me and said in her kindest voice, "Let me take you up to your room." I followed her like a lost child.

There is nothing more left for me in this world.

When the house is quiet I will go into the kitchen and take the arsenic from the shelf where I have seen Betsy put it. Then I will creep out of the house and take the poison to the cemetery. Death will not be painful for me if I lie down by the grave of my child.

Lauren's voice fell silent. Isabelle's story had been told. Justice had been done.

Alice re-rolled the piece of paper and returned it to the metal tube. Then she placed the metal tube back into the folds of the material where it had lain for so long.

Mr Heap, the undertaker, stepped forward and said that it was time to transfer the bodies into the new coffin which they had brought for the purpose. Peter Hart had chosen one in the finest oak with a lead lining and a cream silk interior. Lauren and Tom watched in fascination as the undertaker and his assistant laid the bones in their new resting place, positioned the lid and sealed it in place. Tom and Peter then helped the undertakers carry it to the Hart family vault in the Circle of Lebanon. Lauren and Alice followed behind. Isabelle was to be returned to her family.

As the Reverend Martin Andrews read out the words of the funeral service, Lauren thought about what she had learned of Isabelle's life from the diary. She would need to give the diary back to Peter, it belonged in his family, but first she would ask him if she could finish transcribing the entries. She wanted to keep a record of the woman who had once lodged in her house. One day she would write Isabelle's story.

Isabelle's final resting place was in the grand Circle of Lebanon. Her coffin lay on a shelf in the Hart family vault above that of her brother Nathaniel Hart and his wife Helen.

Lauren glanced across at Peter. There was a look of contentment on his face as if he was glad that his family had been reunited.

The funeral service over, Alice closed the heavy door to the vault and locked it with a large metal key. "I'll go and put the kettle on," she said, walking briskly down the Egyptian Avenue towards the cemetery office. Peter went with her, Lauren and Tom following behind.

At the bottom of the Egyptian Avenue Lauren and Tom turned to look back, one last time, at the Circle of

Lebanon.

A woman was standing beside the Hart family vault. She was wearing a simple white dress and her long hair flowed freely around her shoulders. As Lauren and Tom watched, the figure of the woman shimmered in the morning sun, growing brighter until she was glowing with a white light. Then she faded and all that was left was a patch of sunlight on the ground and a butterfly that disappeared into the trees.

"Let's go," whispered Lauren. "She can rest now in peace."

89

Reflections of Will Bucket, Gravedigger, In the Year of Our Lord 1870, concluded.

It were like this, see. I were kneeling down, cradling her in me arms like a baby when I hears footsteps come running through the cemetery, twigs snapping underfoot and a voice, a man's voice, calling, "Isabelle, Isabelle, where are you?"

I didn't know what to do. I couldn't leave her there all alone but I didn't want to be found with a dead woman in me arms.

But there was no time to do anything. All of a sudden he comes crashing through the bushes, this gentleman, like he's being chased by the devil and he sees me there and sees Isabelle in me arms.

I lays her down quick, but gentle like, and says, "I just found her. I didn't do nuffink. I swear."

He collapses on the ground beside her and starts to weep. "I know," he says. "I know."

When he'd recovered himself a bit he stood up and told me he was her brother and he'd been looking for her all over London. He'd found her too late.

"I'm sorry," I says.

"I will see to the funeral," he says.

Then I makes a decision. It's a bold one. I tells him, "This place was special to her. By the sleeping angel. She buried something here. In secret."

He looks at me. He don't ask any questions but he says, "Then please dig up whatever she buried and I will see that it is laid in her coffin."

"It'll have to be done in secret," I says. I think he understands.

"Tonight. At dusk. I'll meet you here."

I nods. "Tonight. At dusk."

ACKNOWLEDGEMENTS

I would like to thank Catherine for her detailed checking of the manuscript, and Steve for all his support and re-reading of the manuscript at its various stages of development.

ABOUT THE AUTHOR

Margarita Morris was born in Harrogate, North Yorkshire. She studied Modern Languages at Jesus College, Oxford and worked in computing for eleven years. She lives in Oxfordshire with her husband and two sons.

OTHER BOOKS BY THE SAME AUTHOR:
Oranges for Christmas

Berlin 1961. The War is over. But for Sabine the fight for freedom has only just begun.

CONNECT WITH MARGARITA

Website
http://margaritamorris.com

Blog
http://margaritamorris.wordpress.com

Twitter
@MargaritaMorris

Facebook
https://www.facebook.com/margaritamorrisauthor

Pinterest
http://www.pinterest.com/margaritamorris/

Printed in Great Britain
by Amazon